Sex and Music
A Wicked Words erotic short-story collection

Look out for other themed Wicked Words Collections

Already Published: *Sex in the Office, Sex on Holiday, Sex in Uniform, Sex in the Sportsclub, Sex in the Kitchen, Sex on the Move*

Published in November 06: *Sex and Shopping*

Published in February 07: *Sex in Public*

Published in May 07: *Sex with Strangers*

Sex and Music

A Wicked Words short-story collection

Edited by Lindsay Gordon

BLACK LACE

Wicked Words stories contain sexual fantasies.
In real life, always practise safe sex.

This edition published in 2006 by
Black Lace
Thames Wharf Studios
Rainville Road
London W6 9HA

Typeset by SetSystems Limited, Saffron Walden, Essex
Printed and bound by Mackays of Chatham PLC

ISBN 0 352 34061 4
ISBN 9 780352 340610

Contents

Introduction and Newsletter

After millions of years of evolution we've come to this? Leaping about dance-floors like wild things under pagan moons to the beat of hypnotic drums? Thrusting scantily-clad bodies at each other to mimic sexual acts? Holding strangers close with intimate embraces and moving against each other and around the floor, spellbound by a formal waltz? Jumping up and down before a stage as if to catch sight of some messiah dressed in black?

Music does strange things to us, and always has since the first piece of animal-hide was stretched around wood. Even today, music still provides the backing track to fertility rites, remains a prelude and accompaniment to courtship, and since rock 'n' roll swaggered into being, actually imitates sexual passion. And unless it sets out to do otherwise, music is mostly about giving and promoting pleasure.

There are few mediums or substances so effective at impairing our inhibitions and reserve. A great hook-line in a chorus, anthemic guitar riff, or poignant movement in a symphony can instantly unlock a memory or inspire a fantasy. Music is a transporter. Inseparable from the imagination. Breaks us out of the ordinary and inspires. And considering the deification we attribute to pop and rock stars, combined with their clever cultivation of sex appeal, it's no surprise our libidos dance when the records begin to turn.

And our authors have found an astonishing variety of harmonies to eroticise music with. *The Apprentice* and

The Harp feature novel, and even haunting, takes on curious students of music; *Private Performance, Duet* and *Coda* bring admirers and musicians together in unusual ways; *All I Have To Do* and *Sonata* go deep to reveal the erotic influence of memory and melody on an appreciative girl; *Wednesday Sessions* and *Sparrow* reveal the close proximity of talent to sex drive; while *Musical Chairs* and *Siren Song of Birchwood Gardens* do something very unusual with party games and noisy neighbours. So whichever style or genre is explored in these tracks, we guarantee an album full of memorable hits. So turn the page and turn it up.

Lindsay Gordon, Spring 2006

Want to write for Wicked Words?

We are publishing more themed collections in 2006 and 2007 – made in response to our readers' most popular fantasies. *Sex and Shopping* and *Sex in Public* are the next two collections. The deadline for both collections has now passed, but if you want to submit a sizzling, beautifully written story for *Sex with Strangers* (deadline for submissions October 06), please read the following. And keep checking our website for information on future editions.

- Your short story should be 4,000–6,000 words long and not published anywhere in the world – websites excepted.
- Thematically, it should be written with the Black Lace guidelines in mind.
- Ideally there should be a 'sting in the tale' and an

element of dramatic tension, with oodles of erotic build-up.

- The story should be about more than 'some people having sex' – we want great characterisation too.
- Keep the explicit anatomical stuff to an absolute minimum.

We are obliged to select stories that are technically faultless and vibrant and *original* – as well as fitting in with the tone of the series: upbeat, dynamic, accent on pleasure etc. Our anthologies are a flagship for the series. We pride ourselves on selecting only the best-written erotica from the UK and USA. The key words are: diversity, surprises and faultless writing.

Competition rules will apply to short stories: you will hear back from us about your story <u>only</u> if it has been successful. We cannot give individual feedback on short stories as we receive far too many for this to be possible.

For future collections check the Black Lace website.

If you want to find out more about Black Lace, check our website, where you will find our author guidelines and more information about short stories. It's at <u>www.blacklace-books.co.uk</u>

Alternatively, send a large SAE with a first-class British stamp to:

Black Lace Guidelines
Virgin Books Ltd
Thames Wharf Studios
Rainville Road
London W6 9HA

Private Performance
Mae Nixon

When Noel Coward said 'It's strange how potent cheap music is,' just for once, I think he got it wrong. Because, when you think about it, all music's pretty potent, isn't it? It can make you feel sad or help you forget your troubles. It sees us through good times and bad and a few bars of a melody can instantly bring to mind a memory you thought you'd buried long ago. I mean, Dvorak's 'New World' Symphony makes everyone think of Hovis, doesn't it? Even people who've never listened to Classic FM still know all the words to 'Everyone's a Fruit and Nutcase' and 'Just one Cornetto'. And, if you've just broken up with your boyfriend, 'I Will Survive' is guaranteed to make you feel better.

Sad, uplifting, poignant or comic, there's a song for every mood and every moment of your life. The other day I heard 'Papa Don't Preach' and was instantly reminded of standing at the edge of the gym at school discos with the smell of polish in my nostrils desperately trying to pretend I didn't mind being a wallflower. And I only have to hear the first line of Sinead O'Connor's 'Nothing Compares 2 U' and I'm fourteen again, slow dancing with Michael Cox at someone's birthday party wondering if he'd kiss me when the song ended and terrified I'd look a fool because he only came up to my chest and I wasn't sure if etiquette demanded I bend down or he stand on tiptoes.

Pavarotti reminds me of sitting at the kitchen table watching my mum cook the Sunday dinner and Ray Charles reminds me of my dad's old 45s. I lost my virginity to Frankie Goes to Hollywood's 'The Power of Love' (1993 re-release) and first said I love you in a noisy pub with Take That's 'Back for Good' playing on the jukebox.

Like it or not, everyone's life has a soundtrack. But, until I met Peter, my personal score had always been delivered by the radio or the CD player or even, when I was a kid, my dad's cherished collection of classic vinyl. Though I've always loved live music, somehow the pivotal moments of my life had always been accompanied by recorded tunes.

There's something unspeakably exciting and miraculous about live music, isn't there? Some extra little frisson of excitement that isn't there when you listen to a recording. All the instruments in the band play their individual parts, yet somehow – almost by magic, it seems to me – they blend together to create music. A complex blend of harmonies and melodies that somehow evoke emotion. Sometimes I'm completely stunned, overwhelmed, by the sheer emotional power of music. Somehow, it seems to enter my soul. It's like good sex: powerful, primal and all consuming. It heightens my senses and makes me feel more alive, more real somehow. I'm serious. The only experience that has ever matched it in intensity is sex. But it had never occurred to me that the two might mix. Until I met Peter...

Usually on a Wednesday night, I got together with two friends for our weekly girls' night in. We took it in turn to play host each week. But this particular evening, neither of them could make it so I'd decided to rent a DVD and pop into the Chinese on the way back. It had been a long day in the shop and I didn't have the energy to cook.

The video shop was quite busy. I squeezed between a middle-aged woman with a small dog on a lead and a young man with a takeaway in a carrier bag. I could smell the spicy aroma of Thai food wafting up at me. It made me feel hungry. I browsed the titles.

'Hello. You don't recognise me, do you?' The man with the takeaway was looking at me.

'I'm afraid not. Should I?'

'I suppose there's no reason why you should. Though I had rather hoped you'd find me at least a bit memorable. I can't tell you how crushing that is for my ego.' He smiled. His eyes were a delicate shade of blue and his blond hair was short and spiky. He seemed slightly familiar, but I couldn't quite place him.

'We've met, I take it?' I struggled to remember.

'At Giovanni's, a couple of weeks ago? I passed your table and you winked at me.'

'Of course. How could I forget? I've still got your phone number in my bag.'

He shrugged his shoulders.

'But you haven't used it.'

'I haven't used it . . . yet.'

'How long were you planning on making me wait?'

'You know the rules, I'm sure. Long enough not to seem desperate but soon enough to seem keen.'

'But you intended to call, I hope?' He smiled and crinkles formed around his eyes, making him look playful.

'I hadn't made up my mind, to be honest. But you've saved me the trouble, anyway. And I promise I won't forget you again.'

The woman with the dog stepped back, jostling me. I

lost my footing and fell forwards. He put out his hands and steadied me, gripping my upper arms. His hands felt strong and reassuring. Our bodies were not quite touching, my face an inch from his. I could feel his hot breath on my cheek. He released me. The memory of his fingers made me tingle.

'Sorry, what must you think of me? I'm Peter Griffin. Pleased to meet you.' He offered me his hand.

'And I'm Tess Tyler.' We shook hands. His grip was firm, yet friendly. His skin was warm and soft.

'Oh, I know who you are. I've seen you going in and out of your shop in the High Street. In fact I think I was caught in a traffic jam behind your van the other day.'

'You'd better stop there, otherwise I might think you're stalking me.'

'I'm not, I assure you. I'm quite harmless.' His eyes conveyed a mixture of amusement and intensity that made my stomach feel fluttery. His blue eyes sparkled. His mouth was slightly open, his tongue just visible between his teeth. He moistened his lips.

'I'm glad to hear it.' I smiled.

'Are you doing anything this evening?' The timbre of Peter's voice belied the casualness of his request.

'I did have an exciting evening planned with a DVD and a takeaway, but I could change my plans, if there's something more stimulating on offer.'

'Are you hungry?'

'Ravenous.'

'Then I hope you like Thai food.' He held up his takeaway.

'Where do you live?' Much to my surprise, my voice seemed to have grown husky. 'I'm in Park Drive.'

'I live on the corner – you know the old school?'

'Really? I've always wondered what it was like inside. Let's go there, it's nearer.' I took his hand.

Peter's building was a Victorian school that had been converted into apartments in the 1980s. His flat, a former classroom, had high ceilings and plain white walls. One of the walls was composed entirely of windows that started three feet from the floor and finished at the ceiling. It was essentially one long room partitioned at one end to create a separate kitchen and bathroom. Slatted blinds covered the windows, and the floorboards had been sanded to a soft gold colour.

The room had been divided into separate areas. In the centre, there were two sofas, a coffee table and a wide-screen television. At the far end were some bookshelves and an easy chair and some expensive-looking stereo equipment. By the window there was an upright piano and a digital piano.

Peter had divided the takeaway between two plates and poured us each a glass of wine. He had taken off his shoes and sat cross-legged on the floor in front of me. I relaxed back against the sofa, my feet curled under me.

'What do you think of the wine?' He topped up my glass.

'It's good. You have excellent taste.'

'Thanks. I bought it in France last year, direct from the vineyard. It was a real bargain. I've only got half a dozen bottles left now.'

I took another sip of wine.

'Do you play?' I put down my plate and nodded in the direction of the piano.

'Oh, yes. I do it for a living. As a matter of fact, that's why I was in Giovanni's when we met. I was closing a deal with the owner. I'm going to be playing there every Friday night from now on.'

'Really? I'm impressed.'

'It's not as glamorous as it sounds, I assure you. I make my bread and butter as a session musician. Sometimes I spend days and days playing stuff I wouldn't even listen to if I weren't getting paid. I'm building up a bit of a name for myself and there's a record company interested in taking me on, but mostly it's just a job.' Though he was deliberately underplaying his work, I could hear the enthusiasm and dedication in his voice. His eyes glistened.

'I've always envied creative people. I can't even sing.' I smiled.

'But your work is creative, surely? Flower arranging is an art.'

I shook my head. 'It's a technical skill. Anyone can learn it.'

'That can't be true, can it? I mean, you might be able to learn how to choose the right flowers, how to arrange them and what goes with what. But you've got to have an eye for it, haven't you? Flowers are mysterious and magical. Some of them are cheerful and make you want to smile. Others fill you with tenderness at their fragility. Some of them denote sadness and some fill you with passion. You have to understand their innate qualities to make an arrangement really work. And you have to have vision and creativity to even want to do it in the first place. Don't tell me you're not an artist. I simply won't believe it.'

'It's kind of you to say so.'

'Give me your hands.'

'What are you going to do? Read my palm?'

'Give me your hands . . .'

His fingers touched my wrists. He brushed them lightly down the length of my hands all the way to the tips of my fingers. He turned his hands over and held them out to me, palms up. I laid my palms against his. His thumbs caressed the tops of my fingers. I shivered.

'You have the hands of an artist. Look at your long

fingers and your shapely nails. And you have a tapering palm. This is the hand of an angel.'

'Yours are beautiful too. So long and sensitive. I should have known you were a pianist. When we shook hands in the video shop I remember thinking how soft they were.' I stroked his fingers.

'That's because I've never done a hard day's work in my life.'

'That's not true, is it? I mean it might not be manual labour but it's hard work, nonetheless. Moving people to tears is a pretty noble occupation.'

'Oh, yes, I do that all the time. Sometimes they throw things as well.'

'Will you play for me?'

'No, I couldn't. I always get nervous and clumsy when someone asks me that.'

'That's must be a bit of a drawback in your job.'

'I don't mind playing in front of a roomful of strangers; that's not personal. But when I have an audience of one I completely forget how to play.'

'I promise I'll stay very quiet. You won't even know I'm here. Please?' I smiled at him.

'Somehow I just don't seem able to say no to you.'

He gave my hands a final squeeze and laid them gently on my knees. He got up and walked over to the piano. He sat down on the bench and closed his eyes. He sat silently for several long moments.

I could hear the murmur of traffic in the street outside. Somewhere in the flat a clock was ticking. Peter's long fingers were poised above the keys. I could see his chest rising and falling. With his eyes closed, his face seemed at once vulnerable and intense. I felt as though he was reaching inside of himself, seeking something secret and personal to share with me as music.

He began to play, eyes still closed. The tinkling notes

filled the room. Within a few bars, I recognised the melody. Peter was playing a lilting jazz version of Billie Holiday's 'Lover Man', a piece that I knew well, thanks to my dad's old records. Somehow, he seemed to imbue his playing with the same quality of melancholy and hopefulness that I always heard in Billie's haunting voice.

Peter's body swayed with the music. His hands moved along the keys with ease and precision. I couldn't take my eyes off him. The music seemed to inhabit the room like a separate entity. It seemed palpable and solid. I almost felt as though I could put out my hand and touch it. It sank in through my pores. It crept inside my skull, filling my consciousness with its tenderness and beauty.

His fingers flew along the keyboard. His chest heaved. His parted lips were red and puffy. He was smiling slightly to himself. An expression that I could only describe as bliss transformed his face.

I was on the edge of my seat. The music resonated inside me. I could see that Peter was completely lost in his playing. The sounds his fingers produced were far more than music on a page, learnt by rote and recreated mechanically. He was playing from his heart and guts, allowing his spirit to speak to me through the keys. As he played the final few notes and rested his hands in his lap I noticed that I was holding my breath.

I stood up and walked over to the piano. Peter looked up at me and smiled, uncertain of my reaction.

'Give me your right hand.' My voice was gentle and soft, but my tone left no doubt that I expected to be obeyed. Peter gave me his hand, palm upwards. I received it in the cup of my own left palm, supporting its weight. With my right index finger I traced the outline of his hand. I turned it over, examining it from all angles.

'It's hard to believe that just flesh and blood and bone and sinew can create such beauty.'

Peter smiled his thanks then stood up and led me back over to the sofa. 'You enjoyed my playing?'

'I loved it. You have very talented fingers.'

'And they're versatile too. I also moonlight as a massage therapist.'

'Isn't that just something men say as an excuse to get you naked and oily?'

'No, it's true. Before my playing career took off I earned most of my income that way. You'd be surprised how many musicians have a day job. If you'd like it, I'd be happy to give you a free massage. No strings, strictly professional.' He looked into my eyes and I could see he was being genuine.

'Thanks. I may take you up on that. I get pretty tired sometimes, standing up all day in the shop.' I smiled. Peter topped up my wine glass. 'I really like your flat. It's a lovely space.'

'Yes, I think so too. It's airy and light and, of course, the acoustics are wonderful. But what made me decide to buy it was the garden. It's incredible.'

'What garden? It doesn't have one surely?'

Peter smiled and nodded. 'It's got a very original garden. A very special one. Would you like to see?'

'Why not? I'm intrigued.'

Peter got up and held out his hand to me. I took his hand and he led me across the flat to the front door. He put it on the latch and led me down the corridor outside. At the end of the passage there was a door leading to the roof.

'Do you like it? It used to be the school playground.'

I looked around the roof garden. There was a paved area with pots and troughs full of flowers and a tinkling water feature. To one side, there was a seating area with wooden benches and tables and a barbecue. The garden's perimeter was defined by iron railings. At intervals of about six feet, there was a taller railing which terminated in a spectacular decorated finial. Each pointed tip was surrounded by a complicated cage of wrought iron like a crown.

Peter led me over to the edge of the roof to see the view. The city was spread out like a stage set. The green swathe of Hampstead Heath nestled between the buildings. White headlamps and red tail lights made the roads seem like moving ribbons. In the distance, the skyscrapers of the city rose into the air like modern cathedrals.

It was just growing dusk. The sky was a deep, mysterious blue. I could hear the rumble of traffic. I could feel the breeze on my face. It ruffled my hair. I brushed against one of the pots and the air was instantly filled with the scent of lavender.

I turned to Peter. 'This is beautiful. Breathtaking. Especially at this time of night. It's almost magical.'

Peter nodded. 'You see why I had to buy the flat now. I moved in the week before the millennium. On New Year's Eve I came up here at midnight and watched the fireworks go off. It was an experience I'll never forget.'

I could see the passion and intensity burning in his eyes. He leant against the railing with both hands and looked at the sky. His hair gleamed in the light coming up through the open door. His eyes sparkled. I put my hand on his arm and he turned to look at me. He smiled.

I leant forwards and kissed him, gently. His mouth was soft and warm. He cupped the back of my head in his palm and his other hand stroked my back. I shivered all over.

'It's getting cold. Let's go downstairs.' Peter's voice was soft and tender, his mouth pressed up against my ear.

Downstairs, Peter poured us each another glass of wine. I was feeling pretty relaxed by this time. He was easy to be with: gently amusing and undemanding yet absolutely compelling. As we talked, I noticed he never took his eyes off my face. I stared back, more boldly than I normally would, I admit, but he was making his feelings so clear there didn't seem any point being coy.

I noticed that he had very long, pale lashes and his eyes were an almost lavender blue. He had a way of unconsciously running his tapered fingers through his hair as he talked and I found it totally bewitching. But it was his hands that fascinated me most. Years of piano playing had made them strong and dextrous. He'd obviously spent a lot of time in the sun and the skin on his hands and arms was tanned to a pale golden colour. I could see the muscles and tendons standing out in his forearms and his biceps were nicely shaped: muscular but not over developed. They stretched the sleeves of his white T-shirt ever so slightly and, for some reason, this made me feel protective towards him and in awe of his strength at the same time.

He must have noticed me staring at him because he began to gaze quite openly at my chest and, when I leant forwards to pick up my wine, made a point of trying to look down my front. But it was playful and teasing rather than sleazy; as if he was telling me he found me attractive but was to much of a gentleman to take things further without an invitation.

'That's the third time you've done that, Tess. Does your neck hurt?'

'Done what?'

'You keep rubbing your neck and rolling your head from side to side as if you're in pain.' He demonstrated.

'Yes, I suppose it does ache a bit. It's been a long day and my assistant wasn't in this morning so I had to unload the van all by myself. But it's nothing. I'm sure I'll be all right after a good night's sleep.'

Peter got up and stood behind me. He laid his hands on my shoulders. His palms were warm and heavy. A little shiver of pleasure slid up my spine.

'I'll bet you've had it a while. You've got a way of holding your head on one side, did you know that?'

His hands felt heavenly. I closed my eyes.

'No, I didn't. Maybe you're right. I think I'm just used to it.' His fingers began to knead the muscles of my shoulders. I let out a long, low moan. 'You have magic hands.'

Peter laughed. 'I really am a massage therapist, you know. I'm not just spinning you a line. I used to make a very decent living at it.' His fingers located a sore spot and massaged it.

'Mmmm, that's heavenly. I don't suppose you'd give me a freebie, would you?'

'These days I mostly operate on a barter system.'

'That's very practical, I must say. What would you want in return?'

'I'll leave that up to you. I'm sure you'll find a way of reciprocating.'

'As it happens, I give great reciprocation.'

He leant forwards, cupped my face with both hands and stroked my cheeks with his thumbs.

'I don't doubt it.' He looked up into my eyes.

'But, there's only one problem . . .'

'Yes?'

'You don't appear to have a bed.'

He laughed. 'It's on the mezzanine floor. You have to climb up the ladder.' He pointed.

'It's a long time since I climbed up a ladder to go to bed. Not since my sister and I had bunk beds.'

'You get used to it.' He took my hand and led me over

to the ladder. 'Do you want to go first? I'll come up behind you and make sure you don't fall.'

'You can't fool me, you just want to look at my arse.'

'Not just to look. I intend to involve all five of my senses.'

Peter's bed was a futon laid directly on the floor. There was a fluffy white quilt and, a low cupboard at one side of the bed bore a candle, a digital clock and a small CD player. The wall opposite the bed concealed built-in wardrobes behind a panel of mirrors.

'It's nice up here. Sort of peaceful and detached from the rest of the world, somehow. Do you know what I mean?'

Peter nodded. 'I love it, I must admit. It's a very special space.' He stroked my cheek. 'Would you mind if I undressed you now?'

'Is that included in the price?'

'Not officially. In fact, when I was getting paid for it, it tended to be frowned upon. But I'd enjoy it. If you don't mind.' He gazed at me, his eyes shining with need.

'I'm putting myself entirely in your capable hands.'

He untucked my shirt and unbuttoned it with trembling fingers.

'No bra. Now that's a pleasant surprise.' He cupped my breasts and stroked my nipples with his thumbs. They hardened under his touch. His breathing was rapid and loud.

He unzipped my jeans and slid them down.

'And no knickers, either. You're full of surprises.' He got to his knees and pulled my jeans down to my ankles and I stepped out of them. He used his fingertips to trace the curve of my thighs. His fingers moved slowly, exploring every millimetre. His touch was light; his fingers barely brushed my skin. His fingertips were soft and warm. They made me tingle.

He trailed his nails over my buttocks. I shivered all over. He pressed his face against my crotch and inhaled, drinking in my scent. I arched my back and moaned softly.

'Lie down and I'll get my stuff together.'

I lay down on my stomach in the centre of the bed. I felt my body sink into the fluffy white duvet. Peter trotted quietly around the bedroom lighting candles and gathering together the oils he needed for the massage. He selected a disc, slipped it into the CD player and turned it down low. As it began to play I instantly recognised Miles Davis's mellow trumpet.

I relaxed against the bed. I could hear my own breathing, the music and Peter moving quietly around the room. I could hear the ticking clock and, somewhere, in the distance, a police siren.

'I'm just going to get undressed and then I'll be right with you.'

'I didn't realise we both needed to be naked, Peter.' My voice was a husky whisper. 'When I have a massage at the health club, the masseur doesn't undress as well.'

'I haven't got my special white jacket on. I'd get my clothes covered in oil if I kept them on. I'm only concerned about the laundry bills, that's all.' He sat down on the bed beside me and rested an oiled hand on the small of my back. I loved the weight of it, the firm pressure of it against my spine. Peter's skin felt smooth and warm. I closed my eyes and sighed deeply, concentrating on the sensations of his expert hands on my skin.

Peter's fingers slid down my spine in a long, slow *glissando*. I gasped. He massaged the muscles of my back with long, smooth strokes. His hands moved over my skin with the same confidence and accuracy that he had used on the piano.

With gentle pressure he teased out the knots of tension and soothed them away. His strong fingers worked my stiff shoulders. I felt myself loosening, my muscles softening, the anxiety and pressure of the day dissolving.

He alternated the pressure of fingers: sometimes using just the tips in a teasing *pianissimo* and sometimes putting the weight of his shoulders behind it in a satisfying *fortissimo* that made me gasp in appreciation.

I was drifting away, somewhere on the margin between sleep and consciousness. It was heavenly. The rhythm of Peter's hands on my body, the quiet repetition of the music and the wine I had drunk earlier all combined in a delicious sensation of contentment. I surrendered to it, letting out a soft purr of breath from my throat.

Peter's hands were never still. He played fluttering *arpeggios* along my vertebrae. He tantalised me with deep, slow strokes down the length of my back. I felt the tension building in the base of my belly. I was tingling all over. His hands moved constantly, sliding over the slippery skin. On the downstrokes he slid his palms along my sides, causing his fingers to gently brush the outer curve of my breasts. The slow, sensual caress made me tingle all over.

Peter moved his attention to my lower back and buttocks. He moved each hand in a circular motion up my buttocks towards my back, then down again over my hips. Soon his fingers started to stray along the cleft between my cheeks. On each upstroke he trailed an oiled finger up the crack of my bottom, lingering momentarily over my puckered opening.

I sighed. Peter's fingers began stroking the length of my pussy before swooping upwards and teasing my nether hole. I felt moisture welling inside me and combining with the oil on Peter's probing fingers. My breathing quickened and I unconsciously raised my rear end upwards to meet his moving fingers.

Feathery strokes brought me to a pitch of arousal. I wanted the oily hand to concentrate on my swollen clit, to stay there and stroke it firmly until I came, yet I knew I'd enjoy it all the more if I let Peter take control. I felt torn: half of me wanting to beg for fulfilment, half of me wanting to give myself up to Peter's experienced hands.

I wriggled against the bed and let out a soft moan. 'Oh, you're so cruel,' I said.

Peter laughed. He leant forwards and kissed me tenderly on the shoulder.

Gradually, almost imperceptibly, Peter increased the pressure of his fingers. He slid them along my slippery crack, pausing momentarily to circle the hardened bead of my clit. Then he trailed them upwards between the globes of my bottom, teasing me a little by pressing his thumb against the wrinkled opening.

I opened my thighs wider, offering my pussy to him. The moving fingers were concentrating on the area between my legs now, stroking upwards from my clit to my arsehole. Each stroke was a little firmer than the last and I soon felt the familiar sensations of tension and sensitivity which would lead, inevitably, to orgasm. My clit was hard; my bumhole contracted as the slick fingers teased it. I felt Peter's hand slide under my body and cup my mound. His thumb circled my sensitive clit while his other hand slid rhythmically along my cleft, teasing both holes.

A coil of warmth spread out from my groin. My own moisture mingled with the massage oil and made me slick and slippery. Peter's fingers stroked my clit rhythmically and firmly.

Sweat filmed my body. Damp hair clung to my face in

wild tendrils. My eyes fluttered under closed lids. My pulse beat in my throat. My hands clutched handfuls of duvet as Peter fingers coaxed me to a crescendo. I began to moan softly.

I was on the edge now, riding the line between arousal and orgasm. I let out a sharp cry as two of Peter's fingers entered me, quickly followed by two into my arse.

My body began to shudder. I gripped the duvet, my taut body racked with pleasure.

'Peter! Oh, Peter!' I screamed. My thighs quivered. My clit twitched and throbbed under his expert hands. I was coming. Peter pushed his fingers deeper into both my holes, intensifying the delicious sensations.

I never wanted it to end but, gradually, my muscles began to relax. My cunt stopped throbbing and my breathing returned to normal. I wiped my unruly hair away from my forehead and turned to smile at him.

'I bet you got a lot of tips, when you were doing it for a living.'

'I didn't go quite this far in those days. Let's just say that I put in a few extras just for you.' He stroked my back, running the flat of his hand down my spine.

'If I remember correctly, I promised you some reciprocation.'

'Only if you feel like it.'

I pushed Peter back down onto the bed. I rolled on top of him and kissed him. He tasted of wine. I nibbled on his plump lower lip. My nostrils were filled with the scent of arousal. I could feel his heart beating against my chest. I kissed his neck, concentrating on the sensitive spot near the ear. I nibbled. Peter's body stiffened under me. He tilted his hips and pressed his groin against me.

'Patience,' I murmured before moving on to lick the base of his throat. I trailed my tongue over smooth, scented skin. I nuzzled into Peter's hairy armpits, drinking in his essence. I kissed my way across his chest, seeking out a nipple. I teased the hardened bud with the tip of my tongue, barely touching it. I bathed it with saliva then blew on it, causing it to peak and contract even more. Peter let out a low moan.

I loved the way his nipples swelled and reddened when I excited them. I sucked one into my mouth and flicked it with my tongue; feasting on it. I swapped sides and treated the other nipple to the same loving attention.

A red flush of arousal coloured Peter's chest and throat. Sweat made his skin shine. His breathing was thready and rapid. I reached down and started to stroke the length of his torso with my fingertips, feather-light strokes, barely making contact with his sensitised skin. Peter's skin formed into goose pimples in response. I trailed my fingers down his sides. Starting at the armpits, I ran them down as far as the hips, then up again over the belly and chest. I could tell that he ached to have his cock touched. He wriggled his hips, begging to feel my touch. I shook my head.

I continued my exploration of Peter's body. I stroked up and down his chest, my fingers gentle and soft, still barely touching. Gradually I moved nearer and nearer to his hardened nipples. I circled them with my fingertips, knowing how tantalising this must feel. Then I used my thumbs to brush across the swollen buds. Peter moaned with delight.

I slid down his body and positioned myself between his parted legs. Peter was obviously a natural blond. He had a mat of golden pubes which he kept trimmed. His balls were tight with excitement, his scrotum already thickened and taut.

The tip of his cock was wet and glistening. The light

from the candle seemed to make the slippery moisture glow. I inhaled deeply, filling my nostrils with the delicious perfume of man. I used my thumbs to stroke around Peter's balls, then slid down to tease his bumhole.

'Suck me, please,' begged Peter urgently.

I dipped my head and extended my tongue. I pushed it against Peter's helmet and explored him with it. I loved the sensation of my mouth against the silky skin of his cock.

Peter spread his legs wider and thrust his crotch at me.

I tongued his helmet, at the same time fingering his bumhole. Every so often I pushed my fingertip against the sensitive opening. Peter was gasping and writhing beneath me. I knew he wanted me to start sucking him, but I wasn't ready yet. I wanted to work him up to a peak of arousal, make him beg for it.

'Please!' Peter was practically wailing.

I took no notice, but began licking at his helmet. I gripped the base of his cock and squeezed. Peter let out a soft moan and his thighs started to tremble.

'OK,' I said, 'I know what you want.'

I opened my mouth and took him inside. I sucked hard and Peter shivered with delight. I flicked his helmet with my tongue, squirming it into the hole.

The next track on the CD began and I instantly recognised 'My Funny Valentine'. Peter moaned as my mouth made contact. I knew it wouldn't take long for him to come now; he was so aroused. I closed my eyes and relished the sensation of slick, hot cock against my own slippery mouth. I eagerly sucked on his rigid member. His musky man smell filled my nostrils as my nose nuzzled against his pubes. Miles Davis's swooping trumpet solo seemed the perfect soundtrack for this moment. Its dancing cadence somehow seemed to echo the rhythm of arousal, layering and building until the inevitable moment of crescendo.

I sucked hard. Peter started thrashing his limbs and thrust his cock hard into my mouth. I slid my lips up and down his shaft, allowing his cock to fuck my mouth. The trumpet sang urgently.

Peter was moaning and panting now, one hand on the back of my head. I could feel his thigh muscles tensing. I sucked hard, every so often squeezing his cock firmly with my hand. I slid a finger inside his tight arsehole.

The repetitive base beat pounded in rhythm with Peter's excited breathing. His hips rocked to a tempo of their own, grinding his crotch against my eager face. I sucked harder, at the same time circling my finger inside him.

Peter was groaning and mumbling. I felt his thighs trembling, taut with tension. I knew he was close to coming and I quickened the pace and intensity of my sucking. I slid a second finger into his arse and rotated them firmly. The trumpet's restless melody resonated inside me, echoing my own need and Peter's excitement.

My slick lips slid along Peter's shaft. His bottom raised off the bed as he ground his cock against my face.

The song built towards its frenzied, exultant coda. Peter started moaning, shouting almost; meaningless sounds which signalled his orgasm. I held on, struggling to keep my mouth in place as he came. Hot spunk spread over my tongue and I swallowed, relishing its thick saltiness. I sucked hard, coaxing the last aftershocks of orgasm from him as the last note of the song died out.

Finally, Peter stopped shouting and I slid my fingers out of his bum. I placed one last kiss on his cock and rested my head on his belly.

Fifteen minutes later, we had an encore and since

then Peter and I have played plenty of duets together. Sometimes we go for classical, creating symphonies with separate movements and themes, and sometimes we opt for jazz with its raw rhythms and energy. Occasionally, we even do solos, one of us performing while the other plays audience.

A week later I watched him receive a standing ovation after his first performance at Giovanni's. I joined in the applause knowing that I alone would be getting a private performance later on.

The Apprentice Fiona Locke

Master Leighton was right. His apprentice played flaw-lessly after a caning.

Three sharp strokes to the seat of the lad's trousers. No ceremony. Just swift correction for a sour note. And Martin played the piece again. Perfectly.

'Excellent,' said Master Leighton. It was the only time he ever used the word, the only time he ever sounded truly pleased. He wasn't so much praising his apprentice as praising himself for eliciting the impeccable recital.

It was a hard life with Master Leighton, but well worth it. He was the most brilliant violinist in the country and he was extremely selective about his pupils. Strict discipline was a condition of his tutelage, a con-dition that discouraged many less dedicated boys from studying with him. Martin was different.

Alison twisted round in front of the mirror to see her smarting backside. The trousers offered little protection from the sting of the cane. But she was grateful for every stroke. Because she was his apprentice. And Master Leighton did not accept female pupils.

She was eighteen, but her slight build allowed her to pass for a much younger boy. It was no sacrifice to conceal her femininity. Music was her life and anything she had to surrender to pursue it was worth losing. The fact that Master Leighton wouldn't teach girls hadn't dimmed her spirits for a moment. She had simply cropped her hair, borrowed some clothes from her brother and gone to audition for him. That had been eight months ago.

It was difficult in the beginning. Alison worried that he would see through her disguise and send her away in disgrace for trying to deceive him. She fretted about how to walk, how to talk and act like a boy. But with some coaching from her brother she grew confident.

Master Leighton caned his new apprentice on the very first day, ostensibly for some careless error. Alison suspected it was more to establish his authority. She tried to take the punishment bravely, reminding herself with each stroke that she was a boy and boys didn't cry. The caning was painful, but it did not expose her ruse.

Now she no longer had to remind herself not to whimper or cry. Her boyish manners were second nature to her and she accepted her master's correction with the fortitude of any lad.

Alison gently rubbed the vivid tramlines. To her they were badges of honour. They meant she was studying with the genius.

'You're not sawing a tree limb, boy!' Master Leighton would snap, rapping Martin's knuckles sharply with his bow.

He could be tyrannical, forcing his apprentice to practise for hours on end, hammering away at a troublesome musical phrase until it was played to perfection. Eccentric and unpredictable, he was easily offended even by honest mistakes on Martin's part. Indeed, he sometimes seemed capricious, as though looking for any excuse to use the cane, whether it was truly deserved or not.

The rewards were uncountable, though. And when Master Leighton performed, Alison was allowed to sit just offstage and watch, mesmerised, dreaming of the day when she would be the one the audiences flocked to see.

As she crawled into bed, wincing at her bottom's contact with the sheet, Alison pictured her master's handsome face. His features were distinguished – sharply defined and as austere as his manners. But somehow that only made him more appealing. His black looks made her tremble, but they also made her squirm with desire. She cherished his intensity. His harsh criticisms, his severe punishments. She wanted more than anything to please him, to make him proud. Trying to keep her feelings for him under control, she showed as much affection as she dared, as much as would be appropriate from a boy apprentice. But secretly she loved him. And each time he punished her she embraced the pain as proof that he loved her too.

The cane awakened strange feelings in Alison. True, it frightened her. It hurt terribly and made sitting most unwelcome. But it got her attention and it usually corrected what it was meant to. She certainly didn't enjoy it, but neither did she resent it.

Master Leighton was uncompromising. He made every stroke count and her bottom always throbbed and burnt afterwards. But when the pain began to fade to a warm glow she felt her heart swell with even more affection for the man who had inflicted it. There was a strange comfort in submitting to his discipline.

Alison snuggled down in bed, pulling the blankets up to her chin. She sighed with contentment as she replayed the caning in her mind. She had obediently assumed the position he had taught his apprentice that first day: standing three feet back from the door, bending forwards with her feet together and her hands braced on either side of the doorway, back arched and bottom presented.

Master Leighton rarely told his apprentice how many strokes he was going to administer and the suspense was both awful and heady. She clutched the architrave, her knuckles white, counting in her head and wondering if another stroke was coming.

With a deeper sigh, Alison turned onto her side, reaching behind her to savour the heat in her bottom. She had sometimes been tempted to make some minor mistake to earn punishment, but she never got up the courage. The guilty, naughty thrill of the thought was enough to make her tingle, though, and she squeezed her legs together, trying to banish the fantasies.

He must never learn the truth. It was sometimes agonising, and Alison longed to tell him who she was. She wanted to show him the proof that girls could play as well as boys. But she didn't dare raise the subject. If he should even begin to suspect . . .

Master Leighton drew his fingers along the polished surface of the violin, admiring its construction. The instrument was like a dancer. To the eye it seemed delicate and fragile, yet it had power beyond its appearance. Its graceful lines and feminine curves were deceptive, as it could only truly be mastered in the hands of a man.

Martin was like the instrument – soft, lissom, light. The boy's voice showed no sign of changing, though he was well beyond the age when it should have done. He was moody and tender-hearted. Indeed, the music often brought tears to the lad's eyes.

Master Leighton's suspicions had been growing for several weeks, but he kept returning to the one undeniable reality: the boy was a prodigy. No girl could possibly play so well.

And yet . . .

Martin's features were androgynous. He had wide brown eyes that peered out from under long lashes. His complexion was fair, with no trace of facial hair. Long, shapely fingers gripped the fingerboard of the violin and there was a feline grace in his bowing. And music easily stirred him to emotion.

One could certainly never doubt the lad's pluck under the cane. Master Leighton had reduced boys to tears before, but Martin never cried. He took his punishment and was invariably better for it. He was far more likely to become tearful over a string of haunting minor chords than over a flogging.

The master shook his head. It couldn't be true. But the more he pondered it, the more he began to see all the little clues.

It would make perfect sense, of course. He was actually surprised no one had tried it before. Martin was the best pupil he'd ever had. There had never been another so diligent, so committed, so *passionate* about music. Was it possible that was because he had more to prove?

The more he thought about it, the more certain he became. Martin was a girl. But how could he make sure? He had no intention of dismissing the apprentice. Boy or no, Martin had a gift. There was no one who could nurture and refine that gift more than Master Leighton. And, if he was to be completely honest, he was fond of the lad. But it was time to end the charade.

As he looked through the sheet music for the next day's lesson an idea came to him. He didn't enjoy having to punish his pupils. He regarded it as a duty. But if he *was* right about Martin's secret, the idea wasn't entirely unappealing. After all, if the boy really was a girl, she certainly deserved a thrashing for deceiving him.

It surprised him that he wasn't really angry. On the contrary, he was as impressed by the girl's audacity as he was by her talent. But he intended to humble her for it.

He put away the music he had planned to use the next day. It would have challenged Martin, but not as much as what he now had in mind.

He searched through his library for the right piece, weighing Martin's talent and skill against each one. He wanted something difficult, something just beyond his apprentice's abilities. Enough to frighten and frustrate even a seasoned player.

When he found the piece he was looking for he dusted it off. It was a concerto he had underestimated himself when he was a pupil. Its complexity belied the apparent simplicity of the notes on paper. Martin – whatever her real name was – had a rigorous lesson ahead of him. Her.

'Again,' Master Leighton said harshly. 'You insult the composer when you play it like that.'

Alison stared at the music, taken aback by its intricacy. Her master had always told her that no composer exposed the amateur more than Mozart. His music demanded perfection. Nothing less would suffice.

With unsteady hands she began again. Master Leighton stopped her after three measures.

'No, no, no! Like this.' And he played the first movement himself.

Alison was always enchanted by his playing and she could easily lose herself in it. This time, however, she watched him attentively, studying his fingers and trying not to let her emotions distract her. It was impossible. Every colour and nuance filled her with longing as her master teased hidden melodies out of the concerto.

Alison marvelled that he thought his apprentice was ready for such a composition. It was more advanced than anything he'd set her before and she didn't know whether to be honoured or terrified. One thing was certain: she didn't dare tell him it was too difficult. She'd made that mistake once. It was the hardest caning he'd ever given her.

'Now play it again.'

Taking a deep breath, she obeyed, loathing the hesitance in her rendering. She couldn't help it, though. Each time she stumbled over a phrase or altered the tempo her master winced as though she was causing him pain.

'I'm sorry, sir,' she said. 'It's much harder than it looks.'

'I know that. It's not a piece that suffers show-offs.'

She gasped. 'But, sir, I'm not –'

'Are you answering me back?'

'No, sir.'

His features relaxed into an indulgent smile as he patted her shoulder. 'No, you're not a show-off, Martin, but you do sometimes forget that you are the servant of the music and not its master.'

Alison lowered her head, embarrassed. 'Yes, sir.'

'This piece is about melody, not technical precision, though you need the one to showcase the other.'

'Yes, sir.' Bewildered, Alison stared again at the music. Sometimes, after practising for hours, the notes would swirl into meaningless black smears as though someone had spilled ink all over the pages. These notes looked like that now. How was she ever going to master them as their poor, confounded servant?

Master Leighton rose and retrieved his coat. 'I have to go into town for a little while. Practise the concerto while I'm gone. You will play it for me when I return.'

'Yes, sir.'

When he had gone Alison played it through without stopping. It sounded ghastly and dissonant with her myriad mistakes, but she forced herself to stay with it until the end. Then she started again. It was the best way to conquer her fear of it, to show it that she wasn't going to capitulate halfway through because of a wrong note. The concerto was filled with lively little *arpeggios* and tricky phrasing. She could almost believe the music didn't want her to play it. In fact, if she hadn't heard Master Leighton play it himself, she might have doubted whether it was even playable at all. A sadistic composer, was Mozart.

After forcing her way through it five times she allowed herself a small break. Nearly an hour had passed. Now that she was a little more familiar with the music she was ready to focus on it in more detail. Without her master standing over her it was tempting to skip over the easy passages and run straight to the difficult ones, learning them with more care and diligence. She resisted the urge. In his overcritical mood Master Leighton was likely to hear it in her playing and accuse her of showing off.

As she worked her way through the music she listened to the virtuoso inside her head. She could almost tune out the hash she was making with her hands and focus instead on the memory of her master's exquisite performance. Hearing him play so beautifully made her forget how strict he was, how fond of the cane. It seemed incongruous to her that such a hard taskmaster should be capable of such artistry. But the contradiction was intoxicating. His hands were soft and considered with the instrument, yet so rough with his apprentice. She couldn't help wondering how they might be with a lover. How they might feel caressing her delicate, downy limbs, enfolding her in a passionate embrace . . .

Alison shook herself out of the daydream. If Master Leighton came home and caught her staring off into space he'd make his displeasure known. And felt. With a sigh, she lifted the violin to her chin and began to play.

* * *

Her master had been gone nearly four hours and Alison was still struggling with the music. She didn't dare stop playing. It was another of his favourite tests. The violin could be heard all the way down the street, so there was no way she could take a break and simply wait until he drew near to start playing again.

At last she heard the door and she wilted with relief. Master Leighton came in, waving a hand for her to stop. 'From the beginning,' he said, taking his seat in front of her.

Too tired to be nervous any more, she started over, dreading every note. She didn't dare look up at her master; she knew she wouldn't be able to bear any expression of disdain. He allowed her to play the *allegro* straight through and she grew confident when he didn't stop her. At last she finished. She lowered the violin and bow with shaky hands, turning to him in the hope of finding approval in his features.

Instead, he looked at her inscrutably. 'Have you *been* practising?' he asked. 'Or just staring at the music?'

Alison's mouth fell open. 'I haven't stopped playing since you left, sir,' she said, baffled.

'Then perhaps you need another four hours.'

She stared at him in disbelief, not knowing what to say. Couldn't he see that she'd been working hard? Couldn't he *hear*? 'It's a difficult piece, sir,' she said weakly. 'I just need more time.'

'Then you shall have it.' Master Leighton rose from his seat, deliberately. 'I'm going back out. While I'm away you will learn this piece. You will practise until I return and I don't care if your fingers fall off, boy. Then I expect to hear you play it properly.' He left the threat unspoken.

Alison hung her head. 'Yes, sir.'

'I can only think your mind is somewhere other than on your studies.'

Miserable, Alison assured him that she was as dedicated as he could hope.

'We'll see about that,' he replied. And with that, he left again.

Alison blinked back her tears and looked at the clock. It was nearly two and she hadn't eaten. Her stomach was complaining and her hands would begin to shake if she didn't eat something.

'No,' she told herself disgustedly. If something as trivial as hunger could distract her, then she wasn't focused enough. She'd actually known her master to *forget* to eat. And it was only when she suggested it to him that he realised he was hungry at all.

Armed with fierce determination to prove herself to Master Leighton, the apprentice took a deep breath and began the concerto again.

It was another four hours before Alison allowed herself a break. She was exhausted. Her neck was stiff and her wrists and fingers ached in a way they hadn't since her first gruelling day of apprenticeship. She had a permanent bruise from the chin rest, but the unremitting practice had deepened it so that the slightest pressure was agony. She couldn't believe the violin strings hadn't cut through her fingers. The deep grooves burnt and tingled from the pressure of the fingerboard. But for all that, she'd forgotten her hunger.

She was beginning to wonder if her master would ever return. She went to the window and peered down the street. There was no sign of him.

A sudden, terrible thought seized her like an intruder's hand. What if something had happened to him? Tears sprang to her eyes at once and she swallowed her panic, trying to calm herself. It wasn't unusual for him to disappear for hours at a time. No doubt he needed his space from her. She didn't suppose that the company of his apprentice was as captivating as that of his acquaintances in town.

Or lady friends.

The image was unbidden and unwelcome, but once seen, it couldn't be unseen. It had never occurred to her before. She had always taken it for granted that he was too consumed with music to have time for a relationship. But now Alison was forced to confront the possibility. Was he off amusing himself with some exotic creature while his poor apprentice slaved away in his absence?

Alison tried to resume her practice, but the feelings wouldn't dissipate. She couldn't banish the thought of her master in the arms of an alluring paramour, laughing and enjoying her stimulating company. Her playing suffered for the preoccupation. Frustrated tears were beginning to sting her eyes when she finally heard the door.

At first she didn't know whether she was relieved that he was unharmed or angry that he'd deigned to return from his tryst. She looked up at him, weary and confused. He didn't notice.

'All right, let's hear it, lad,' he said without preamble. He sat in front of her and crossed his arms expectantly.

Alison couldn't read anything in his tone or his expression to tell her if her suspicions were true. Resentfully, she played the *allegro* for him. In her own eyes her performance had all the colour and passion of dishwater, though she hadn't missed a single note. A hollow victory, she thought bitterly.

Master Leighton stared at her for a long time, his brow furrowed, as though trying to puzzle out the change in his apprentice. He seemed to be searching for something to say.

'I didn't miss a note, sir,' Alison supplied, making no attempt to disguise her bitterness.

Her provocative tone made his eyes flash and he straightened in his chair. 'Indeed you didn't,' he agreed. 'But I doubt if that would have impressed Mozart.'

Alison lifted her chin a little at this slight. She ground her teeth to keep from responding in kind. She was frightened by the intensity of her feelings. She knew better than to cross swords with him, but she feared things were about to come to a head.

'You will therefore play it again,' he continued. 'And you will keep playing it until I'm satisfied. You will not be dismissed until then. Do you understand? My master set me this piece when I was your age and I had to play it over and over until I got it right.'

It was too much. All the confused emotions that had been simmering below the surface erupted in a flash of fury. 'Your master was as much of a sadist as you are, then!' she snarled, lashing out at the music stand with her foot. It fell with a clatter on the floor, scattering the sheet music. The pages fluttered around them and drifted to the floor with a loud papery flapping as Alison realised what she'd done.

Master Leighton was staring at her and she thought there was something triumphant in his eyes.

Several seconds passed in excruciating silence while she watched him, terrified.

At last he spoke. 'Right.' It was just one word, but the cold and precise way he enunciated it made her shudder.

Now she was for it. He'd once given his apprentice a dozen strokes just for questioning him; this outburst had to be worth three times that.

'Fetch the cane.'

It was amazing, the way those simple words could

make her regret so much. The stress of the demanding practice had made her reckless and insolent. And jealous. Who was she to question her master or make assumptions about him?

Hanging her head in shame, she brought him the cane as she'd done so many times before. He nodded towards the door and she went there, her feet dragging.

'I've clearly been too lenient with you,' said Master Leighton. 'I've allowed you the protection of your trousers whenever I've caned you. But in showing me such blatant disrespect you've lost that privilege. Take them off.'

Alison's eyes were wide with horror. Oh, what had she done? If he caned her without her trousers he'd uncover her deception. Then he would turn her out.

'I'm waiting.'

Alison had no choice but to do as he said, silently praying that he would let her leave her underpants on. Their scant cover would offer no protection from the cane, but they would keep her secret. Perhaps Master Leighton wouldn't notice anything amiss.

With great reluctance, she unfastened her trousers and pulled them down, slipping them off. The air in the room was hot and dusty; nonetheless, it chilled her as it touched her bare legs. She felt more exposed than she ever had before. Blinking back tears, she leant forwards to take hold of the door frame, pressing her legs tightly together.

She heard his step on the wooden floor behind her and she gritted her teeth, expecting the first stroke. Instead, she felt his fingers in the waistband of her underpants. Before she could draw a breath to protest, he had yanked them down to her ankles.

Alison froze. She waited for him to denounce her. Instead, she heard the low whistle of the cane as he sliced it through the air in preparation, making her jump. He hadn't seen anything.

Mustering all her willpower, Alison locked her legs and rooted her feet tightly to the floor. Maybe if she was perfectly still, if she didn't twist or squirm too much . . .

Master Leighton was behind her. 'Now then,' he said. 'Let's see if we can teach you some respect.'

Alison had never felt the cane on her bare skin before and she flinched at the cold length of it against her flesh. She uttered a little squeak, but kept her knees and ankles pressed together as tightly as she could. The cane tapped gently, each tap getting harder and harder, leading up to the first stroke. Her master didn't usually draw it out like this. He believed in summary punishment with no frills. But she had really angered him this time.

She held her breath as the cane drew back and struck her with a meaty smack. Hard. She gasped, but stayed in position as the pain began to flower in a savage line across her bottom. She never thought her trousers afforded her much protection, but feeling the cane without them as a barrier, she realised just how wrong she'd been.

Again the cane rose and fell, cleaving the air and then her backside. Alison hissed through her teeth, but focused all her energy on preserving her secret. If she could survive this, she'd never give him cause to cane her again. Then he would never know she was really a girl.

The caning grew more intense with each stroke and, while she managed to keep her legs straight and together, she was unable to keep from crying out. That wouldn't give her away, though; any boy would yelp from such a caning.

When Master Leighton stopped she released the breath she'd been holding. He occasionally paused in the middle of a severe caning. She never knew whether it was over or whether he was deciding how much more she deserved. This time she didn't dare to hope that he would stop there.

He stood directly behind her, inspecting the damage. She heard the creak of the floorboards as he crouched down to look more closely.

Suddenly, there was the cool touch of his finger as he traced the weals left by the cane. Alison shuddered. She could feel his breath on the backs of her legs.

'Mm-hmm,' was his only response.

He stood up again.

'You know what comes next, boy,' he said. 'Feet apart.'

This was a command she'd always dreaded, even with her trousers on, because of the way it tautened the fabric across her backside and opened up new areas for the attack of the cane. Now she dreaded it for an entirely different reason. She opened her mouth and turned her head to plead with him, but he cut her off.

'Feet apart.'

Well, this was it. He would see now. She inched her feet apart and waited for him to discover the truth.

Instead, the cane sliced into her again. And again. And again. He didn't allow much time between the strokes and she barely had time to recover from one before the next fell. Each one hurt terribly, but the torment of knowing that any second he would learn the truth was far worse than the pain.

'Wider,' he said gruffly.

The inevitability was agony. How could he not see? Could he possibly be so focused on her bottom that he just didn't notice? As a girl Alison was very pretty. And unclothed, it was inconceivable that he couldn't tell. Her plump bottom, shapely legs and girlish figure should have been apparent long before now, not to mention the obvious. But no. The cane continued to do its worst while she yelped and cried under it.

She had lost count of the strokes. It was well over a dozen, possibly even two. She was dazed. As much by confusion as by pain. So dazed, in fact, that she didn't even realise when he stopped.

Master Leighton was silent for a long time.

Alison's heart sank. It was over. He'd seen. Tears streamed down her face. She refused to make a sound, though. She wouldn't disgrace herself any further with hiccupping, childish sobs.

She clung to the architrave as though letting go of it would also mean letting go of her dignity. The punishment was over. The charade was over. Her life was over. She couldn't move.

The floorboards creaked and she trembled. He was inspecting her again. Not the marks this time, but her sex. No doubt he was shaking his head in disgust over her folly. Reassuring himself that he was right about the inferiority of female musicians. The feeling of exposure was hard to endure, but she dared not move until he instructed her to.

But instead of cursing her and ordering her out, he traced the lines of the cane again. Slowly. Thoroughly. As though savouring each one. Alison shivered in spite of herself. So many times she had wanted him to touch her like this. Now it was to be the first and the last time.

But there was something odd about the familiarity in his touch. It was soothing and gentle. Not the touch of a master examining his punished pupil at all. It was the touch of a lover. The finger trailed over her burning flesh, coming to rest in the centre, near her bottom crease. Then, one by one the pads of the other fingers descended until his entire palm rested lightly on her bottom.

Alison was afraid to breathe. One breath could disrupt the stillness she never wanted to end.

The hand patted her and then continued down to the cleft between her cheeks.

She closed her eyes.

Then the hand cupped her firmly between the legs and gave a little squeeze.

A jolt surged through her at his touch.

The hand between her legs told her more than words ever could. She gripped the doorway, arching her back into the sensation. Her legs felt as though they would give way beneath her. The warmth in her bottom spread through her body, unfolding like scrolls.

Her master softly smacked the insides of her thighs with his fingertips, urging her legs further apart.

Blushing, Alison obeyed, painfully aware of the dampness between them.

He stroked her softness, drawing his fingers across the little slit as though teasing music from it with his bow. He smoothed the moist folds and drew closer to her.

He took away his hand and she tensed. Then she felt his own arousal as he pressed himself against her sore bottom.

Her knees threatened to buckle and he took hold of her wrists and prised her from the doorway. She sank into his arms and he turned her around to face him. She couldn't meet his eyes. He didn't force her to. With a sigh she let herself go as he unbuttoned and unlaced her boy's clothes and led her to his room. He guided her to the bed and she sat down, wincing at the freshly awakened discomfort in her bottom.

Master Leighton smiled. He pushed her down on her back and she looked up at him for the first time since the caning. In place of his usual temperamental scowl there was a tender expression she had never seen before.

Then he kissed her, pressing his mouth into hers with firm, gentle force. He cupped her small breasts, squeezing them gently, tweaking her nipples until they stiffened.

Her body surrendered as his hands explored her, acquainting him with her femininity. She wrapped her legs around him, urging him closer, tighter. He moulded her curves to his angles as he took possession, driving himself deeply into her wetness. The roughness of the bed beneath her punished flesh wrenched a muffled yelp from her. But she absorbed the rising notes of pain, grinding her hips into him greedily. Her mentor, her master.

She was unprepared for the sudden spasms of pleasure that consumed her, overlapping like the notes of a swirling symphony. He clutched her tightly, urgently, as he filled her with the hot jets of his own climax.

Satiated and spent, she panted for breath, her head resounding with the music of release.

After a languorous, breathless silence he smoothed a damp lock of hair away from her forehead and kissed her there. He was smiling. 'What's your name?' he asked.

She flushed. 'Alison, sir.'

He repeated the name, as though tasting a new wine. 'Alison. You are as lovely as your playing.'

They were words the long-suffering apprentice had never dreamt she would hear from him. Tears shone in her eyes. 'Thank you, sir,' she whispered.

He chuckled. 'I don't think it's necessary for you to call me "sir" any longer.'

Alison turned on her side and reached back to touch her tender bottom, to reawaken the sting. The pleasure was so much sweeter for the harmony with pain. 'I know,' she said. 'Sir.'

The Harp Monica Belle

'You play well, I've not heard any man play harp music half so sweet. Not outside of Ireland.'

He'd sat down opposite me as he spoke, placing a glass and a bottle in front of him. I smiled, unsure if I wanted him to go away or pay me another compliment on my playing. He didn't speak again, his full concentration devoted to pouring the stout he'd bought from bottle to glass. I couldn't help but feel a bit put out at having a complete stranger sit down with me, and I suppose that's what brought out my awkward streak.

'Surely, even if we allow that Ireland produces the best harpists, which I don't, then they'd play just as well here in London, or in Timbuktu for that matter.'

After a moment to ensure that the very last drop of beer was in his glass he looked up to reply. 'Now that's where you're wrong, and I'd have thought you'd understand this, you being a musician. You can have all the talent in the world, but it's nothing unless you have the soul to make your music speak, and it'll never speak so clear as when you're in your home country. Now I'm biased, being born and bred in Dalkey, which is south of Dublin if you didn't know, but if you think you'd be the equal of an Irish harpist, playing in an Irish town, I'd put a thousand pounds on the table to say you'd not, and you can name your jury.'

For a moment it occurred to me that he might be trying to con me into taking some elaborate bet, which I would inevitably lose, and I was going to tell him I wasn't quite as stupid as he thought, but after a swallow of beer he went on.

'Do you know where the oldest harp in the world is?'

'I think there are some from Egyptian tombs.'

'I mean a Gaelic harp, the *cláirseach*.'

'There's the famous one at Trinity College, which is fifteenth century, I think.'

'Wrong, by the best part of a thousand years. The oldest Gaelic harp is that Guaire Aidni Colmin, King of Connaught, ordered to be made for his bard, Seanchan, who was at the time *Ard-Filé*, or chief poet of Ireland.'

'And this still exists? In what condition?'

'As good as the day it was made.'

'Where?'

'Kinvara, where it's always been, in the crypt beneath St Coman's church. I'll give you the full story, if you'll keep my glass full.'

I'd been expecting something of the sort, but it seemed a fair exchange, even if what he was saying clearly needed to be taken with a large pinch of salt. At the bar I secured four bottles of the stout he was drinking and lined them up in file on our table, which put a grin on his face. I'd had my own glass filled and sat down to listen, telling myself there were worse ways I could pass the rest of the evening until my lift arrived.

'What you need to know is the character of Seanchan. He was a jealous man, very proud and very jealous. It wasn't enough that he was *Ard-Filé*, he needed everybody to know it, and to prove it over again. For that reason, every third year he would call an *eisteddfod*, to show that nobody could compete beside him. So it went, until one year a girl arrived to compete, nobody knew where from, or who her folk were. Nathaira, she was called, and her hair was as pale as sea foam and her beauty as delicate and as fresh as the rain.'

He stopped to refill his glass, leaving me to build up the vision of pale beauty he had drawn in my head. Only when he'd refreshed himself did he continue, now sat back in his chair, completely at ease.

'She played, this girl, she played on Seanchan's own harp, which was stringed with silver, and she played well enough to move King Guaire to tears and his nobles with him. Even Seanchan was moved, for no man could resist the sounds she drew from that harp, not for one minute. And when she was done she sat aside, speaking no word to anybody, and Seanchan came to his harp.

'Now whether it's true that the instrument was bewitched by her, or that she'd bewitched the king and his nobles, or if she was the better player pure and simple, or if it was just that some of the nobles thought it was worth buttering her bread, if you follow my meaning, nobody can tell us. What I can tell is that King Guaire and all the others who were judges said she was the better, and that she took the prize, a purse of gold put up by Seanchan himself as he thought he'd never be beat.'

Again he paused to drink. When he'd finished, he leant forwards across the table and went on.

'You can well imagine Seanchan would be angry, being the man he was, and you'd be right. He flew into such a rage he was chewing the rushes on the floor, and spitting curses, for a while at least, until he took off swearing that if they preferred her music they could have it and welcome, but he'd not be back until she was gone. Now that would have been a fine thing, you'd have thought, to be rid of the miserable bastard and have a pretty girl in his place, but not all of them that were there thought that, and least of all the witch Aoife, who loved Seanchan, and perhaps wasn't best pleased at all the attention Nathaira was getting from the men folk.

'So in the night she made a great curse, Aoife did, and when the folk came into the hall the next morning Nathaira was gone, but where the pillar of the harp had been a plain curve of stone when she played it, now it was fashioned in the form of a young woman, which is what Aoife had done to her, bound her to the harp, and which is why sometimes today the pillar of a harp is shaped as a woman's body.'

He took another long drink, emptying his glass before he set it down, then went on.

'And that's the long and the short of it, except that the local priest took charge of the harp, and because it was witch's work, he walled it up in the crypt under St Coman's. There she remains, poor beautiful Nathaira, until the day somebody plays her harp better than she did that night, or so it's told.'

A man had come in the door and was looking around, presumably the driver come to collect myself and my harp. My companion had once more begun the methodical process of pouring out a bottle of stout, but spoke again as I rose to go.

'I'm not done, not quite.'

'Sorry, I have to go, that's my cab, but thank you very much, and enjoy your beer.'

I left, sure he'd spun me a cock-and-bull story but quite happy with the bargain.

Over the next couple of years I thought of the conversation we'd had quite often, although more what he'd said at first than his story. In a sense he was right, in that familiar surroundings and an appreciative audience make it easier to play, but I wasn't prepared to accept that not being Irish, or even Celtic, put a limit to my abilities. I'd be the first to admit that Bromley isn't the most romantic place on earth, but music is innate in the individual, not where they come from.

He wasn't the only person to make the same assertion either. I heard it often enough at recitals, and more often at competitions, always delivered with that same infuriating mixture of certainty and condescension, as if it hardly needed to be said, as if they expected me to accept it as a limitation I could never hope to overcome, like only having ten fingers to play with. That drove me to practise longer hours, to learn every nuance of my art, to read every book and speak to every fellow harpist. I even ordered a custom-made instrument, hand carved from a single block of willow and strung with brass in the ancient style.

I felt driven to try my hand in Ireland, but didn't dare for fear his words would be proved right. Only when I placed third in Builth Wells and couldn't understand a word the jury was saying did I begin to think I might really be good enough. The woman who won was beautiful too, and very pale, with an ethereal quality to her face, which reminded me of the story for all that her hair was flame red rather than pale. That night I decided to go.

My Irish debut was at the Ormond Hotel in Dublin, two days before Bloomsday, so the place was packed with American tourists. They made up over half the audience, and I've seldom had such appreciation. There was no prize to be taken, but it lifted my spirits, and secured me an invitation to compete in Galway City a fortnight later.

I came to Galway City with rain driving in off the Atlantic, but in the morning the land was fresh and green, with every surface and every blade of grass sparkling wet. My hotel was on the promenade, looking out over the sea, with the hills rising across the bay against a sky of the clearest eggshell blue I had ever seen. Only there did I really begin to understand what my companion had meant about the soul of a people being tied to a place, but it only made me the more determined. That night I took the prize.

All through my dreams and when I was awake the next morning the harp music was running through my head: my own and those I'd played against. I knew Kinvara wasn't far, and it seemed as if the music was calling for me to go there. So I went.

I took my lunch in the village pub, where they directed me to St Coman's church. Perhaps it was the second pint I'd taken with my lunch, but as I walked up to the church the sense of place had grown stronger still and I was sure I could really hear harp music, on the very edge of consciousness, and no tune among those from the night before.

I didn't know the church was a ruin. Just three walls still stood, grown thick with ivy and heavy with moss, as were the tumbled blocks in the nave and the fallen tombstones around it. Still I could hear the music, sweet and melancholy at the same time, always on the edge of my senses and yet never loud enough to be sure it was there at all. Never had I known so magical a place, and I sat down among the stones to think, and to try and capture the haunting melodies. The music was ancient, built not on chords but on alternating drones, a version of what has come to be called sleep music, but of fantastic variety and subtlety.

How long I sat entranced I do not know, only that the sun had begun to move down the western sky, striking in among what I had thought were shadows among moss-covered stones, but proved to be the deeper darkness of an opening into the ground. Immediately I remembered what had been said about the crypt and moved forwards to find that a recent fall had unblocked the arch of a tight, spiral staircase, from which the music seemed to rise, stronger than before.

How could I not investigate? The air was cool and still, but there was light, filtering in through ivy-covered fissures to one side, rich and green and dim, so that once I'd felt my way down the stairs I had to stand with my eyes wide to make out the space I had entered. Only slowly did the shapes emerge, and as they did, so my hope rose. There in front of me was a dark mass, at first only vaguely harp shaped, but clearing gradually until I could distinguish sound box and neck, strings and pillar, the last carved into the form of a woman. I had met Nathaira.

She was tiny, little taller than a well-grown child, but clearly a woman, her lithe, delicate body completely naked, with the soft feminine swell of her breasts and belly and thighs captured in exquisite detail, while her face expressed beauty and pain. I could have stared at her forever, but, although she was cold, ancient stone, to have touched would have felt like the grossest of intrusions.

At last I managed to tear my eyes away to investigate the design of the harp. It was ancient, that much was plain, the form classic but simple, the carving on the sound box and neck of a style at once primitive and elegant. There were 22 strings, as I would have expected, but they were silver, not brass, and so had stood the corrosion of time, blackened but still taut.

I could no more not have played that instrument than will my heart to stop beating, but to do so meant taking Nathaira in an embrace, and with that expression of pain and longing on her exquisite face the thought made me start with guilt. For some time I hesitated, trying to tell myself that she was only stone and that I was being foolish, yet unable to push away the sense that I was about to take an unpardonable liberty. I also saw that I was not the first. A great square block of stone had been dragged in front of her to make a player's seat.

With that my resolve grew firmer still, for if one man had held her, why not I? I sat down, but before I could take her in my arms and put my fingers to the strings, I looked into her beautiful stone face and spoke. 'I am sorry, Nathaira, but I must do this. Please understand that it is for the sake of your music.'

I moved close, pulling myself to her until my hands could reach the full width of the harp, which left her tiny pointed breasts pushed hard to my chest and the smooth roundness of her belly against my own. Her face was close to mine as well, against my neck, as if she was nuzzling me, her stone lips touching my bare skin.

The strings were as taut as if they had been set that very morning, and my first touch drew a plaintive note, strangely resonant in the stone sound box, but in perfect concord with the music running through my head. I began to play, my eyes lightly closed, following that same system of drones, clumsily at first, but soon in exact match. Each touch of my fingers became the reflection of what I could hear inside my head, until the two had merged to become one, a sad, sweet music not played or heard for hundreds of years.

From the moment I began to play I was lost, oblivious to all else but the sound of the harp, the feel of the strings and Nathaira's stone body against my flesh. It was as if she was playing with me, somehow making the strings move even as I did, and indeed, it was the curve of her back and thrust of her chest that kept them taut. I began to imagine her as real, held in my arms as

I played, her lips pressed to my neck and her breasts to my chest, seduced by the beauty of my music.

Yet it was her music, not mine, and with that thought I changed my style, adding modern nuances, chords and harmonies, which seemed to flow from my fingers with greater ease than at any recital. My confidence grew, to change the mood from sleep to joy, and as it did I felt sure her lips moved against my skin, a gentle brush like the most timid of kisses, yielding and yet unsure. I closed my eyes tighter still, lost in the dream of beautiful Nathaira making love to me as I played, her body now warm and willing against mine, unable to resist my music as I drew her from cold stone to vital flesh.

The joy of my playing grew greater still as she pressed against me, her breasts now firm yet yielding, her nipples hard, but in arousal. I felt her arms come free, wrapping around my neck as her kisses grew hot and eager, her tiny, sharp teeth nipping at my skin in growing abandon. Her legs came forwards too, first pressing softly to my thighs, then higher, wrapping around my back to bring her body onto my lap, with the heat of her sex directly against my own.

Now she was mine, enslaved to my music, unable to hold back the needs of her body. I responded to her kisses and then allowed my mouth to find her neck and down to the twin mounds of her breasts, suckling on her nipples to make her sigh and shiver against me. She began to speak, her words unintelligible save for an echo of what I'd heard in Wales and Ireland, and yet her meaning clear enough.

I never stopped once, playing as I have never played before, with ever rising passion and at ever greater pace. With every note she grew more eager still. One tiny hand sought out my crotch, fumbling for a moment at my zip before she had me free, hard and proud already. She was urgent, rubbing my stiffness to her sex and moaning with passion into my open mouth as we began to kiss once more. I felt the wet of her sex, and the mouth of her body, seemingly too tight by far, but yielding as every woman does, to take me deep within her.

She cried out as I filled her body, a sound as full of joy as my music. Once again our mouths met in an unrestrained kiss as she began to move on me, her tiny, resilient bottom rising and falling against my lap as she took her pleasure. I began to push back, struggling to concentrate in my rising ecstasy and with her urgent body pushing me away from the harp.

I had to hold her, to feel that silk-smooth skin under my fingers and the softness of her body, and yet I feared my dream would dissolve the instant I stopped playing, until she herself reached out to pull my hand to her back. With that I gave in, abandoning myself to the pleasure of her body. My hands went beneath her, to cup the perfect orbs of her bottom, the spread of my fingers easily encompassing her. She clung tighter still, wriggling against me and biting at my mouth as we kissed with ever rising passion.

Yet the music never stopped, not in my head, surging around us, ever faster and more joyful as we made love. It had been she who was unable to resist, climbing onto me and taking my body into hers because she could not do otherwise, but now it was me. My lust was too powerful to be held back, and I took her, there on the dank stone floor, rolling her onto her back and mounting her as she clung to my neck with desperate energy. With that I allowed my eyes to open and she was real.

She was more than real. She was Nathaira, Nathaira as she had been described to me, elfin in her delicacy, ethereal in her beauty, but also hot with need, for me. Her hair was as pale as sea foam, her skin as smooth and white as alabaster, her eyes the limpid grey of pearls and misty with arousal. Never had I known a woman so beautiful, nor so passionate, and at the sight of her I lost my last vestige of control.

I became like an animal, knowing only the pleasure of my body. She was the same, biting and scratching as I thrust into her, clawing at my back and her own breasts, which only served to drive us both to greater frenzy. I put her on her knees and enjoyed her from behind, my thumbs holding her tiny, perfect bottom wide and her head thrown back in ecstasy. I used her mouth, pushing myself deep as she struggled to take me, as eager as I or more so. I licked her sex and her anus too, with her enthroned on my face and babbling entreaties in her ancient tongue.

Even as she rode me I could hear each and every note of the harp, a sound still joyful, but also full of power and vitality, a perfect mirror to our straining, heated bodies. I could hold back no longer, and nor could she, swinging around to throw her legs across my hips and once more ease her body down on mine. As she rode her hair was flying around her face, now set in fierce, wanton ecstasy such as I have never seen in a modern woman.

I gave to her as she gave to me, pushing hard into her, and ever faster as the music rose, picking up both pace and sound until the air trembled in time. She began to scream, and it was as if she was singing, a song of joy and freedom and triumph all at once, and as her song and the music came together in a perfect crescendo I too reached climax, erupting within her as shudder after shudder of uncontainable ecstasy ran through me.

She'd thrown her head back as she came, setting her body in the same tight arch she'd held for so long as the pillar of the harp, perfectly still, as I ceased driving into her from below, as pale and smooth as if she were carved, her tiny breasts thrust high, her belly pushed out to mine, her face once more set in anguish and still the most beautiful I had ever seen.

Only as she came back into my arms did I realise that she was real, living flesh, as warm and vital as any other, her lovely skin lightly speckled with sweat from her exertions, her breathing still fast, her heart hammering against mine. She was smiling too, happy to be alive and to be able to take her pleasure in my body as I had taken mine in hers. Only her eyes betrayed any other emotion, a curious melancholy as if in doing what she had done she had lost something.

It was there for just a fleeting moment, and then gone as her eyes closed and she moved her face to mine. Our lips touched in the most delicate of kisses. She said something, her tone sweet and gentle yet infinitely sad, and her hand rose to my face, to close my eyelids, as the sound of the harp once more faded to the music of sleep, so faint I could no longer be sure if it was there at all.

With her touch a great weight seemed to have settled onto me, a tiredness I could not resist any more than I had her body. I let myself be overcome, falling asleep to that distant music and the sound of her singing in a voice almost as quiet and full of sadness.

How long I slept I do not know, perhaps just minutes, as when I came awake she was still there, standing at the base of the stairs in the rich golden green light of the afternoon sun. She was no longer naked, but dressed in my clothes, ridiculous in the outsized shirt and rolled-up trousers, but as I made to laugh I found I could not. Nor could I move, my senses alert but my limbs without feeling, set in solid stone as the pillar of the harp.

All I Have To Do
Nikki Magennis

Remember home-made mix cassettes? The ones that lovers used to make for each other, shyly choosing tracks that hinted at all their furtive desires without using the actual words. Songs that made you smile, made you swoon. A gift that you puzzled over, wondering if they really loved you or just wanted a little carnal adventure. One of those sweet little gestures that seems so innocent now, now we're all grown up and too tired for games.

I found one today. With my name on the outside in red pen. The songs listed on the paper insert, your writing small and scratchy.

I remember getting it, that day in June, so long ago. The parcel in the post arriving with a delicious thud on the doormat. Before I was fully awake. Sticky with sleep, I bolted to the door to find what well-wrapped present you'd sent, heart fizzing with nerves, as hopeful and desperate as a kid on their birthday. I remember everything about that summer, even the light. It was as though even the sunshine had its own particular yellowy scent, the dusty stones warmed by sudden light that seemed to break open the city and promise endless, sweet freedom. I was living on air and white wine then, full of a vivid energy that carried me through my crummy office job and sailed me quickly from weekend to weekend. Yes, it was like sailing. A sea full of light, insubstantial water, a huge open vista of parties and dancing and smiling young men, eyes glittering with that electric look that meant sex.

Everything was bright, and everything was moving so fast you couldn't touch the sides of your life. Dizzy. And in amongst the sweaty clubs and drunken grinding of a hundred lost weekends, I met you, with your white smile. Your chocolate-smooth voice. Your fine, long fingers and your delicate frame, built to craft melodies. I could tell from the way you moved the air around you that you were someone who created things. You seemed to promise something vast and expansive. We danced without speaking, lurching slowly round the slippery floor in that way that lovers do, trying to press body parts as close to each other as possible, feeling wonderful bulges that begged further exploration. Hanging round the dark corners, interlacing fingers in a gesture that means: as I push my hands into yours, so I will fuck you. On a wave of booze, lust and music, we swayed. Later, five in the morning, with the glow of dawn chilling us quietly, you sang to me.

The Everly Brothers. A song like honey, like being wrapped in sweetness. You held my wrist and stared into my palm, like you were looking for something. While my hungry young pussy was clamouring for attention, something in the way you sang reached deeper, turned even my heart into a puddle. After the song finished the room seemed changed, as though the low timbre of your voice had altered the world. Made a space. Wide with possibility, heavy with intent. More than fucking, your singing promised that I would be utterly explored, utterly turned on.

And then you were gone.

There were phone calls, and I'd tangle the phone cord round myself like I was wrapping myself in your voice, coiling it round my ankles and wriggling. Letting you tickle my ear with your laughter. Listening to the sounds in the background, the landscape of your life, so distant and alluring. You sent letters too, written in the same red pen, sheafs of creamy paper tucked in parcels that had the aura of relics, the sense of you folding them and slipping them inside like little secrets.

You were so far away, so unreal, that my whole body ached for you. I became super-sensitive, shivering at the sound of your voice at the end of the phone, as though you were touching me just by speaking. I pictured you moving around in your city, making songs in your room, trying out notes on your keyboard with those gentle fingertips, striking the keys with that suggestive weight, that playful touch. I wished so hard to feel you touch me that way that sometimes I felt the slightest bump against my neck or shoulder, as though some phantom hand of yours had reached out somehow across thousands of miles and made contact. I'd jump a little, and feel the warm tingling spread over me, like the liquid swell of post-orgasm. Like you'd turned your thoughts to me and made a mysterious, psychic fuck happen in my head.

Meanwhile, through my obsessive haze of your voice and words, I was hurtling through real life. I had the hysteric, vivacious hunger you get from losing something before you'd even got to play with it. I found a club that played soul, the songs so loud they warped the air and made the floor thud. I stuffed myself onto the inferno of the dance floor, squirmed through the tightly packed bodies till I found a boy with a cute face or a tight ass, thumped up against them and danced like a whore. The music was bottled sex, dirty and funky and delicious. You couldn't listen to it, only dance, and dance like you were coming right there on the crowded floor.

Shooting fish in a barrel. I'd always leave with a boy's

arm draped over my shoulder, sometimes two. A trail of phone numbers was scrawled on hands, on beer mats, on flyers. Lipstick and eyeliner smudged the numbers – sometimes made up, sometimes real. And then there were hotel rooms, and foreigners. Sweat and body hair and tights with holes ripped in them. The kisses of starving people, so hard they made your head spin. Clothes shed like confetti, clumsy manoeuvres towards the bed, the shock and wonder of a strange tongue in your mouth, love bites tattooed down your neck. I loved that cocktail of tastes, the concentrated essence of men and decadence that was so heady and strong it was better than drugs. Almost addictive.

It got so easy to spread my legs for strangers I felt like a wild beast – a connoisseur of cocks and body hair, tasting their aftershave like vintage wine as they shoved their hands eagerly into my more-than-willing pussy.

Those brutish, fast and messy nights would leave me tender and satisfied, my body bruised like a piece of fruit and my skin all humming with the friction of men's hands, stubble, cocks. I'd wake on a Sunday morning and pass the day in a happy daze, the dirty sheets and hangover a glorious reminder of each new conquest. I'd lower myself into a scalding bath and let the water sting at my poor chafed parts. Relish the humming sensation of a body that's been well fucked.

In the evening, you'd call. The phone would ring gently like a cat meowing, and I'd pick it up carefully, take the receiver and hold it to my ear and receive your 'hello' like a kiss of benediction, a warm salve to wash away the night.

It was a slight, nothing-much of a love affair even in the beginning – both of us too shy to say anything blatant. A whole ocean to keep us apart. The more sweet and distant you got, the more wild and lascivious my week-ends became. Booze, fellatio, cocaine, threesomes. One long summer of lust. I felt like that mythical woman the sailors used on long voyages – made of rubber; flexible; indestructible. And all along our chaste, dreamy conversations, little gifts, a longing that stretched out like aeroplane trails over the blue skies.

I racked up enough lovers to develop a kind of world-weary demeanour. Became so careless I didn't even try to remember their names, or cherish the battle scars. A skilled slut, I learnt how to lose people and how to enjoy even the slight ache of loss, the possible heartbreaks. I'd think with pride how my tits had been fondled by an army of men, enough almost to make up for the lack of you.

Time's passed, since then; the inevitable seasons come and go. I grew tired of debauchery and moved elsewhere. Your phone calls quietly stopped.

I got a house, a job. Took care of my lovely pussy and decided I would no longer hand it out to every cute guy I happened to dance with. After a long while, I hung up my dancing shoes altogether. I got a husband.

No more soul clubs, no more gut-vibrating beats to get my mojo going. No more long-distance phone calls and foreign parcels. No more love letters. Instead, I pay my bills and post thank-you letters. My hair got longer, and these days I wear less make-up. I still love fucking, but sex has become more comfort than dazzle. A way to knock ourselves out before sleep, grabbing for that pleasant buzz from each other like eating a slice of heavy cake. All those exotic and horny young men, left behind like my sweaty nightclub dancing clothes. Life built up around me like a piece of self-assembly furniture, surprisingly graceful as it fell into place. As I learnt how to be a human being. I watch the world pass now from behind large clean windows. I smile at the shopkeeper when I buy milk; I ignore his glittering eyes, the raised eyebrow. It seems you become immune to all the little signals, kind of dulled. As though there's a secret world of signals and scent and glances that gets left behind as you age, overtaken by more important languages. Subtler, saner conversations. All my friends got fat. We got money and started sagging at the edges.

Sundays these days I wake up with a clear head and take a walk in the park. I climb the hill and look down on the city, lying there like a vast jigsaw puzzle: mapped, tattered, understandably complicated.

I live within familiar patterns. Supermarket. Kitchen. Chop spring onions with a matchstick in my mouth to stop the tears. Hoover. Wash. Consider the wall colours.

Still, no matter how organised my life is, I have shelves overflowing with junk, cupboards full of things that lurk in the dust and murmur to me. Make me feel guilty.

So this afternoon I started, gingerly, pulling open old boxes and sifting through the detritus. On my own in the bedroom, husband collapsed next door under the papers, I unfolded pieces of ancient history, touching them quietly so as not to disturb the patina of age, the weight of forgotten history. I found stashes of old love letters, cringeworthy teenage adulation spilling from the pages. The thousand lies of old boyfriends, recorded forever on blue onion-skin paper. Kneeling on the bedroom floor with the sisal rug making ribbed dents in my flesh, I got submerged in all the preserved pieces of time past. Stashes of photographs emerged. Pictures floated into my field of vision, images of a more colourful time. Those days I wore bright lipstick and listened to music so loud it infuriated all the neighbours. It was all brighter, harder, more desperate and more furious, days when you flung yourself into things. Your whole body. Your whole self.

I was lost in wry and pretty memories when I found that tape. Small and plain, it was a little bomb that set something off in me. All the blood rushed to my head and I felt my heartbeat pounding like I'd swallowed a clock.

Without making any more noise than I had to, I slipped it in my pocket and carried it into the study. Closing the door behind me, I walked straight to the Bang and Olufsen stereo and slid the tape in the slot. I settled in the big faux-leather chair and felt myself sink deep into the cushions. I put on the big padded earphones that smell faintly of aftershave. I pressed play.

There was a hissing noise, and it suggested the sound of that summer, the interference pattern that played as background music to all our coy telephone conversations. The sound of distance, of hunger and of unspoken, aching, aching longing.

When the piano chord struck, it hit me right in the chest, with a strong taste of bitter pleasure, like you'd laid your hand on me. That stereo is so perfectly tuned it seems that the music originates inside your own head, delivered straight to the most tender part of the mind. The part that responds instantly, overwhelmingly to sound. As though you were right next to me, close enough to touch.

And though the tape had lain untouched and silent for years it played with such ripe and vivid melody I could have wept.

Resonating, playing slowly up the scale, I felt your touch running over me again, fingertips brushing the side of my face as softly as new spring beech leaves. My lips were buzzing to feel you, to taste you. That lemon-tinged flavour of yours that echoed so faintly – I knew it was just on the edge of my tongue – then the song started, the words, and it was as though your voice was in my mouth, like a deep kiss. I might have expected to be moved – the bittersweet pang of long ago is one I'm accustomed to. What I hadn't counted on was that I'd be aroused. Eyes closed, I felt the song as much as heard it, felt your voice like silk over me, creeping into my ears and lulling me with those sweet words. 'Baby...' you crooned, and it was pure hell, pure hell and pure heaven all at once, as you insinuated yourself into my body all over again. I felt the lack of those lost days so strongly it hurt.

You sang about wrapping me in your arms, and I hugged myself, rocking, feeling at the same time the low beat of the drum bump along like you were bumping your hips against me, felt my nipples stiffen up as though you were nuzzling into my neck. I was leant back in the chair, the afternoon sun lying on my legs, warming me slowly, and the rest of the house started falling away, obscured by the lush and seductive sound of the music.

The strangest of feelings, being fucked by a song. My breath was heaving. Between my legs my cunt was undeniably buzzing, getting the slippery way it does when I'm anticipating sex. The desire was growing in me again, all the hazy, delicious desire of that long summer unfolding from within and multiplying like a psychedelic dream of pornographic detail. I felt myself swell and fall, my limbs grow heavy, my knees weaken. That wanton, reckless girl I dimly remember as my younger self seemed to awaken. The tug of sex stirred under my clothes, and I shifted in the chair. An old touchpaper was lit, burning quickly from my pussy and rising in my chest. I was sure that somehow I had grown young and juicy again, lips redder, tits magically prouder and as full as a bowl of fruit. I rubbed my thighs together, letting the crotch of my jeans agitate my clit. For once I felt mischievous, inflamed, vivacious again.

By now my clothes were all starting to itch and all I wanted was to strip and somehow bathe in that song, be naked in the sound and let it penetrate me, soak into my skin, pour into my ears and cunt. While you played, I could hear the deep breath you took before singing a line, and I swear I could feel a cold draught of air as you did so, your inhalation brushing over the back of my neck. With one finger I traced a line from my throat to my breasts, to the outline of my jutting nipples, crying out to be tweaked.

Just the way you would twang a guitar string, I flicked at myself, coaxing little shocks of pleasure from the hard tips. I pictured you doing it, with that half-smile of yours, the lazy lopsided way of looking at me with your head tilted and a splash of black hair over your eyes. When you wrote this, I thought, you were standing, one leg half bent to hold the guitar. Your hips angled forwards, and every note would send a vibration down the neck to shudder against your cock. I wondered at the thought of that sensation, the feel of the instrument between your legs, making you a little stiff, a little horny. At the image of your cock hardening, I let my legs spread wider, like you'd gripped my ankles and tugged them gently apart.

Was this what you'd wanted? When you wrote this song, were you imagining me lying back and slipping my hands down the front of my knickers? Was that low note you sang a way of courting me, like a songbird singing his mate into a state of readiness? Maybe you knew that the ache of this song would seduce me, maybe you wrote it with your cock in your hand while you imagined fucking me across oceans. Knowing that the notes would turn me liquid, would send me, writhing, on a voyage of erotic intent.

It was working. I was working on myself. One hand crawling inexorably down my belly towards my sex, my hips bucking in time to the suggestive drumbeat, biting my own lip to give it the stimulation of pain, if not the blessing of your warm skin.

It occurred to me that all the excesses of that summer might have been prompted by your innocent-sounding voice – the undercurrents of sexual want propelling me towards those dark basement clubs, into the arms of a different man every week. All the time I'd been enthusiastically sucking and writhing in the beds of strangers, I'd had the maddening want for you, for a night in your bed with you whispering dirty words in my ear. I worked my way through all those various cocks in a search for your elusive, beautiful presence. An echo of your melody-soaked possibility.

As I thought of this I was still pawing at the front of my pants, feeling the rough scratch of hair at the V of my thighs and knowing I had to bring myself off or go crazy listening to this heart-rending music.

A three-minute song wouldn't give me the drawn-out mindfuck I really craved and, realising I was halfway through the middle eight already, my dirty hands suddenly plunged right in, desperate to wring an orgasm out of this song, to come while you breathed a melody in my ears. It was burning heaven to feel fingers against my clit, frantic, hot as lava and as resounding as C major clanged out on a Steinway. Reviving. At the same time, I felt weirdly as though you were present, watching me, cheering me on with the rising chorus of your song. A performance as intimate and shocking as masturbating in public, and I felt my cheeks burn as though I were onstage, exposed as a slut yet unable to stop.

I rubbed that hungry pussy like I was strumming chords, loving the feel of it but still craving more. I felt the huge absence of your cock within me as I tensed my muscles. Panting, I rolled from side to side on the recliner in desperation to press myself against a firm surface, to feel friction, heat, the thud of satisfaction as the song rushed towards the climax. I knew it was foolish to think the bass beat was some priapic, rutting creature that had me impaled on its rhythm but believed it still in my delirium. Hanging on to your voice and the smooth growl of your lyrics, I spun myself tightly, thrusted upwards onto my hand and twisted, pressing, bringing at last and just in time a long, swooping rush of sweet gunfire hammering through my head and breaking open in a full-on orchestral clamour – you screamed, the last refrain, I moaned, I made a sound like I was breaking into tears as the guitars clanged, clanged, clanged. I came like a car crash, full speed and so hard I forgot to breathe for a minute, gasping, convulsing, curling over and letting the song carry me with it as it unravelled in a glorious, tangled crescendo.

And faded. I was holding tightly onto my pussy with one hand as the last chords softened and faded, a little reverb echoing sadly in the way one clings to a lover's neck, like the tide going out.

So I was left lying there like something washed up on the beach, flushed and mildly ashamed of my stolen tryst. How would one explain something like that? I just got fucked by a guitar, by a bass and a piano. True, what sent me spinning into lustful fantasy was mostly your honeyed voice, but in a way I felt I'd just wanked with a crowd of strange men as they played their instruments.

Had a sordid fling with an imagined lover. Was this a common perversion? Teenage girls screaming at The Beatles, wetting their knickers with excitement. Kissing the pin-up posters on their bedroom walls. I felt like some obscene groupie as I pulled my clothes straight and let my heart thump out the last post-orgasmic beats. I'd given in to that old lust, the voracious appetite that used to send me spinning out to find a conquest. Still there, after so long. The desire for that pageant of sex. The fast motor of my libido had suddenly been jump-started so hard I was shocked by my own feelings. Like a wound-up teenage nymph, not a sober adult doing her Sunday housework.

The shakiness of afternoon sex made my movements uncertain, and I staggered to my feet with the head-phones still attached, like a tethered animal, disoriented, suddenly come to from a lurid daydream.

It was when I turned to switch off the stereo, which was playing a hissing wail of white noise, that I realised I'd been caught. A shadow caught my eye.

Husband, hands in pockets, leaning against the radia-tor. His eyes fixed on me, on my crumpled clothes and flushed face.

Awkward moments between a married couple are something to savour. When you've spent so long deep in each other's lives, breathing the same air, it's almost a gift to find yourself suddenly screaming with shame, humiliated in such a thoroughly shocking way. What did he see? Me writhing on the recliner, hands in pussy, face twisted in painful ecstasy, lips bitten. I searched wildly for an excuse, for a reason to explain why I was locked in rapturous union with the headphones, a thief caught red handed. Stealing a fuck from the distant past, com-mitting adultery with my own memory. I was guilty as sin.

He could have left me hanging there, stewing in my own painful embarrassment while I tried to recompose myself. But it's at times like this when I realise one of the reasons I marched up the aisle with this man. One of the reasons I hang around and play house with him. Standing there, acres of space between us on that Sunday afternoon, he gifted me with one of those beautiful lopsided smiles of his. A splash of black hair in his eyes.

He traversed that vast space like it was nothing more than walking across the room. Pulled at my dishevelled clothes and laughed at me. With his voice like chocolate, like silk in my ear, he put his mouth to my ear and sang to me. It's always taken my breath away, how he forgives my lurid excesses with a shrug and a tease. How he can turn me on just by talking to me, but most especially by singing to me. Those Everly Brothers songs. When you sing 'Dream', it still turns my knees weak.

Duet Maya Hess

Northdean Manor, 25 June 1815

My dearest cousin Charlotte,

The heat in this airless valley is drying my ink before it even touches the paper, making my urgent correspondence all the more frustrating. Hardly much use for relating my exciting news! How I wish your summer visit was upon us and that we were taking tea on the lawn in the hush of the whispering beech trees. My desire to regale you with all the happenings here at Northdean Manor is peaking in an unbearable fashion. Let me begin at the beginning, dear cousin, so that you may not become as befogged as your older relation.

Whilst in London during March – recall the endless visiting that our mothers forced upon us, the hapless afternoons spent in dull conversation with fat and old gentlemen nearing the age of forty? – well, there was one such afternoon that now affords me sweet reverie even though it was in the company of Mr Leighton, the biggest bore in the entire town.

The afternoon was barely there at all due to the veil of drizzle that took away the street scene beyond Mr Leighton's drawing-room window. My fingers were numb from the chill and I was slow to remove my muff and pelisse. Then, unlike the fine posture that Mother and my undergarments had between them thrust upon me, I clamped my arms around my bodice in an ungainly attempt to warm my bones. At once I was surprised (and, cousin, don't be shocked) by the ampleness of my bosom as it knowingly pushed up beneath the lace frill of my new spring dress. The exhilaration and delight that such a fleeting occurrence gave me at once warmed my cold blood. And that is not to mention the sudden stare of Mr Leighton, which had soon enough heated parts that a young woman oughtn't to recall when out visiting on a dull March afternoon.

But Mr Leighton's lecherous intent (and with Mama only two feet from my side!) was the least of my surprises during my visit. True, my host's stare made frequent returns to my bosom to catch sight of yet another rise of pink flesh, and true also that I rewarded his faithfulness with several more displays, one of which perhaps went a little too far because Mother issued her own stare, causing my bosom to shrink away.

Our conversation was set on its usual track and, after Mama insisted I play the piano (to impress our host), the discussion focused briefly on my feeble attempt at a Sonata in G minor on the undeserving polished Broadwood beauty. Then there was talk of Mr Leighton's country estate which, as it happens, is six miles from our Northdean Manor. He admitted to longing for the end of June, when he would take a break from the city toil. Who, I asked, can refuse the lure of the clean air and the scent of roses or an early morning promenade? Yes, Mr Leighton was keen on summer, especially so, he informed us, because of his prized house guest who would be residing at his estate from late June until the middle of August.

'Oh, do tell of your guest!' I squealed and, to hasten his reply, I feigned a chill once again and clamped my arms around my breasts (which were by this time becoming quite tender due to all the clamping). He responded, after a fond visual drink from my cleavage, by cussing the servants for not rendering the drawing room warmer that afternoon.

'Do not fuss on my account, Mr Leighton,' I said and by this time Mother was thankfully in conversation with an elderly woman with whom I was not familiar. They were discussing something not nearly as exciting as what Mr Leighton was about to reveal. 'I am of the opinion that to suffer a little chill will keep one's health refined.' And again I embraced myself, which caused a grumble in poor Mr Leighton's throat. When he had resumed his composure, he made the announcement I was keen to hear.

'Make no doubt, Eliza, that I will be sending a multitude of invitations to you and your family in order that you may fully acquaint yourselves with Mr Henry Barrington, the most upcoming and popular composer in all of Europe and my personal musician for the summer, if you please.' His face bulged with pride.

'Oh, I do please, Mr Leighton. Your kind offers will be gratefully accepted, I am sure.' I was outrageous in tone, mainly because the afternoon was the dullest on record in terms of climate and company and if it hadn't been for my keen breast then I might have fallen asleep. Besides, Leighton's musician sounded intriguing and I wanted to learn all about Mr Barrington happenchance he be in possession of a good fortune and *not* in want of a wife – or indeed at least willing temporarily to overlook the one he currently may possess.

(Dear heavens, it must be something in the country water that has touched my senses so. Such candid talk between cousins is acceptable, surely? Be certain to show no one my ramblings and conceal my letter well within your room, my Lottie. As long as we each take a little heed, there is no reason to cease communicating our private thoughts to one another.)

Now back to the dull afternoon three months ago. 'Mr Leighton, are you to keep me waiting until summer itself arrives before you tell me details of your guest?' Instead of pressing together my mounds of flesh, I next did something that if Mother had seen she would surely have fainted. I touched my finger to the end of my bosom and allowed it to remain there for an entire breath. Then I dared to meet Mr Leighton's eye as he stared at what he must have initially thought was an accidental passing of my hand against my body. However, the lingering action of my forefinger and slight parting of my lips gave away my intentions until I began to pity him and the redness of face that he now wore.

'Would you like a glass of water, Mr Leighton? You have become suddenly flushed.' I was a terrible tease that afternoon but if only the wretched man had talked of the mysterious Mr Barrington sooner, we could have deemed our visit terminated.

Finally, he acquiesced and spoke of his plans. 'Mr Barrington is currently studying in Vienna under the auspicious care of Mr van Beethoven. Unfortunately the great composer, who was due to perform in London with the British Philharmonic and accompany my guest on his journey back home, is currently suffering from poor health and therefore Mr Barrington will be travelling alone.'

Would this not be the ideal chance, dear Lottie, for us to improve our musical skills, especially as I have since heard that Mr Henry Barrington is leaving a trail of fainting females in his travels around Europe due to his unusually rakish good looks?

And do you now want to know the sheer luck of all this? Forgive me for sounding so harsh but as of the last few days, our poor Mr Leighton has been struck by some vile illness that has sent him to the south coast to take the sea air for a month instead of to his country estate. Can you believe my joy when Father announced we would be playing host to the musically gifted Henry Barrington for the entire summer?

I must rush, Charlotte, to make ready for his arrival tomorrow. Hurry to Northdean, sweet cousin, that you may keep sensible watch over me and that you may take note of the interesting gentleman for yourself.

With love and anticipation,

Your Eliza.

Northdean Manor, 27 June 1815

Dearest Charlotte,

If this mailing ever reaches your eager fingers then my heart will droop with sorrow for it will mean that you are still in London indulging in the summer season. As it is, if you have yet received my earlier mailing, our letters will cross paths on their way. But I can scarcely write fast enough to regale you with recent happenings at Northdean and even though you may not receive this for weeks until your return home (I pray each day that your carriage is on its way), I have to release my innermost thoughts lest I go as mad as the King!

Firstly, Mr Henry Barrington chose a fine time to arrive at Northdean when not a servant was to be found to attend to the gentleman's needs. Can you imagine the disturbance when in the dead of night there was a certain brawl in the house? Dressed only in my nightgown, I ran to the top of the staircase to witness a most unusual scene in the reception hall. Papa was fiercely brandishing a fire poker at a rather surprised yet overly handsome young man who was positioned on the threshold of our home. Meanwhile, the dogs were tearing at his breeches, which were soon ripped between their hungry teeth, and at the sight of Mr Barrington's exposed thigh flesh I felt quite giddy. The man's skin was as creamy as my own!

Only when I descended into the fracas did the dogs release their hold and my father lower the poker. A simple demand for his identity revealed that the assaulted gentleman was none other than our house guest, Mr Henry Barrington. At once I looked to his fingers and saw, as true as I had heard, that they were long and elegant and would surely make for the finest pianist in Europe. Indeed, they appeared as brittle and underworked as any feminine hands. His face, at close range, was honest and fair and was framed by his unkempt hair – as black as a raven and worn longer than the current fashion, which added to the wayward charm that I had immediately noticed – and he kept flicking it away from the most piercing blue eyes I have ever encountered.

So, dear cousin, what a rag-mannered dandy we are to host over the coming weeks and, despite his ill-considered behaviour in the dead of night, I suddenly wished to escort him to his room in order to bathe his scratched leg in rosewater! But, while I stood motionless and dumb, our guest flowed towards me with a musicality that proved how lithe the rest of him was, and indeed he was about my height so our faces were perfectly level. He took my hand, Lottie, and then pressed it to his lips and I inhaled his scent until daybreak because I simply couldn't sleep that sultry night. I am convinced the demons have got into me and now I have another shock for you, Lottie dear, so seat yourself lest you faint.

My freshly perfumed hand took a mind of its own those next few hours as if all my senses had departed. I am ashamed to say that I touched myself down there for fear that I was suffering from a strange feminine fever, such was the burning between my weakened legs. With every tentative exploration of silky flesh, my sickness grew stronger until I cried out in convulsion and pushed my face into my pillow with a prayer that it might transform into Mr Barrington. I found myself longing for all I was worth that he be lying next to my panting, feverish body but what, aside from catch the sickness himself, would he be able to do for me?

It is a strange passion with which I am stricken but as I write these words in the early hours of yet another sweet summer morning, staring out across the striped lawns through an eiderdown of low mist, I can only hope that upon waking Mr Barrington's music will be as sweet as his unusual entrance.

Until soon,
Your Eliza.

Stanthorpe Mews, London, 2 July 1815

Dear Eliza,

I also wish that I were taking tea with you on the sweeping lawns of Northdean Manor and I have been dreaming of my visit for many weeks now, especially since your recent letter! Alas, our journey north will be delayed by another few days while Father takes care of business matters, which leaves me, your quiet cousin, even quieter as most of London society is busying itself with balls and dinners to which I have not been invited due to my planned absence.

You can be assured of privacy and I can hardly read my own words as I write of similar desires. How I admire you that you played with Mr Leighton's senses that March afternoon. If only you had told me this in an earlier correspondence, I would have had something scandalous to think about other than Mother's constant need to find me a husband.

My correspondence is short for now and perhaps my

arrival at Northdean will occur before the delivery of your reply. Your seductive thoughts will keep my spirits high.

Yours, in anticipation,
Lottie.

Northdean Manor, 6 July 1815

Dearest Charlotte,

It has been well over a week since the arrival of our Mr Barrington, or perhaps I can now write Henry, as it should be noted (and I will tell the delicious details shortly) that we are now on very familiar terms! And also a week overdue for your arrival at Northdean. There is so much excitement currently in my life that to share it with you via ink and paper is nothing short of frustrating. Here is my news.

That first morning of Henry's visit was one I shall never forget. I scarcely expected to see him for breakfast due to the lateness of his arrival and Mother and Father were taking advantage of sleeping late due to the night-time disturbance. So I ate alone in our dining-room with Sarah waiting table as she usually does. Just as I was taking my egg, someone entered the room and my heart skipped at the sight of our new guest taking a seat opposite me.

'Good morning to you, Miss Lawrence.'

'Mr Barrington,' I replied coyly although fancied I might try a small clamp of my breast to see the outcome. I replaced the silverware and wrapped my arms around my body.

'Are you in a draught, Miss Lawrence?' he asked while unfolding a napkin.

I replied that I was perfectly warm and not once did he stare at my breast. I continued with my breakfast with our conversation limited to such pleasantries about the weather and poor Mr Leighton's demise.

'Will you allow me to play for you?' Then Henry leant across the table (he leaned to me!) and whispered so that Sarah may not hear. 'Your beauty inspires my fingers to make music and they itch for a chance to entertain you, sweet Miss Lawrence.'

Dear Lottie, can you imagine my surprise and my near fainting from his forwardness? I was stricken almost immediately by that same fever deep within my dress and fidgeted so awkwardly to ease my strange discomfort that our house guest soon began to laugh, exposing pure white teeth between the reddest lips I have ever seen on a man and set within a smooth, clean-shaven face.

'What amuses you so?' I asked, trying to cease the movements that had served to increase my fever.

'Guide me to your music room. Tell me, what kind of piano does your family possess?' Henry Barrington rose from his chair and took my hand. I had no choice but to follow.

Imagine the music room scented with the intoxicating smell of summer jasmine and a gentle breeze entering through the French doors. Imagine, too, Henry Barrington seated at our pianoforte and me seated (at his insistence) immediately next to him on the lucky, lucky stool! It was fortunate that no one disturbed us that fragrant morning for if I had been discovered alone with a gentleman then my downfall would have been immediate.

Anyway, dear Lottie, I can assure you that as soon as Henry struck forth his tune, the sweetness of summer dissolved because nothing was as sweet and pure as those notes. I swear that I spied semi-quavers floating up from the keys and the stave of the music simmering within his perfectly azure eyes. And my condition was now so intolerable that I was eager to excuse myself to take stock of my person but Henry, while still playing his trill tune, noticed that I might not be well.

'Is it my music,' he enquired, 'that causes you discomfort?' His voice was soft and caressing, like his piano playing.

'Oh no,' I replied directly to his face, which was a mere hand-breadth from mine. 'It is not your music that troubles me.'

'Then what is it?' He was almost singing his concern as he played the compelling melody which my limited knowledge tells me was in the key of E major with periodical flourishes in the minor. Quite my favourite! I lowered my head and gazed at my fingers.

'Your reputation, sir, and my current proximity to it makes me ill at ease.' Never before had I been so forthright.

'And what reputation might that be, Miss Lawrence?' His fingers stumbled momentarily as they danced a silken *arpeggio* for my enjoyment. His breath, having taken not an ounce of breakfast, was a morning breeze on my cheeks.

'That you are known not only for your compositions and recitals.' I swallowed and felt my face flush. 'That you have also created a trail of fallen ladies on your travels through Europe.' Then, Lottie, I clamped and Henry could not prevent a glance.

'And you believe this?' He banged a series of vehement chords to punctuate his words and moved even closer so that our shoulders brushed together. Despite the volume of the bass notes that he hammered (which must lie sorely against the grain of his training with Mr van Beethoven), his voice remained unusually light and free from the male tones of anger. 'And what of the young lady beside me? Is she fallen?' He tipped a slender forefinger briefly under my chin and if Mama should have seen...

Then, shockingly, Henry permitted his talented finger to trace a line from my chin to the curve of my breast and tap out a brief but exhilarating beat. The fainting of ladies I can now understand, because if I had not allowed myself to lean against the gentleman (if indeed I can call him that) then I would have toppled off my seat.

'I admit that it is taking much strength even to remain seated adequately on this stool, Mr Barrington, and of course I am fearful for my well-being –'

'I insist you call me Henry,' he interrupted. And then, dear cousin, he continued to play while I doted on his swift and agile fingers caressing the keys.

But I was continuing to suffer inexplicable discomposure. A relentless seepage was occurring (oh, Lottie, tell no one but it was because of my hand and its illicit behaviour the previous night, I am sure!) and my cleavage sparkled in the most devious fashion like the wind was brushing my bare skin or (the thought!) that Mr Barrington was stroking my flesh due to my frantic bosom clamping. (I was not aware of what a decent cleavage I could procure.)

After a long appreciation of his person and nimble recital, and of course lest Mother or Father should enter, I retired to my room and immediately rid myself of my dress. In desperation, I took to my bed but my mind was tainted with the image of Henry's clear face and precise features. I removed my stays and chemise and lowered my petticoat and pantaloons, of course making sure that my bed sheets were pulled high over my body should Mama enter in search of her ailing daughter.

The only relief I could gain was by vigorously massaging the territory at the top of my legs (previously an untouched area, dear Lottie) and also by stroking my aching bosom. However, it should be noted that despite the frantic rubbings I bestowed upon my person, even after I exploded with convulsions, the respite from discomfort was only temporary.

Quite simply, cousin, I fear that something within me has been misaligned and the only person who can heal me is Henry Barrington himself. As it is, I now have to return to bed in order to stroke my womanliness in order that I may be well in time for tea. We are having guests to show off Henry's delightful talents although I fear his other skills to be more dangerous than his music.

Your bed-bound Eliza.

Stanthorpe Mews, London, 6 July 1815

Cousin,

Having received yours of the 27 June, today I can only offer a mere note from one who is still terribly stuck in town. Papa is struggling with his business affairs, while it seems, dear Eliza, that you are struggling with your own. And quite alone, I might add, when your cousin should be by your side to guide you.

Now, an alert from one who cares. I have been doing a little investigating on your behalf and it seems that you are not the only lady to have fallen sick from Mr Barrington's presence. Perhaps you already know this news by now but alas, the gentleman's reputation as a rake and a fribble even surpasses his reported outstanding musical ability. Beware then, Eliza, that your sickness does not become your total demise when in the company of this utterly fascinating character.

I can only pray that my subsequent communication with you will be in person.

Your loyal Lottie.

Northdean Manor, 6 July 1815

Sweet Charlotte,

The hour is late and the light fairly dim but write to you I must! It was only earlier this day that I penned of my sickness, which I am now convinced can be mended by our dear house guest. Henry has even confirmed his willingness to see me entirely well!

Tea this afternoon was taken in the company of Jane, the parson's daughter, and her brother Edward, who eventually acted as chaperone due to Mama's absence and the parson's wife's indifference. (I wonder, has she caught the same sickness?) After our intake of the usual offerings and several cups of a refreshing brew beneath the copper beech, it was decided that a gentle stroll would be in order, even though Jane's mother was not of a walking disposition and decided to remain at the tea table. Imagine then Edward and Jane, Henry (who had remained thoughtful and silent during tea) and myself strolling and winding between the rose bushes and box topiary with not a care or thought from anyone – even Jane's mother, who was busy melting in the severe afternoon heat.

But no matter to that. In brief, dear Lottie (be seated for my news), Henry requested that in order to be fully mended, I must take his company in the quiet of night (he is fond of the night hour!) and therefore liaise with him in the music room when my clock strikes two. He promised, during that sweet, heady walk through Heaven's garden, that through the magic of music, he would heal me.

How thankful I am for the generosity of our guest! Should I be fully recovered at dawn, I will write to you with my news.

Excitedly, Eliza.

By hand, 6 July

Dearest Eliza,

Forgive the intrusion of this letter slipping beneath your door but I see that your light is burning and believe this particular communication safer than if I steal myself through your door before our time together this night.

Such was the thrill of your presence this afternoon, and virtually unaccompanied, that my heart now beats hard for more of your secret company. Already a tune is forming in my mind that can only hope to capture a glimmer of your unique beauty. I will transpose the notes to the stave in order that you may hear the music of my heart forever.

Gentle Eliza, have no fear of the stories that you hear of my life in Europe. I can tell you that not a single soul in the continent knows a scrap of true detail about my person and how shocked they would be if they knew the complete contents of my mind!

Firstly, I am a musician and my life's dedication is to become as great a composer as Mr van Beethoven, while of course being true to my own inspiration. And secondly (although it is as full in my mind as the entire universe) I must admit that my taste is for a certain young lady that, if my desires should be discovered, then her own reputation would be at stake.

Dear Lord, there is so much hidden that, if discovered, I would be forced to pledge my soul for eternity!

With this in mind, please be assured of my commitment to put right the malaise you believe I have caused you to endure.

With utmost respect and anticipation,
Henry.

With stealth, eleven thirty

Dear Henry,

I fear that treading the creaky boards in this house will foil our tryst although pray the structure will take pity on us as we approach our assigned meeting place. The piano will be our anchor as you soothe my discomfort and, if I could trouble you to ease my guilt also for stealing this letter under your door, then the Lord will look favourably upon our liaison, I am sure.

Pray, what is it that would cause you to pledge your soul for all eternity? You have lit my curiosity in so many ways, dear Henry.

Until my clock chimes two,

Eliza.

Midnight

Eliza,

My person exudes for you, more than you will know. There are mysteries about me that would be sweet decadence for you to discover and yet I fear will remain concealed.

Forgive my haste and scrap of paper. Any communication with you is too addictive.

Your Henry.

Northdean Manor, 10 July 1815

Dear cousin Lottie,

I cannot determine if I am fallen from society, no better than a wayward chit, or if indeed I have risen to new heights and would, if the truth were exposed, be the envy of all the young ladies in England. It is a perplexing conundrum because etiquette suggests one thing while my heart believes truly another. My news is as follows.

That moonlit night, that sultry eve when I waited for

my secret tryst with Henry Barrington, seems like a lifetime ago but I know that it is only three days past since our union. And what a union!

True to his word, Henry was toying gently with the piano keys (how gentle his fingers would become!) and I flowed silently through a moonbeam to stand at his side, after having sealed the music room door of course. Henry's smile and passionate gaze again set alight my discomposure while his piano playing offered a promise of respite from my ailments. His stare drew me beside him onto the piano stool and our flesh was touching, albeit through the layers of our clothing (under which my skin danced), and for a while I listened intently to his music.

What dainty notes he struck, all perfectly bound within the key of G. Henry's music contained the flavour of summer with the mystery of winter wrapped up in a dreamy and quite seductive piece that he later dedicated to me. During the refrain, he bid me to intervene with my own hand, promising that a duet would provide unimaginable pleasure. After a brief moment of coyness, I dipped my fingers onto the keys and touched an appropriate harmony. I could see immediately that Henry was pleased.

We played like this for some time but then our music (which I prayed would not wake the entire household) ceased and Henry's face came close to mine. How used to my faithless ramblings you must have become, Lottie, but will you believe me when I tell you that Henry then kissed me, fully on the lips with a mouth that was not so much dissimilar to my own and with a delicacy that I can only liken to morning dew.

'Dear Lizzie,' he proclaimed. (Note his sudden familiar address. Such passion!) 'Since I first saw you, even as the dogs were tearing the clothes from my bones, I loved your tender eyes and cherished the way your breast rose and fell like the tide.'

At this I blushed and thanked heavens that I had discovered the art of clamping.

'Oh, Henry,' I proclaimed back. 'Your creamy flesh, even as the dogs were ripping your breeches from you, ignited my desire in a way a young lady should not be ignited. It has given me a terrible discomfort.'

'Where is that discomfort then, dear Lizzie?'

Now, Lottie, if you had witnessed the honesty on Henry's face then you too would have had no hesitation in showing him your discomfort. The worst was that, as I lifted my skirts, my right elbow crashed the treasured piano keys in an ungainly mess. I do hope he does not associate such a noise with what I showed him.

'Here is my trouble, Henry. Right here.' I lowered my pantaloons there on the piano stool and waited with static breath as Henry assessed me.

'Oh my,' he eventually declared. 'If I could examine you further ... do stand, do raise your skirts higher.' His ensuing silence was sweet agony.

Can you visualise, Lottie, me with my dress pulled high and the caring Henry Barrington, renowned musician, peering thoughtfully at the place that had been receiving so much of my own manual soothing recently, while my rump played a deaf melody on the keys? This is the unusual truth, I swear!

'For how long have you been in this state?'

'Since your arrival,' I declared. 'There is nothing I can do to ease my dilemma. Can you please help?'

'Of course, if you will only allow me the intimate moment of touching your parts that I may assess how deep your affliction runs.'

I said nothing to encourage Henry but (and it felt most unladylike) I simply parted my naked legs so that he may take easier access. It did not occur to me initially that the dear man was attempting to kiss well my difficult body. Such had been the dampness in the area anyway that it did not strike me immediately how Henry was applying his mouth to my flesh.

Oh Lottie, what a clever gentleman he is! His skilful lips and tongue soon aroused my fretting into pure delight and I found myself desiring to ease any discomfort that he may possess. He lapped at my body as greedily as any thirsty hunting hound post-chase and it took much concentration on my part not to slide off the piano keys that were resounding behind me.

'You do me wonders,' I proclaimed and then he had the good thought to transfer his attention to my bosom and neck. This caused a coincidental ripple of what I suspected was the broken chord of F and suited the frolicking nicely. 'What a talented man you are!'

It must have been my encouraging words that caused Henry to remove his jacket and unfasten his breeches and, at the time, I assumed he must also be suffering from the affliction. He perhaps longed for my remedy.

'Please don't think that by touching me in return you will be surrendering your decency, dear Lizzie.'

'How so?' As it was I was grappling with such thoughts although my errant body was winning as I reached a hand to Henry's shoulder. Any reply that may have come from my lips was thwarted by the insertion of Henry's gentle fingers (recall I mentioned how gentle he was?) into the narrow space between my legs. The piano became my support entirely as I lay back across the ivories and what sweet din I made!

'It is unusual for a young woman to conduct relations with a gentleman outside of marriage,' he panted while fondling me internally.

'An entirely despicable thought!' I replied with a

laugh. It was too late for me and I knew it, dear Lottie. I had surrendered completely to Henry without a care for the penalty.

'But you need never suffer such consequences for I . . .' Henry pressed his tender mouth onto mine during his sentence and then took my hand in his and pressed it to his chest as if I were to swear allegiance. With hindsight, cousin, I think that it was not my allegiance that was bothering him. I believe he was trying to tell me something that I was too naïve to notice immediately.

'Oh Henry,' I gasped and needed no more encouragement to sweep my hands over his lissom body until they also found his intimate places. And what intimate places they were! At first, I was concerned for the anatomy of my dear Henry but as he removed his clothing and revealed gentle curves of pure, creamy flesh that undulated in familiar places – so similar to my own – I began to laugh and delight at what I saw.

'How beautiful you are!' I exclaimed and immediately pushed my face into his small breasts. His nipples drew up like the polished pebbles I have seen in the stream and below his slim waist, hidden in the folds of his brown breeches, was a sweet pocket of nectar just so similar to my own that when I slithered off the piano to take a taste, I could have believed I was devouring myself.

'You are not surprised?' Henry's voice seemed to rise by several tones, as if a great weight had been holding it down.

'I am delighted, dear Henry, that my conscience can now remain clear and I will never be accused of being anyone's bit of muslin.'

'Then call me Henrietta, my dearest Lizzie, in that we may continue our sisterly games without secret from each other yet keep our indecent tricks from the world.'

Then the piano quivered something quite tuneful as Henrietta, now completely without clothing, sat atop the keys and spread her slender legs so that I could take a decent look at what I myself must appear like in that region. Slipping my lips onto her was as thrilling as my first touch of the piano many years ago and the occasional note sang prettily beneath her as she vied for space on the keys. And later, nothing could have prepared me for the noisy crescendo that followed her gentle lapping from my rear as I leant forwards over the useful piano. Our music took no applause as we lay in each other's arms and watched the sun rise.

Cousin, allow me to tell you that we fixed each other properly that night and indeed each night since. Henrietta plays for me during the day, and then with me during the hours of darkness.

Now hurry yourself to Northdean that I may share tales of my sweet Henrietta with you, or indeed the musician herself!

Your Eliza.

Stanthorpe Mews, London, 10 July 1815

Eliza!

I write with great urgency and warning. I have heard from a reliable source that Mr Henry Barrington is a charlatan. Seat yourself, poor love-struck cousin, for I am about to tell you that your dear musician is none other than a Miss Henrietta Wells. A woman, would you believe!

I can feel your pain and disappointment even as I write and later today I will begin my journey to Northdean to comfort you any way you desire. Be brave, poor cousin, until I am able to soothe your ragged spirits.

Your loving Lottie.

Going Down on the Blues
Carmel Lockyer

I've always been a wham-bam kind of girl. Or just a Wham kind of girl, if you want – George Michael could always do it for me, whether before, during or after we all found out that he likes boys. Well, I like boys too. But one day I woke up and realised the boys were all men, and 'Wake Me Up Before You Go-Go' didn't mean so much when you were 29 and you had to get up, make the bed, go to work, pay the mortgage, come home, get dolled up and go and find somebody else to mess up your bed for the night.

I talked to Jason about it. Jason was probably as big a Wham fan as I was – although he was also a big Duran Duran, Boy George and Steve Strange supporter. He was into that ruffled shirt and male mascara stuff when we were at school together, before the terms fag hag, gender bender and civil partnership were ever invented. But even Jason had found himself a live-in lover – by the name of Cedric – while I was still pretending 'Freedom' was my big thing.

'Chrissy, love,' Jason said, 'you've got to move with the times. You know, play it a little cooler, a little slower.'

I blinked at him, then topped up my margarita from the pitcher and turned to Cedric. 'Do you know what he's talking about, Ceddie?'

'I think what the man was sayin' was that you're comin' on like the Material Girl and that's what the guys are pickin' up on – but what you're lookin' for is somebody you can rely on, yeah?'

'Cedric, you're drunk!' Jason took the plastic tumbler out of Ceddie's hand and pushed him towards the kitchen. 'Go and make us some nibbles while I introduce Chrissy to the world of the blues...'

Cedric vanished in a haze of alcohol and Jason leant towards me.

'Chrissy darling, I've known you since you were eight years old – trust me when I tell you that as long as you move to a disco beat, your men are going to last as long as a summer hit – if you want staying power, you've got to start thinking about what works in the long-player market.'

So I went home in a taxi with half a dozen of Jason's CDs and woke up with a stinking headache. It was Saturday, thank God, so I just brushed my teeth and sat on the sofa with a cushion on my lap to listen.

First up: Billie Holiday. I listened to three tracks, went into the kitchen and made a big pot of coffee, poured a slug of brandy into my mug and then headed to the bedroom. I pulled on my old black coat with the fun fur collar, a black lace teddy and a pair of high-heeled red suede stilettos, then I went back to sit on the sofa again, with my brandy coffee, and crossed my legs, letting a lot of thigh show in the gap between the sides of my the coat. Billie sang, 'Ain't Nobody's Business If I Do' and I sang along, gazing at myself in the mirror over the fireplace. This was cool, this was slow, this was ... sexy! By the time Billie got around to 'All the Way' I was feeling the need to go all the way myself.

About six months ago, I'd picked up this guy in a bar who actually had a little leather case in his car, full of the kinds of gadgets that men just love. On a first date I was never inclined to give a man the chance to express

himself through technology, because you can never tell
when an unknown lover is going to move from playing
the fandango with a rabbit vibrator to playing hunt the
disarticulated female corpse with a circular saw, but on
this one occasion I had gone as far as toying with a glass
dildo because it was so pretty. When we were kids, Jason
and me, we'd played marbles, and this glass shaft was
like a grown-up fantasy: marbles for lovers. It was
swirled with amber and gold patterns like phoenix feathers, and when the guy showed me how well it warmed
up, by dipping it in a bowl of hot water – well, I'd kind
of taken to the glass bauble, more than I had to its
owner, although he was gentleman enough to leave it
behind in the morning.

Glass wasn't like plastic – I didn't have to think about
my little gizmo rolling off some filthy conveyor belt
somewhere in Taiwan; instead I could imagine a dark-
eyed Hungarian gypsy pursing his lips and blowing into
a ball of molten glass, shaping it and teasing it out and
curling it into just the right shape, smiling all the time
as he hand-made the perfect phallus just for me. That
was one fantasy, anyway. Today though, I oiled my glass
love charm with pure almond oil and just slid the tip
inside me. Then I took a big mouthful of smooth coffee,
feeling the hit of the brandy on my empty stomach, and
lay down across the sofa so my head hung off the front
with the fur collar of my coat framing my face and my
legs were stretched up the back of the cushions. I was
looking pretty flushed and rosy, I thought, as I watched
myself in the mirror. I bent one leg to allow me to slide
the dildo a little deeper, and then let the music wash
over me while I twisted it gently in place so I could feel
it warming inside me. Slow, the blues were all about
slow. I bent the other leg, letting the stiletto heels hook
into the top of the sofa and slid one hand inside my coat,

pushing the strap of my teddy off my shoulder so that my left breast slid out of the lace and the nipple just peeked out from under the fur. I licked my finger and ran it around the areola, which tightened. I looked in the mirror – I thought I appeared extremely decadent, not a kiss-me-quick Wham kind of girl at all. I slid the dildo a little further into me, feeling the pleasure of the smooth surface. I let my left hand pinch and twist my nipple as my right hand began to pump the glass shaft in and out. Then I slipped my left hand inside the coat to sneak its way down to stroke my clitoris. Billie sang and I came – slowly.

It was a good start to the day and things could only get better.

I packed everything pink and sparkly that I owned into a box and slid it under the bed. I threw my fake tan and anklets in the bin and dug out my old suspender belt and a couple of pairs of black stockings. I parted my hair on one side and slicked it down with gel. I looked in the mirror: slow, cool and gorgeous, I thought.

That night I went to the Blues Garden in Camden – there was a jazz/blues band playing, called the Symposium. I felt really out of place, even in my black on black outfit and my new cool but sexy persona. I couldn't even think of anything to drink when I got to the bar. Normally I'd have whatever was blue, or pink, or came with an umbrella in it, or a two for the price of one offer on it, but suddenly that didn't sound cool enough.

'Bourbon,' I said, eventually. Billie had sung about it, so I would drink it. The barman lifted his eyebrow but poured the drink. It tasted like cat pee, to be honest.

I turned round to look at the band, bending my knee and letting my foot in its high black heel rest against the bar behind me. I was showing less cleavage than I'd displayed at any time since I got my first training bra, but an observant man would be able to spot the telltale shape on my raised thigh that showed a suspender belt concealed beneath the simple black dress. If there were any observant men – I noticed that although the crowd was better dressed than the one I usually mixed with on a Saturday night, it was also mainly couples, and the few men who were solo were gazing intently at the musicians rather than at me. Then I saw him – the Blues Brother of my dreams. Imagine Robert Redford dressed like Jools Holland, smiling like George Clooney and talking like Michael Caine – and you're not even close to Paul Gilcoyne. He played the saxophone, and stepped forwards to introduce each song. Why wasn't this bar packed with women straining to get at him? I asked myself for about ten seconds. Then I ran to the ladies', touched up my lippy, hauled on my bra straps to bring my cleavage right up under my chin and hitched up the skirt of my dress to flash a little flesh above the stocking. But I remembered what Jason had said: 'a little cooler, a little slower'. I left the lippy as it was, but lowered my bust to a less prominent angle and shimmied the skirt back down to its proper length. I walked back to my place at the bar slowly, very slowly, and stood with my back to the band. Within a minute Paul made eye contact with me in the mirror behind the bar, and I turned slowly, very slowly, and lifted my glass to him as he raised his glowing saxophone to me.

There's something incredibly sexy about a man who plays sax – think of Bill Clinton, for example. A man who's prepared to spend so much time getting his lips and tongue in exactly the right places, well ... a girl is going to recognise that as dedication to a good cause, isn't she? So as Paul serenaded me with his golden horn,

I sipped the cat-piss drink and reminded myself I didn't have to grab my opportunities, I could simply wait for them to come to me.

An hour later we were in an alley outside the bar. I could feel the cold bricks against my spine and Paul warm against my front, as he whispered in my ear, 'Chrissy, what a beautiful name.'

I wanted to skim my skirt up so he could get his fingers inside me, but even if we managed to get that far, we'd never get any further because we'd have to negotiate the long buttoned flap of his coat, his shirt, his trousers ... bloody hell, this cool and slow stuff could be a nuisance at times. I could tell, though, that he was going to be worth waiting for – he was so focused and deliberate and he had a quirky little half-smile that lifted one corner of his mouth whenever he made me gasp or sigh, which he was doing fairly frequently. Long warm fingers too, which had managed to find their way swiftly inside the scoop neck of the dress, and were now tickling the back of my neck. They then moved down slowly but confidently to circle my breasts. He dragged his nails slowly across my ribs and made me shudder with desire, before sliding down again to grab my haunches and pull me into him. I pushed my shoulders against the wall and thrust my hips forwards. I lifted one leg to wrap around his arse and pull him closer so I could grind into him. Feeling how hard he was, I bumped and rubbed my groin over one of his thighs until I thought I could almost come ...

'Chrissy, sorry, my darling, time for the second set.' He stepped back, adjusting his jacket and running his fingers through his dark curly hair, then reached for my hand. I let him lead me back into the bar. I was on automatic pilot. Second set? We'd hardly made it past first base!

Musicians. They're a different breed. Here's a blues joke. What happens if you play a blues record backwards? Your wife comes back, your boss tells you that giving you the sack was a mistake and your dog doesn't die. Laugh? I nearly started. Shall I tell you what's really funny about a blues joke? That blues musicians tell them to each other – and laugh. The second set meant that they were on stage again, after their drinks break and this time, instead of just instrumental music, there was a singer, a black girl called Maryze. I tried not to look daggers at her, in her sparkly red dress, but it was difficult. She was onstage with my man and I wasn't happy about it. She could sing though, I had to give her that much.

When the second set was over, Paul came straight to me. 'Chrissy, I have to help the band break down. Give me your number, I'll call you. No, even better, meet me tomorrow. We've got a lunch-time gig at the Third Tun in Greenwich – I'll take you to dinner afterwards.' He smiled his melting smile and I smiled back, but inside I was crying. I was going home alone. He was going to help the band break down, and I was going to go home and break down all on my own.

That night I sat on the sofa, drinking Southern Comfort and listening to Janis Joplin. 'Oh Lord, Won't You Buy Me a Mercedes Benz?' she sang. There's a line in the song about the Lord buying her a night on the town – I smiled bitterly when I heard it. I'd had my night and I wasn't happy at all at how it had ended.

In my mind I kept seeing Paul with his sleeves rolled up, lifting speakers and carrying them out of the bar, while Maryze coiled snaky grey leads and packed them into a box. Whenever she bent down, the split in her dress showed everything from the South Pole to the equator – and she had worryingly good legs.

Janis got it right, I decided – she'd got no help from her friends and neither had I. A week ago I'd been a happy, if somewhat lonely, party girl; today, thanks to Jason, I was a downright miserable woman, shot through with jealousy and without a second head on my pillow for the night. I pulled the glass dildo from its cushion of cotton wool in the drawer but even that couldn't tempt me. I had the blues, did I ever have the blues.

The next morning though, the sun came up, I still had a job (as far as I knew), and I didn't have a wife to leave me or a dog to die, so I got on with life. I depilated my legs so I could give Maryze a run for her money in the smooth stakes and, while I was wandering around bow-legged in an old T-shirt, waiting for the cream to take effect, I sorted through the CDs I'd borrowed from Jason. I came up with Aretha Franklin's *Respect*. It was feel-good music, so I cranked up the CD player to maximum volume, put a hot oil conditioner on my hair and pulled open the wardrobe door. I needed RESPECT all right, and I was going to get it!

An hour later I was in a taxi on the way to the Third Tun. I'd pulled the fur collar off the black coat and tacked it onto an old Chanel knock-off suit in houndstooth check – the way it was cobbled together wouldn't last long, but it wouldn't have to. The skirt was short and tight and, remembering what Jason had said about being cool, I'd set aside the suspender belt. Instead I'd opted for sheer black tights and, over them, shiny black boots. The shirt I wore was brilliantly white and crisp – I'd sprayed it with so much starch it could have cut butter. I'd found a deep-red lipstick and some pale matte foundation; together they gave me the vampy face of a 1920s film star. I looked sharp, I looked cool, and I was ready to sing the blues.

When I walked in the pub, every head in the room

turned. I watched men looking me up and down, and up again, and I felt a warm glow in my soul and an even warmer heat between my legs. So much admiration was more than an aphrodisiac, it was like sexual rocket fuel. I could feel I was giving off vibes that had guys adjusting their clothing and pulling down their shirts and sweaters to hide their hard-ons. I might be cool, but to these men I was hot! I ordered a gin and tonic – no more cat-piss alcohol for me – and sat down at a table near the stage. When I crossed my legs, I heard half a dozen men gasp and splutter.

One of the Symposium appeared on stage, twiddled a few things and then disappeared. A few seconds later I saw Paul looking out from the stage curtains, but I pretended I hadn't noticed – cool and slow, cool and slow. One of the men who'd been standing at the bar shuffled over. 'Is anybody sitting here?' he asked, indicating the chair next to me. I looked him over slowly: on any other day he would have been a good catch, but today I wanted Paul to feel like I'd felt last night so, although I smiled into his eyes and said, 'Doesn't look like it to me,' I was watching Paul from the corner of my eye and saw how his mouth tightened as the guy sat down.

By the time Paul made his way out front, my companion had become bold enough to ask me if I was 'Uh, like, a big kind of, uh, blues fan,' and I'd told him I was really only a beginner but willing to learn; I could almost see the steam coming out of his ears. Paul appeared behind me, with his sax slung over his shoulder. 'Chrissy,' he said, bending down to kiss me on the side of my neck, 'how wonderful to see you, and how wonderful you look.'

I let him lead me to the back-stage area, waving goodbye to my former table mate as I went. But before we got to the changing room, Paul dragged me into a gloomy corner, already inhabited by a dusty fire extinguisher. He started to kiss me and I joined in enthusiastically. As I'd already gathered, he was an expert smoocher, no tonsil strangler, but one of those men who snogged slowly and thoroughly, as though kissing was the point of the exercise, not simply a stage on the journey. I let myself slide down against the fire extinguisher, it was getting difficult to stand up properly and I couldn't see the point in wasting my energy on it when I could devote myself to enjoying Paul's mobile lips and the way his fingertips were working their way inside my jacket, unbuttoning my shirt and easing their way under my bra straps, pushing down on the elastic fabric to free my breasts. His head descended and I felt the heat of his mouth travelling my neck and down until his teeth nipped gently on my right nipple. I was more than ready, and I was already hoisting up my skirt and reaching for Paul's flies when I remembered the tights. There was not a hope in hell of getting them off elegantly, not in a corridor anyway, and I didn't fancy hopping around in semi-public view, trying to extract myself from my hosiery, so I did something I hadn't done for years – I pushed Paul away. His eyes were dark with lust and my red lipstick was around his mouth as though he'd been eating cherries; it looked bloody sexy, to be honest. But I took a deep breath, shrugged my bra back into place and smiled up at him as I wiped the lipstick off his chin.

'Didn't you promise me dinner?' I said.

His smile was hungry. 'Of course, my place, after the show.' He brushed his fingers across my face and headed down to the changing room, from where I could hear other members of the Symposium bickering. I turned around on my spaghetti-weak legs and sneaked into the women's toilet to adjust my face and clothing. Once I

was in a cubicle, I allowed myself to think about what
had just happened: Paul's gentle insistence, his delicious
kisses, the appreciative way his fingers lingered on my
skin ... it was all a bit much and I pushed the horrible
tights down around my ankles as I leant against the
cubicle door and felt the cold air on my thighs. It
wouldn't take long and, once done, I'd be able to face the
punters in the pub more easily. The idea of sitting out
there now, watching Paul on stage, while I was this hot
and troubled, was too much to bear. I leant forwards,
lowered the toilet seat, and put my bag on it to be safe
from the kind of sneaky bastard who steals from your
bag if you put it on the floor in a toilet cubicle. Then I
slid both hands up my thighs, feeling my inner muscles
jump and flex in anticipation of what was coming next
– me!

There was one trick I was rather fond of, which I have
to admit is not your usual, but each girl to her own, and
right now I wanted some fast, furious and above all
complete gratification. So I pulled up the tights again,
unlocked the cubicle and scooted to the basin, where I
ran cold water from the tap over my right hand until it
was red from the chill. Then I went back into the cubicle,
where I locked the door, leant against it, pulled down
the tights with my left hand and – whammo! Three icy
fingers, like Jack Frost: chilly, thrilling, fucking wonderful. It feels like somebody else's hand in you, that's the
first thing, and the second thing is that it scorches –
don't know why, but it does, burns like fire, even though
it's cold. It's a gorgeous feeling, but you have to be swift
so you get off before your fingers warm up. No problems
there though, the problem was going to be hanging on
long enough to get all the pleasure I wanted. I let my
hand move a little, sliding in and flexing, preparing
myself for what came next. I let my left hand drift over

my bikini line, as if I really wasn't sure I was going to do this and then let my left index finger slip and slide down, until it hovered just over my clit. My right hand was throbbing as it began to warm up, which wasn't suprising, given how hot I was, and it was going to take only the tiniest touch, the merest little caress, for me to come.

Then I heard the main door to the lavatories open. I bit my lip. Somebody came in. I could feel my fingers getting warmer and I really wanted to come now – whoever was out there might spend ten minutes doing their hair or fiddling with their make-up; I should know, I'd done it often enough myself, and I wouldn't, couldn't wait that long. I pulled my bottom lip deep into my mouth, pressing my teeth into its inner cushion and let my left index finger circle my clit. I didn't groan, although I wanted to, but I did inhale pretty sharply. I pressed my head back against the cubicle door in an attempt to stifle my responses and the woman outside began to sing quietly. It was Maryze. It was pretty unmistakable, not only because she expressed herself in a beautiful deep bluesy voice, but she was singing a famous old Etta James song – probably the only blues song I could have named before this week – 'I Just Want to Make Love to You'.

I wasn't going to let Maryze deprive me of my rightful pleasure, so I waited until she hit the big line and let herself go with a rolling 'love to you … love to you …' and I pushed deep with my right hand and circled with the fingers of my left hand and bit back even the slightest sound that might have given me away as I came. Then I stood silently until my legs stopped shaking and my breathing returned to normal before pulling up my panties and tights and unlocking the door. At some point Maryze had stopped singing and left the place, but

I'd been too lost in the aftermath of my orgasm to notice exactly when it was. I washed my hands and repaired my face and headed back out into the bar.

I took my seat back at the table and watched Paul perform. Whatever relief I'd given myself, he'd been denied and, if I still felt horny, he must be positively insane with lust. At one point, when the Symposium moved into 'Blueberry Hill' and he came forwards to play a solo on his golden horn, I was glad I was sitting down. His eyes were fixed on me and when he knelt down, tipping his head back and lifting his saxophone high, it was exactly as though he was on his knees in front of me. I could almost feel his tongue inside me, so it was no suprise I was finding it hard to sit still.

I couldn't wait for the gig to be over. Even when Maryze appeared and started to sing, I barely noticed – all I could think about was that we would soon be on our way to Paul's flat.

It seemed like Paul couldn't wait either. There was no waiting around at the end of the second set, or helping the rest of the band to break down: he handed his saxophone to the bass player, stepped down into the audience, took hold of my elbow and led me straight out of the bar, even before the punters finished applauding.

He drove a canary-yellow MG. Well, what else? It was a sexy funny car for a sexy funny guy. On the way to his flat he told me musician jokes, except musicians call themselves musos, not musicians. I smiled, but really I was wondering how long it would take to get to his place and whether I should let my hand creep up his thigh, but he was driving so fast I was nervous about distracting him and, although he talked fluently, he never took his eyes from the road.

He lived in West Kensington – a little mews flat with a tiny garden, which I glimsped out of the window before he grabbed me by the shoulders. I stared up into his eyes while I shrugged out of the little Chanel jacket with its big fur ruff, and undid the cuffs on my shirt. Then I lowered my eyes to my front as I began to unbutton the crisp white front of my shirt. I heard him make a sound, like a little growl, and then he picked me up and half threw me onto his squashy sofa. It wasn't a cool move, or a slow one, but I was past caring – I pulled him down on top of me.

There were a couple of seconds of confusion while I tried to continue undoing my top and he tried to help me, and then he got the idea and started to pull off his clothes with one hand while tugging at my skirt with the other. I leant forwards to unzip my boots and he lifted my shirt off my shoulders. Then he pushed me backwards again with his lips nuzzling into my breasts. I reclined, trying to lift my leg in the air so I could remove my boot, while developing a sudden inclination to breathe deeply and a total inability to focus or concentrate: he really did have the most amazing mouth!

Finally though we got ourselves sorted out. I got both boots unzipped and my tights off, he struggled out of his jacket and shirt and then scooped me up again and carried me to the bedroom. I was a little peeved, to be honest. I quite fancied making whoopee on his cushions, but once I hit his big white bed, with him working his way with fingers and tongue down from my cleavage to between my legs, I forgot to be anything except achingly wet and completely pleasured.

Paul took everything slowly. He crept his way down, pausing every few seconds to revisit some tiny fraction of my flesh that had got a more than usually vocal response from me. I could feel myself melting underneath him – I'd never really known what 'melting' was before, but if the fire brigade turned up now and told us the building was on fire, they'd have had to carry me out in a tub, I was too liquid and boneless and without a will of my own to do anything.

The first orgasm happened before I'd even unzipped Paul's trousers. There was a moment when I remembered myself enough to get on with trying to give him back some of the fun he was handing out to me, and then his tongue hit exactly the right place and exerted just the right kind of pressure at the perfect speed and I was riding a wave of absolute physical glory. Even then, Paul didn't let it happen fast. He kept me there, right on the edge of coming, until I thought I was going to scream like a steam train whistle, and then he let me tip, slowly, over that edge. I did scream. At least I think I did. I can't remember too much about what I did; I was too busy being overwhelmed by what I felt.

The next orgasm I did remember more clearly. It came when I was on top of Paul, having slid him inside me as soon as he'd fitted a condom, which he did with expert speed; he was a man whose fingers were pure gold. I was kneeling over him, smiling down, and he was grinning up at me. 'Is this dinner?' I asked.

'This is simply the appetiser,' he said, and I started to giggle, and the action of laughing started something off inside me that he spotted immediately, and he began to thrust a little faster, while guiding my hand between my thighs. I leant forwards even further, so my breasts were rubbing against his chest, and let my fingers dabble against my clitoris, and then, just as I began to come, he pulled down and away from me, leaving me hovering on the brink of orgasm again. Over and over he brought me right to the screaming point and held me there, and then finally, when I thought I couldn't bear it any more, he tipped me over so we were lying on our sides facing each other. He pushed my hand away, replaced my fingers with his own and then made me come, gazing into my eyes as he did.

The third time I came, he was on top of me, kissing and biting my neck as I arched my back to push myself against him, and the fourth time we were beneath the covers of his bed, making a slow weaving rhythm of our bodies in the increasing darkness of the early evening. I drifted off to sleep to the sound of a blues tune being hummed in my ear.

When I woke I asked him what it had been.

'"Things 'Bout Coming My Way", by James Young-blood Hart,' he said.

I pretended to swat him, but I was too exhausted and happy to make the blow connect.

'I have actually got some dinner,' he said. 'Tapas stuff from the deli and *dulche de leche* ice cream for pudding. I thought you looked like the kind of woman who would enjoy ice cream.'

I nodded.

'I'll put the tapas on a tray, shall I? We can eat in bed. Um, I wondered if you'd like to come to Dublin next weekend? We've got a gig over there.'

I nodded again.

While he was in the kitchen I thought back to the past few hours. The sex had been fantastic. It would be even more fantastic when I could persuade him to use the time between sets to invest in some quick and dirty knee-trembling behaviour, but there was no rush – we could take things cool and slow.

Sonata A. D. R. Forte

The notes of a piano sound over the drumbeat of the rain, plaintive and primal running together, falling and fading. I adjust the volume down, just enough that I can hear it without drowning the song of rain patter. Then I turn from the stereo and go to the sofa, where I sit and curl my feet under the warm velvet of my skirt. I can see nothing through the downpour. Water obscures the world outside, washing it away while I look out from this refuge of glass and latticework. Piano and rain.

I run my fingers along the windowpane, following the path of the rain. Lean my head on the glass and close my eyes, slip back into the semi-sweet place of memory.

It was pouring then too; a summer thunderstorm full of thud and bluster, the air pungent with the smell of rain. I'd sought shelter in a doorway, leaning against the dirty red brick wall in an effort to stay dry even though the wind still did its best to spatter water into my refuge. I didn't mind the rain, not much. Eventually I'd make the mad dash for my car and get there soaked and out of breath; turn the heat on full blast while I tore off damp scarf and jacket and ruffled my hair up cockatoo style. But for now I was content to stay dry until the worst of the downpour had vented.

And then I heard Mendelssohn. Trio No.1 muffled by concrete and brick, audible only in bits and starts over the drone of rain, the splash of car tyres in puddles and the screech of brakes. I went still. Listening.

Somewhere within the building a door squeaked, banged. Voices murmured. Yet still the music carried on, unfaltering. Tireless and fluid with the ease that comes from true passion for the craft. It wasn't until the side of my head began to hurt that I realised I was straining to hear with my ear and cheek pressed against the damp wood behind me.

I thirsted for that sound.

The hallway looked like the inside of every other campus building once I entered. Struggling fluorescent tubes that lit dingy concrete once painted beige. Creaking wood floor and greyish-brown linoleum. The musty smell of ancient carpets and filing cabinets.

But the sound of the piano pulled me on, drew me in past rooms and offices filled with dusty instruments, scribbled-upon whiteboards. Occupied by grey, colourless people who typed or talked, oblivious to the emotion bleeding through the tired hallways with every note.

I walked past them. How could they not hear? How could they remain so insensible, pacing through life like this? Like horses with blinders, trotting past open fields; never seeing or knowing what they were missing. Never thinking about what could be.

The piano answered me, indifferent to anything but its own joy and its own wild pleasure. *Appassionato*.

At the room itself I halted outside. I wanted the music and what it promised: the careless longing, the sensuality. I suddenly didn't want to see the player, just another miserable human eking out an existence except for this one instance of unrestrained joy. So I leaned again against the room doorway and listened.

I let the music beguile me, charm and whisper to me of golden damask sheets, of pillars twined around with vines, of red velvet and wine-sweet kisses. Of those aching, powerful moments of feeling that happened too few and far between the stretches of ordinary life. A look or a smile in the aftermath of sex. An unexpected touch. An instant of understanding without words.

There in that fusty little building with the mouldy ceiling lowering at me, I knew desire. And then it ended. Left me like a lover urgently called away. Chagrined, I bit my lip and frowned at the ceiling.

I told myself I should at least thank the piano player. He or she might be just a humdrum little person, ignorant of the voice and the longing in the music, but I could still show gratitude. A little moment of kindness on my part. So I pushed away from the wall and turned to enter the room. And found my way blocked.

He looked down at me and we said nothing at first, for there was nothing to say. I'd seen his face before, across impersonal, busy spaces among too many people. Somebody not part of my world. Somebody I had no reason to make part of my life, even though I had looked and looked again at that face: long proud nose and full mouth. Dark, rebellious waves of hair. Eyes the pale green of ivy leaves.

Now I looked full into his gaze and I spoke, and brought him into my world. 'I heard your playing.' I didn't add that it was lovely, that it was rapturous. That it was any of the hundred foolish, mindless compliments I could have uttered. And he understood.

He smiled and lifted the fringed edge of my scarf; let the silky, woollen strands glide through his fingers. Hands like pale ivory, but with no hint of fragility. I was caught by that sudden, unlooked-for touch, netted like a stray fairy in a wizard's garden, and I should have known then any chance of escape was lost.

'I'm lucky you did,' he said and let the scarf fall.

Such intimacy and such arrogance, brazen in his defiance of convention. But since he had stepped out onto thin air and dared me to follow him, I did. I took his arm as if we were old friends. We left the building, careless of the stinging rain that fought for our attention with each cold gust of wind. Now there was no reason to hurry. I wanted to savour the minutes and the rain chill and his warmth at my side.

We found a café; spent hours talking over something. Coffee, sandwiches. It didn't matter. What mattered was his hands rubbing my wrists, his thumbs covering mine before tracing the lines on my palm. His pulse warm against mine. His green eyes and his smile.

But he didn't kiss me that first night.

We circumvented each other for a long, wasted time, keeping our interactions chaste because we could rise above things like animal desire. All we needed was the meeting of like minds. We wanted nothing but long conversations and tranquil silences.

We shared confidences and thoughts and books. Traded recipes for stuffed mushrooms and chicken pot pie. He taught me how to make English trifle, and when my custard didn't set and I fretted, he laughed and fed me strawberries. We drank all the sherry, ate the entire bag of walnuts and stayed up until morning.

I listened to his fears and he listened to my frustrations. He played for me while I sat beside him and listened, my head on his shoulder, my eyes closed. We promised each other that was how it would remain between us. Never would we fall into the trap of wanting too much.

There were promises to others: expectations and plans we could not simply throw to the winds.

'Never,' we said.

We were so stupid.

* * *

But he came to me first, after an evening of too much wine and too much poetry. After hours of meaningless social pleasantries; of mingling and smiling and small talk about nothing. Of listening to the party's hostess read Neruda while we pretended not to notice each other. Ignored the heat when we stood too close. I told myself it was the alcohol, the crowded room. Told myself it was anything but his eyes following my every movement, or the way he looked at me and smiled for no reason at all.

He took me home and stayed, shrugging off his jacket and hanging it up in the closet as if it belonged there. Letting the dog out and then coming to find me where I stood, arms folded, beside the darkened garden windows. Always that's how it was. I can look back now and see that I was ever the one to pull away first. To run.

Yet that night, when he rested his head on my shoulder, slipped the straps of the evening dress down and kissed the hollow just below my shoulder blade, I yielded without a thought.

'I've looked at you all night. I've wanted you,' he said.

I nodded, unable to answer, and he kissed the pulse beating in my neck. He cupped the dark-rose satin dress over my breasts and stroked the flesh through it. My nipples responded to that steel-ivory caress and rose to meet it, wanting more. I was his instrument and his art, craving his touch. Craving him.

I turned and pulled his mouth to mine. I kissed him and stopped halfway though, confused. There was no demand in his response, no bid for power. Instead, I felt him relinquish control; all that he was and felt and knew into my keeping. He gave himself to me that night.

Hard cock. Hard, tensed muscle in his legs. Soft hands. Soft skin on his thighs, his stomach, his ribcage: everywhere that I touched and licked and sucked. Naked and offered up for my taking.

I made him suck my fingers and ran them – still wet – over the head of his cock. Stroked it. He licked the tangy drops of his own arousal from my skin before I slid my fingers into him, and then I caressed him from the inside while I teased his cock with my tongue and my lips. He cried out with pleasure and arched his hips upwards, fighting release.

'I want your wet pussy,' he said. 'I want to fill you.'

'You will, love,' I said. 'Be patient. You will.'

I fucked his ass with my fingers and I sucked his sweet cock until he came, thick and hot on my tongue, and then I licked the sweat from every inch of him until he rose again for me. He had his wish then, filling me and stroking my breasts, my neck, my shoulders while I knelt over him, my hips moving with his rhythm. And I wondered through a haze of orgasm and joy why I had ever, ever thought I didn't need him this way.

That first night. Such magic. Every night was magic, every morning and afternoon and instant of time I was in his arms. It was the times in-between. When we worried about who was watching and what they thought. Disapproving glances. Curious, harpy stares from those who styled themselves colleagues and acquaintances or, worse yet, friends.

I glowed when he touched me, but I cringed when others saw it, when I saw their lips curl in mockery or disdain. I didn't understand envy; I was too ashamed of my own unruly weakness. We both were.

Only the music tore away barriers. Listening to him play in the hot, navy-shadowed dusk, I closed my eyes and forgot the outside. I forgot reputations, and the now obsolete romantic attachments that still clung and brought twinges of guilt. I didn't think about the wasted expectations and the gossip left in their wake.

While he played, I was inside the music. The raw notes left me tired. Only his playing could pare me down like that, and strip away my pretences. His playing. And his fingertips on my skin.

Until the last day. It should have rained that day. There should have been skies of steel with an icy wind or perhaps russet, falling leaves whispering of loss. Something poetic. Instead we had humid air, muggy with the aftertaste of smog. Traffic and lines at the airport. Tasteless coffee in green and brown plastic cups with white lids.

He sat quiet, drinking his coffee and watching the planes inching by beyond the windows. Not sulking, merely accepting when he knew any more opposition was just a waste of time. He reached out, touched my shoulder, his eyes focused on the lace at my collar as if he contemplated an unfamiliar instrument.

'I'll miss you.'

Simple. Stated without guile or motive. Just a fact.

I looked up, trying to seem brave and matter of fact, trying to hold back treacherous emotions. 'Yes. And so will I. But . . .'

His fingers moved to cover my lips. 'You don't need to explain it any more, love. I already know.' A sad smile. 'I hope you're right, I hope it gets better with distance.'

The intercom pinged. We listened to them call my flight for the last time.

'It will.'

But even now, here in this house that still seems strange to me, I find that neither time nor distance has healed the wound. I was wrong. All I thought I knew turns out to be nothing.

A space of silence while the CD changes. A click before the music picks up again, filling the emptiness. Mendelssohn. I lower my head onto my folded arms on the back of the sofa. I don't want to see the rain. I don't want to remember. I don't want to hear those chords, stirring the ache inside, the futile longing for kisses and knowing fingers. I am too strong to cry and too proud to pick up the phone. So I sit here with only the sounds of piano and rain.

And then I hear the muted snick of the front door, opening and closing. I did not lock the door. This place, a little town in a distant country, doesn't warrant locked doors. Amazing, I think, that such a place should still exist. I look up, expecting to see a neighbour, or maybe the vet's girl with the week's prescription. But instead my heart leaps and somersaults like a schoolboy on the first day of summer. Even though I cannot command a single other muscle to move.

He stands in the doorway, raindrops caught in his hair and on his clothes. We look at each other, saying nothing. I, because I think he can be nothing more than a figment of my imagination. He should be a world away. It's where I left him.

He walks forwards, staring at me with such intensity I don't know whether I want to run away and hide, or let myself be pulled into the storm promised by that icy green gaze. He sinks to the floor at my side, rests his cheek on my thigh, and closes his eyes. A penitent and a pilgrim come through fire and trial, overcome at the shrine for which he has so long searched.

His hand rests on my velvet swathed knee, and I shiver as if the cloth did not exist. As if his musician's fingers, fine boned and strong, touched my bare skin. A touch both electric and sensual, like cold white wine drunk too much and too fast.

'You came all the way here. Why?'

He looks up at me, apologetic and burning all at once and I regret the sharp edge to my tone, the tinge of resentment that I've been without him, without even the consolation of his words or his voice so long. No matter that it was my own fault, my own wish that the break be clean and final.

'I tried, love. I'm sorry, I did. But I can't forget how it feels.' He sighs, shifts. 'I need to talk to you; I need to fuck you. I can't do this.'

I look out at the watery world, trying to ignore the impulse to stroke the droplets from his damp hair, to curl my fingers in the darkened strands.

'We broke the rules before. We broke them and didn't care,' he says, frowning when I turn to him.

'And part of the reason I left was to stop . . .'

'But it's hurting us. You told me it was an addiction, like any other kind. So why should we care about what the right thing is now anyway? Why?' His voice rises, quavers in frustration and pain. Throwing my own demand to know back at me.

'Good question.'

I know he's still looking at me, stung by the indifference in my voice, but I avert my gaze. Find safety in watching water run in a haphazard trickle over some irregularity on the window frame. I'm still fighting the longing, fighting him. And I don't even know why.

'How can you be this cold?'

I shake my head. The rain falls in staccato needles, and a harp has joined the notes of the piano still pouring from the stereo speakers. I think I will break apart from longing and guilt.

I feel him move and I close my eyes. I know what will happen; it doesn't matter how cold or cruel I try to be. Yes. Yes, love, this is an addiction.

His hands turn my face to his, and my limbs betray me, taking me to the edge of the sofa, my arms going around him. His lips are rain cold and sweet; his clothing damp and chilled. But heat rises within him like a song, growing in tempo and sound.

He opens me. His hands search beneath my skirt, find the silken edges of my panties. He pulls them to my thighs, my knees. He slips them off one ankle and then another and, still kneeling, holds my feet together in his lap. Beneath his jacket and shirt his stomach is warm, vulnerable, and I rub my toes against that yielding, intimate space. He closes his eyes, cups my calves and massages them slowly.

It hurts to be shut out, even for a moment, and I whisper to him to look at me. I've already shut myself out for far too long. He smiles, obeys and bends to kiss my knees, trailing kisses down to the ticklish skin at the arch between knee and calf. Licking tiny, wet caresses up the undersides of my thighs as he pulls me forwards. As he takes my skirt off with practised ease. Tosses the cloth aside and turns to my belly. Water drops from his hair and piccolo kisses falling on the curve under my navel, the curve of my waist, up to the edges of my ribs.

This time I cannot help burying my hands in his hair. Arching under him and crying out as he makes love to me with these simple, soft kisses. Art without effort. But no, this isn't lovemaking; this is far beyond the simple, carnal weakness I was so afraid of once. This is worship and sacred song. It's as close to magic as I'll ever know.

His kisses are falling lower now, notes spiralling into a powerful melody. His tongue parts the folds of my sex, dancing over my clit, searching out the entrance to my pussy. Moving within me like a song of flame.

I lift his head and bring his lips to mine to kiss the fragrant, glistening moisture from his mouth. Tasting myself on him; taking myself back from him because all this while he's kept me safe while I ran. He runs his fingers up into my hair and down the back of my neck left bare by the short strands. He grasps the collar of my linen shirt and I hear the fabric tear, feel the touch of air as he eases the ruined garment down my arms. He kisses my shoulder as if to apologise for his impatient passion.

And I don't know how or why I should deserve this. Deserve him.

I lie naked on the sofa, watching him undress, and I think that he belongs here; his figure before the old-fashioned window, framed by bookcases and hand-carved chairs, that of a hero in a Regency romance. Body hard with muscle, hair long and tangled, the edges just brushing his chin. Serious and sensitive and melodramatic. All that I've ever wanted.

My fingers search between my legs to answer the need fuelled by the fantasy, by the longing. He is naked now too, but he stands still to watch, his full cock quivering as he takes in the sight of my spread legs, my fingers moving over the folds of my sex like a maestro's over ivory keys. He strokes himself, watching me, his gaze moving from my body to my face that I can feel is flushed with heat. In his eyes, I am Beauty.

'Don't stop,' he says as he comes to my side. He kneels and cups one breast in his hand.

The tip of his tongue brushes the nipple and the flesh between my legs thrums in answer. Another gentle lick and I'm melting in moans and sighs again. I tap my fingers faster against my swollen clit, fluttering movements driving the crescendo while his tongue plays accompaniment on my nipples, my belly, my parted lips.

He straddles my body, hand still moving along his cock, lips red from my kisses. Like a priest-king in some archaic ritual, waiting to offer his seed and his power to the priestess beneath him. Male and beautiful. He rubs the shaft of his cock along my sex and I'm ready to explode with sensation. Yet it's the thought of what he does – the way he does it, intense and deliberate – more than the action itself that puts me over the edge.

And while I'm still coming, still crying out with the satisfaction of orgasm, I feel him enter me. Feel the muscle of his cock sliding into my pussy, awakening even more feeling, taking away all pretence to decency. I forget the man and can think only of the delicious hardness driving into me.

But then he leans forwards and says my name, voice rough with arousal, and I remember the man. I remember why I have wanted him. All the days and nights of longing, the memories of forbidden trysting. All that I know now. The turmoil of emotion and thought joins the song, intensifying it, and helplessly I'm caught up in it while our bodies move.

The rain has become a torrent, beating itself wildly at the glass. Free and not free; trapped by bonds that cannot be seen. By duty. Obligation to fall. And so it falls with relentless passion.

We whisper to each other in short, breathless fragments. Things we should never say: desperate, filthy, loving. We leave bruises and bite marks. Something tangible to last, to prolong what is over too soon in a final burst of motion and inordinate cries. And then I clutch him to my sweat-soaked body, my breasts crushed by his weight, my legs folded tight about his. I press my face into his shoulder, breathing his scent. I'm surrounded by him; filled by him, inside and out. Safe.

The piano wafts sad and sweet over the subdued patter of rain. The music is always free and untethered by fear. The music will always win out over that which threatens to mute its voice. I promise myself that I won't run any more.

'How long do you have?' I ask, *pianissimo*.

'A few days,' he mumbles into the hollow of my neck. He lifts his regal, tousled head. 'Unless you let it be more.'

His tone is quiet, asking for nothing, but his eyes plead. I look away; I still can't give an answer. I know now that I'll do anything for him, but old habits and old fears are hard to let go of.

'Love . . .'

I shake my head, pulling his back down to my shoulder where I cannot see that gaze of longing. I'm giving in; it's only a matter of time. The music is weaving its spell and soon I will have no defences left. But not yet. He sighs and sinks into my arms, but he knows it too. The sounds of the piano and the rain run together, lull us to sleep. When we wake, he will make love to me again, and I will say yes.

Wednesday Sessions
Siondalin O'Chnoc

Eileen McCafferty scooted her chair left to make room for Conlin and his guitar, making a horrendous racket over the worn linoleum tile of the White Cockade's back room. She felt the rough wooden chair leg snag her pantyhose, and muttered a mild oath in Gaelic. The fact that she would now have to stop for new hose before work tomorrow morning capped off a day of grinding irritations. And why was Conlin setting up over here, anyway? He always stood on the other side of the room, straight across from her, the gentle bobbing of the seven-piece cap drawn down low on his brow holding her steady and true on the beat.

Crossing her ankles and tucking her low-heeled pumps back under the chair in the hopes that no one would notice the run in her nylons, she realised the whole session group was staring in her direction, waiting. Blood rushed to her cheeks, bringing a wave of heat to her face in the cold damp winter air.

'Sorry,' she murmured.

A nudge on her shoulder made her look up. Conlin O'Doherty towered over her, the wrists of his long arms awkwardly escaping his sleeves as he thrust her wobbling music stand in her direction.

'Sorry,' she said again, bow clattering to the ground as she reached out her hand.

Sheets of music peeled off and floated around her feet

as she manoeuvred the stand's three legs between the chairs. She heard Conlin sigh, felt without looking that he lifted his guitar strap over his head and set the instrument on the stand behind him.

'Right then,' Eamon Hand, the session master, continued. 'As I was saying, we have a new guitarist joining us tonight, Sean Thomas, who was born here in Slieve Bloom, but has been long away in America, where he tells us that sessions are alive and well but of course we shall all believe that when we see it. In any event, welcome, Sean. Shall we get started then? "The Maid" set, start with "Drowsy Maggie" into "The Maid Behind the Bar", a-one, two...'

Eileen bent awkwardly to the floor to pick up her music. Aware of her blouse pulling out of the back waistband of her tweed skirt, she hoped that her jacket was covering the bare slice of skin. She tried to reach through the line of chairs in front of her to fetch her bow, her legs swinging out to hold her balance as she stretched. Conlin knelt down next to her. His long arms stretched to grasp the pearl and ebony frog of her bow, slid it back across the floor, and picked it up. She clasped the papers to her chest as he handed it to her.

'You know you have a run,' he whispered.

She looked up blankly. His eyes glowed in a soft chestnut brown under thick black brows, the ring of gold around his pupils bright in the shaft of late-evening light coming through the high transom window; his graying hair escaped his cap and curled around his ears in a most unruly fashion. He smelt of lemon-scented laundry soap and starch. The fingertips of his left hand touched the back of her extended calf, and Eileen's hand froze on the bow, her intake of breath arrested in her throat.

'Just there,' he said, and, with his eyes locked on hers, his hand moved slightly, the flesh of his middle finger sliding over an inch of her calf under its torn nylon, swiftly pressing at her skin like a wooden match struck along the side of its box. Eileen's body flared with an unexpected lightness, her jaw dropping as she struggled for something to say, something of her usual witty and caustic nature that would cover this odd and overwhelming sensation, but Conlin quickly stood and turned his eyes to his tuning pegs. The space on her leg where his hand had been tingled. Eileen's papers dropped again, and she ducked her reddened face to collect them.

'Hold up, then, hold up,' Eamon said, and the group squeaked to a halt. 'I say, are you ready then, Eileen? Are we interrupting you here?'

She shook her head, arranging her music on the stand, refusing to look up. She started to speak, but no sound came out. She cleared her throat and tried again. 'Sorry, Eamon. Sorry, everyone. Off day. Go on, then.'

Eamon sighed and started the count again. Eileen's bow plunged into the opening on a five-note roll and slid up into the three-note cross bowing on the minor phrase, then settled into a gentle rocking motion that pushed the A part of the tune into its characteristic lilting, lifting form. Beside her, Conlin thrummed the rhythm with his fingers against nylon strings, the hollow body of his Martin pulsing time, serving as a matching bookend to Biddie Harper's gentle bodhrán in the far corner. Out of the corner of her eye, Eileen could sense the fingers of his left hand switching chord formations on the fretted guitar neck; the very same fingers that had moments before flickered across her calf. She turned her head slightly, briefly, and took in an image of his hand, long and slender, pale and supple, dancing across the ebony fingerboard. Unbidden, she felt them again on her leg, and sucked in her breath with a start. This was Conlin, she reminded herself. It was not as if she had not sat with him in these Wednesday night sessions for over a decade now.

Around the A part again, Eileen felt herself sinking into the familiar bouncing rhythm, the day's frustrations – her cat pissing on the laundry in the morning because she hadn't changed the litterbox; running out of all but decaffeinated tea; her error at the register at O'Hanley's shop earning her a wicked scolding from the manager – sloughing off her neck and shoulders. The lines beside her blue eyes softened; her thin lips eased into a peaceful posture that was not exactly a smile, but at least relatively pleasant.

She slid her left hand up the violin neck to third position as they rolled into the major key B part, and looked up to see that Tom Gallagher had done the same, but old Kevin MacMillan was frowning his disapproval at them both. 'Never was a fiddler in my day used third position,' he would be railing over a pint later, 'and there's no need to start now. It's not traditional. Like those guitars, too. Shouldn't be here.'

'Fie on your tradition,' Eileen would answer in their customary banter. 'The fiddle's not even traditional. They didn't start playing it in Ireland until the fifteen hundreds. You'd have us all on gut-strung harps and wearing togas if you had your way, Kevin MacMillan.'

Eileen's lips parted a bit more in the direction of a smile as she thought of it, then her eyes flew wide open as they saw something she never thought she'd see: Kevin MacMillan's fingers tripping to a stop as they dropped back into the A part of 'Drowsie Maggie' for the second go-round. She'd never seen Kevin hesitate for an instant on any song, much less one he'd been playing probably every day for the better part of the sixty years since he first picked up a fiddle. The sight of it made her skip a turn of the bow. She quickly threw in a triplet bow shake to get turned around and saw Eamon shoot her a quizzical look. She shrugged and kept playing, her attention returning to Kevin.

He'd stopped, stock-still, the fiddle perched at his shoulder. Then he lowered it, slowly, tucked it under his right arm, and folded his arms across his chest. Eileen saw his grizzled face darken with more than his ordinary grouchiness. He looked downright mad. She followed his eyes to the far side of the room, and gasped out loud.

It took a minute for her ears to hear what her eyes were seeing. The new guitarist, Sean Thomas, stood in Conlin's usual spot wearing blue jeans, a pair of gym shoes and a black T-shirt with some kind of rock-band logo on it including a large marijuana leaf. He picked the steel strings of his flame-finish Ibanez, eyes closed and near-shaven blonde head lolling back, chin poking the air garishly in exaggerated time. The guitar swung back and forth as he rocked his hips, his fingers flying through the melody, filling in rills and off-licks at the ends of each phrase. As the group slipped up to the B part once more, Sean fingers tapped down the fretboard, first in harmonic thirds, then into a walk-down counter melody.

By the third time through, Kevin MacMillan looked like he was about to explode, and Eamon looked fit to be tied. Perhaps he'll even out on 'The Maid Behind the Bar', Eileen thought. She glanced up to Conlin and saw him staring at Sean with detached interest, marking the movement of his hands like a man might look to see where the other boats seem to be headed in the morning before deciding where to fish.

She looked back at Sean and tried to fix her face into the same look of disinterested detachment, at the same time thankful that Conlin was at her right ear keeping a steady beat. On second look, Sean had a fine square jaw, and the T-shirt was stretched over a fine set of lean, rounded shoulders that, together with the lightness of his hair, left her assuming he had been working out of doors, on the docks perhaps, or building things. His bare arms looked startlingly naked amidst the buttoned-down shirtsleeves and tweed coats of the sessions group. Naked, and tanned. She glanced away, but felt her eyes drawn back to the swathe of bare skin that was his right arm draped over the lower body of the Ibanez. As his fingers moved, the muscles of his forearm twitched and bulged and rolled under blue veins and a fuzz of soft hair.

Conlin cleared his throat pointedly as they soared into the third go-round of 'The Maid', and Eileen realised she'd fallen off pace. Her fingers stumbled, and she felt the flustered look cross her face. Conlin turned in his chair to face her, his hands firm in their steady, unchanging pace. Eileen nodded her thanks as she turned sideways to face him, and felt more than heard the vibration of the Martin's soundbox like a soothing heartbeat echoing in her chest. She breathed in deeply and focused, the pattern of the music filling her lungs, and caught back up with the group as they rolled into the B part of 'The Maid' with its long athletic *arpeggios* running across all four strings.

She watched Conlin's hands stroking their percussive beat, and suddenly she refocused to a different plane. There, across the face of his guitar, lay the shadow of her hands. Her fingers beating their tattoo on the shadow neck of the fiddle, her wrist down in its non-lazy classical playing grip; the dark line of the shaft of her bow sliding over Conlin's right hand, dipping down into the soundbox, then up again and over his thumb. She stared, entranced. She'd never watched herself play before; a workshop teacher had once suggested that they all go home and practise bowing in the mirror, but her bathroom was too tiny to even get a full bow stroke in from one wall to the shower door, and the whole idea had struck her as rather silly. This was like a mirror, and yet different. Were those her hands, those dark shapes sliding over the spruce top, over Conlin's ceaselessly moving fingers in a ghostly caress? Did he know? Could he even see it?

She looked up and found his eyes fixed on her own left hand, neatly cradling the shaft of the violin neck. His nostrils flared slightly as her hand slid back down to first position, and Eileen became aware of the throb of his Martin's soundbox humming in her breasts as her violin rose and fell with her breath. She became conscious of her nipples pressing against the nylon lining of her Marks & Spencer sale bra, and an image raced unbidden across her mind's eye, of her flesh encased in something racy and lacy and silky under the neatly pressed placket of her shopgirl's blouse, and Conlin's fingers dancing across the embroidered threads, plucking at them, playing her body.

Before she could sweep the image out of her mind, the swelling sound in the room split in two, and Eileen looked back at the session group, startled, ears racing to make sense of the cacophony. There, Kevin MacMillan had stopped altogether. Biddie Harper played on her bodhran without missing a beat – she was half-deaf anyway, and probably didn't notice the change. Tom Gallagher and the other fiddlers and two flutists had moved to the last tune of the set, 'The Shy Maid', but another melody line was cutting through the rolling progression, and Tim O'Brien on his accordion was bouncing back and forth between the two, face scrunched up in utter confusion.

'I know this one,' Eileen muttered aloud, sliding her index finger low on the A string then flicking an E with her pinky. She lost the progression, closed her eyes, and found it again. '"Pretty Maid Milking Her Cow"', she said to Conlin, whose hands had stopped mid-stroke on the guitar, his lips turned downwards in impatient concentration as Eileen caught the rolling change into the major key on the B part.

The other fiddlers dropped away as the tune rose to the E string, then down again, Eileen's spirits rising with it. She looked across the room to find it was down to her, Biddie Harper and Sean Thomas, his mouth widening in a broad smile with his pick clenched tightly between Hollywood-white teeth, his bare fingers plucking the melody and a running line of interceding drones at the same time. The tune rose back to its apex, a high A on the E string, and Eileen slid her hand up to catch it with her first finger and give it a roaring vibrato instead of the usual fourth-finger roll, the plucked notes of Sean's guitar flying through the roll beneath her like cherries tumbling beneath the smooth glossy surface of a butter-crusted pie. They bounced down, down through the minor thirds and back to the D string, the middle section of Eileen's bow bouncing in hard dramatic swipes, then they rose again, together, their blue eyes locked to one another across the room.

Eileen could feel the stares of everyone else in the room, and found to her own surprise that she didn't care. Let them watch, she thought. Let them look at me. I can do something they can't do. For once.

She felt Sean pulling her along, felt his eyes piercing into her, the bulging muscles in his forearms pulsing for her and her alone, his fingers playing her, this tune that only she knew, from some depth that she wasn't even aware of. Rolling down the minor thirds again Eileen felt her shoulders swaying, then lifting, her body rising straight on the upbeat, breasts pushing outwards, hips rocking back ever so slightly in her chair, her weight moving forwards between her thighs, then falling sharply on the third beat of the measure. The scent of warming rosin began to rise from her violin as her bow moved faster, the sharp pine taste of it drying the back of her throat.

The rip in her nylon began to run, stitch by stitch popping up the back of her calf, behind her knee. Eileen moved harder, eyes closed, deliberately circling her hips in small movements she hoped would go unnoticed, riding into the sheer unexpected pleasure of the cool hard chair seat pressing against the sliding rhythm of her cunt, slipping under layers of nylon panties and slip and skirt lining, the scratchy wool tweed of her skirt stubbornly encasing it all, tugging her hips back into a more respectable line at every stroke. The hem of her skirt crept upwards, the fabric bunching thicker and thicker into the bending gap between the top of her thigh and the curve of her buttocks.

She felt the end coming up, but her body didn't want to let go of the tune. Her hips moved more sharply, the pressure of the ridge in the centre of the chair seat teasing her, rubbing between her vulva but not quite reaching her swelling clit as she twitched forwards and slid back with each measure. It called to her, pulling the tune down through her from the curl of her fiddlehead to the congested wet flesh beneath her, something that she wanted, something just out of reach. Maybe if we went around again, she thought, her breath pulling in short dry bursts against the roof of her slightly open mouth. But no, this is it, it's ending. Last time through.

As the B part rose to its final cresendo, the run in her stocking let go and flew up her thigh and over the curve of her ass to her waistband. Then they were there, and together, abruptly, with three crisp strokes, it was over.

Sean gave her a big wink as she lowered the violin from her shoulder and felt her face break into a wide warm smile.

There was a scattering of handclapping, a murmur of 'what was that,' and Tommy Gallagher stood and announced he was going for a pint.

'I think I'll join you,' Conlin said loudly. He looked pointedly at Eileen. 'It seems I'm not needed here at the moment.'

'Five minutes, five minutes only everybody,' Eamon shouted as chairs scraped and cases clattered for an unexpected run to the bar. 'And Mr Thomas, for future reference, that's "The Shy Maid" we run into on the end of that set, and what was that odd piece you were playing?'

Eileen stood and stretched, and looked to catch Sean's eye, but his back was to her, and he was deep in animated conversation with Eamon. She glanced towards the bar, saw Conlin standing head above the rest, his profile placid as he passed pints of amber and brown liquid back to the other musicians gathered around him. She felt a jostle and found Sean and Eamon edging past her to join the others.

''Scuse me,' Sean muttered, not looking in her direction. The smile faded from Eileen's lips, and she plopped back down in her chair. Laughter and chatter drifted through the door from the White Cockade's tap room, and she knew without looking that Sean was in the centre of it. Feeling foolish and empty, she leant her forearms on the back of the chair ahead of her and buried her face in the crook of her elbow, willing herself to snap her violin case shut, stand up, and walk out the door, down the sidewalk, and up the lane to home. Sean's voice was chanting the cadence of some elaborate tale in the other room, which rose, then cracked into a round of shouts and laughter. Cigarette smoke and warm beer drifted through the air.

She gave a little jagged breath, not quite a sob, her mind drifting back to the run in her hose; she could buy new nylons when she stopped for kitty litter on the way home tonight, but that would mean lugging bag and baggage back to her apartment, or else walking home, getting the car and heading back out again in the dark of the night. She felt drained, and quite alone.

'Hello there,' Conlin said.

Eileen jumped, and found him sitting, straddling the chair in front of her, holding out a pint of golden red ale. She smiled gratefully, took the glass, clinked its rim to his and took a long thankful draught.

'Quite a performance,' he said, standing and pulling off his jacket. He stopped mid-movement. 'Do you mind?' he asked. 'It's suddenly warm in here.'

She laughed at his excessive politeness, waving her hand in graciously exaggerated permission. He draped the jacket over his seat and straddled the chair in front of her again, facing her.

'Now then,' he said, unbuttoning his left shirtsleeve. He looked into her eyes, slowly rolling the shirtsleeve up to his elbow. 'What was that piece you were playing?' He rolled up his other sleeve, his eyes never leaving her face.

'"Pretty Maid Milking Her Cow"', she said, as he reached for his guitar, his face unmoving. 'It's really a song. I've heard the words in Gaelic but I don't really know what they mean.'

He flicked his fingers out in a quick stretch, then cracked his knuckles and leant back, neck taut against the guitar strap, bare forearms wrapped around the hollow body of the Martin. With the middle finger of his right hand, he traced the curves where the spruce top

WEDNESDAY SESSIONS **125**

met the side walls of the instrument. 'Lilt it for me,' he said mildly.

'Oh, I can't really sing, Conlin, you remember that from choir, don't you? What a disaster that . . .' Her voice trailed off as she saw his eyes widen and his lips part slightly.

'Please,' he said, voice dropping to a husky whisper. 'Lilt it for me.'

She nodded, tentatively, and cleared her throat. She started in, soft and unsure. Conlin's fingers began to move, following her voice as it grew stronger, his left hand tapping the melody along the fretboard, his right hand still hovering over the polished wood of the sound box, circling it, just touching the strings. The second time through he began to pick out the notes, his thumb darting along the strings for the lower thirds and fifths above the melody line.

'Ready for the B part?' she asked.

'Oh yes,' he murmured, shifting in his chair as she started in. 'Wait, pick up your fiddle. Show me what you were doing with it. No, you don't need the bow, just hold it there and let me see your fingers moving.'

She watched the tendons on the backs of his hands flexing as he followed her silent fingers slip over the shaft of the fiddle, her voice warming in her throat now, finding the key and the rhythm. She slid up to the third position high A and heard him gasp as she slid back down to first. He lifted the guitar slightly, pressed his body deeper into the chair towards her. Beneath the chair back rail, she could see the pleats of his khaki trousers straining, his long hard cock pressing upwards against his instrument. She gave a little cry and stopped, seeing now in his eyes his unmistakable hunger.

'Don't stop,' he said, and the tip of his tongue darted to touch the centre of his upper lip.

'Conlin,' she whispered, pulling her fiddle tightly between her breasts, 'I had no idea. I . . .'

He lifted his right hand from the strings, moved it in aching slowness towards her face. She lifted her chin to press into his palm as his fingers met her skin, the fold beside his thumb falling over her lips. She opened her mouth and grasped the wedge of flesh between her teeth, then slid her tongue up and over the tip of his thumb as it pressed into her mouth, then deliberately pulled outwards as Conlin drew a ragged breath. His wet thumb drew a line down the centre of her chin; his fingers traced her jawline and slid down to the base of her throat. He stopped at the deep hard V below her larynx and pressed, gently but persistently.

'Lilt it for me,' he said again. She began to hum, her voicebox caught within his curling fingers, his thumb firm against her airway. His lips curled back with desire as the vibration filled his hand. 'Oh, Eileen,' he breathed.

He released her neck from the grip of his fingers and dropped his hand lower as she sang, his thumb still pressing hard against her as it fell between her breasts. His fingers spread wide, cupping her, finding her nipple hard and squeezing it between his third and fourth fingers. 'Why do you think I've been coming to these God-awful Wednesday sessions for fourteen years?' he said, eyes piercing hers, smiling, then catching his lower lip with his teeth.

Eileen pushed back her shoulders, lifting her breasts towards him as he opened the top button of her blouse, and the next. 'I don't know,' she said. 'I just thought you liked the music.'

'You are the music.' His palm warm against her flesh, he slipped her bra strap from her shoulder. His left hand wrapped around her neck and pulled her mouth to his as his fingers slid back along her ribcage under her blouse, then pressed upwards into the soft hot pulsing of her underarm. Eileen felt her heartbeat straining to meet his demanding fingertips.

Her lips met his, hard and eagerly, and she sucked his tongue between her teeth. The familiarity of all these years washed over her: the smell of his skin, the sound of his voice, the movement of his fingers on the strings all intimately known to her. Now all that she had missed of him rushed through her: his lips and tongue and fingers on her body, in her mouth and her cunt, the feel of his long naked legs intertwined with hers in pale grey morning light. Her hips moved on the chair again, inching towards him, needing to engulf him.

The carved ridge down the centre of the wooden chair seat tormented her aching wet cunt, no longer abstractly pleasuring her as it had when she was playing minutes before. This time she knew just what she needed to come, and every cell in her body cried out for Conlin to fill her, to let her come rubbing just like this against his thighs, his ass, his hips, the tall thick cock that she could see straining to burst free of his clothes. She reached out her left hand and found its tip beneath his zipper, tugged at it between her thumb and forefinger and felt his first damp drops seeping through the twill khakis under her fingertips.

His hand moved to her bare breast and wrapped around it, his calloused thumb setting the tip of her nipple on fire with rough circling strokes. He pulled his lips away from hers and slid them down her throat towards her nipples. His wet tongue was seeking to cool her burning nubs, when voices burst back into the room. Conlin leapt up, his uncomprehending eyes trying to refocus as Eamon and Sean walked in with their arms draped around each other's shoulders, in rousing chorus of a verse of 'Seven Drunken Nights' he hadn't heard before. He rearranged his guitar, trying to hide his bulging crotch, and moved into his chair, his legs awkwardly unco-operative.

Eileen hastily replaced her bra strap on her shoulder and started to rebutton her blouse.

'Don't,' she heard Conlin whisper. 'Leave it just like that.'

She glanced down: the open buttons left her bosom covered, though the swell of her cleavage was apparent, at least to someone sitting higher than her, as Conlin was. He would be watching her then, watching her skin as they played. She lifted one hand to her throat, sliding her fingers where his had so recently pressed against her, and shot him a fiery look.

They both fumbled self-consciously with their instruments as the rest of the group filtered noisily back into the room, buoyant from the drink and the camaraderie. As they began to settle in, strings plucked and turned, notes blown to warm up fipples and fingers, Conlin leant near her ear.

'Let me drive you home,' he whispered.

Suddenly it all flooded back to her: her cold, messy apartment, the litterless kitties, the job in the morning. 'I . . . my apartment . . .' she started.

'I meant my home,' he said. He cleared his throat. 'It so happens that for fourteen years, I've done my cleaning and laundering on Wednesday afternoons. Just in case I might, you know, have company. Embarrassing, really.'

She raised her eyebrows, then realised with all her body that he was completely serious. 'Yes,' she said. 'Yes, yes and yes. Oh, but I have work. Tomorrow.'

'O'Hanleys,' he said. 'I see you there, sometimes. I'll call you in sick.'

'How can you do that?'

'Actually, I recently purchased the place. I developed a sense that they needed a new manager.'

'No.'

'Yes.'

'I say again,' Eamon said loudly over the buzz. 'Now settle down, people. I say, what shall we start with?'

A bevy of replies flew through the air, from hornpipes to airs. Eileen tore her eyes from Conlin's face and squared her shoulders. 'I've got a piece,' she said. Heads turned in her direction, voices dying away. 'I've got a piece,' she said again. 'Something I've been working on. An original composition. I think it's ready to be presented here.'

'Jaysus, Mary and Joseph,' Kevin MacMillan exploded. 'Have you gone stark raving mad? We can't play a new composition! It's not traditional.'

'How do you think the traditional tunes got started, Kevin?' Eileen retorted. 'There's a first time for everything. Do ya think "The Kesh Jig" was never played for a very first time somewhere?'

The group erupted into indignant chatter again. Eileen leant close to Conlin. 'Don't worry,' she whispered. 'I'll sing it again for you. Later. Very, very slowly.'

He closed his eyes and pressed against the back of his guitar, his hand tracing once more its sinuous wooden curves. He opened his eyes and smiled at her warmly.

'All right then,' Eamon shouted. 'This is the strangest Wednesday session I have ever attended. But, Eileen, if you must, then go ahead and lilt it for us.'

She closed her eyes and tilted her head back, took a deep breath, feeling her flesh between the folds of her open blouse rising and falling in the cool air, the eyes of the session group on her in rapt anticipation, Conlin beside her longing to fasten his mouth to her nipples and plunge his body between her thighs. Strong and clearly, she began to hum.

Sparrow Primula Bond

The first time I heard the applause, I came. I mean really *came*. No denying that creeping pleasure, pussy lips pursing, urgently but oh so uselessly, to stem the delicious rush. Sweet juices springing there and catching between my legs after the soft explosion. I could feel the stickiness, because under the velvet I wore no knickers that night.

There I was, pinned on a little stage down a little alley. Dazzled by spotlights while invisible hands clapped and invisible lips whistled. I'd done it. Jake was right about that. I'd been the jazz singer, slinking and strutting across the stage, that he said I could be.

Have you ever felt it? It's electric. The applause. They wanted more, I wanted more. This wasn't me miming into a hairbrush. No joke. Not some reality show. The punters had been minding their own business until I came along, had come into the club for a quiet drink, maybe a background cabaret, and got me. Now they were loving me. Who wouldn't want to linger, lapping up that frantic approval? And the louder the encores, the hands clapping in my ears until I tingled, the faster the crescendo of triumph rose inside me like a long, lovely fuck.

It was a climax in every sense of the word, you see. But it was also the beginning.

A week before that first night Jake Fagin was locking up his club. It was sunrise, the dawn chorus erupting. He heard me singing on my way to buy flowers for my stall.

Early mornings are awful for the voice. I know that now, six years later, especially after a rough night, too much booze or fags or boys. These days I'm rarely out of bed before noon. But my voice was clear as crystal then. Anyway Jake liked what he heard. The high brick walls of his alleyway echoed with churchlike acoustics. Which was perfect, because would you believe that day I was singing the 'Pie Jesu'.

'Sod the voice of an angel,' he said, blocking my way. In a Hollywood movie he'd be waving a recording contract. 'That sound could sell sex to nuns.'

You're easily flattered when you're at a dead end. He badgered and bullied, and finally bribed – I wasn't a total fool. I agreed to do it, just the once, so long as there was no stripping involved.

He introduced me to the band and later to the world as the cockney sparrow he'd found in the gutter, his Edith Piaf. He even renamed his club La Mome (slang for little or sparrow – sounds better in French) but it was all bollocks. I'm posher than him. I was your archetypal convent girl for heaven's sake, bringing tears to the eyes of congregations with my searing soprano. I'm no more cockney than Julie Andrews.

Pete the pianist was hostile, the band was knackered. But they kept me up all night rehearsing. Then Saturday night came and I was glugging vodka in the cramped wings. Jake handed me a spliff and I took a toke, or toke a took, and then he jammed his hand into my back and shoved me out on to the podium.

'Diana Krall eat your heart out.'

And then Pete picked out the intro. My throat was zipped tight. As he reached the last languid notes, slowing to a pause, the dope seeped in. I swayed like a proper diva in my borrowed dress. The silver microphone waited for me, glinting under a single spot.

Was that a squeak? I loosened my throat, swelled my chest like the sparrow I was meant to be. Felt the velvet pull against my breasts, stitches straining down my sides, the dress running into slits up my thighs as the breath filled me. I lifted the mike out of its cradle, brushed its rounded head against my mouth, tasted the metal mesh. My mate in this adventure.

'Summertime,' I crooned into my silver phallus, holding the first syllable till the audience hushed, sat up, took notice, 'and the livin' is easy.'

I never knew that success and relief could be so physical. When the repertoire was over I was jelly. If I tried to walk or curtsy, I'd fall over. That's why I stood there, embracing Pete's piano and, when at last they started the applause, I had a private orgasm in front of a couple of hundred people in a little nightclub somewhere in Fulham.

'Wow! She has fantastic legs as well as a voice that could shatter glass.'

I spin round, holding my kimono closed. Too late. It stops at my fanny, and he saw it all. 'Who the hell are you?'

He holds his hands up. Long hands, very long fingers.

'Oh, I'm Louis. Your pianist.'

'I didn't order another pianist.'

'You have pianists on a menu?'

'Good thought, but –' I turn away and grip the edge of my dressing table '– where's Pete?' The face in the mirror is powdery and ashen. Where did those grooves come from, the lines etching down my mouth, tugging at my eyes? I'm older than they think, but not that old. 'I can't sing without Pete.'

'Smacks of the workman blaming his tool?' The guy's still in the open doorway. He looks more like a rock star than a piano player. Messy blond hair falling over his collar. Looks somehow poetic over the white tie and tails I insist my accompanists wear.

'If you're headlining a show like this, you're entitled to smack whatever tool takes your fancy.'

'Spoken like a true diva.' He lets out a really dirty chuckle and I have to fight the amusement. No one these days dares tell me to button it.

'And what are you? Stevie Wonder?' I point at his dark glasses.

'No. Just affected.' He laughs again. 'I heard you fired poor Pete. Like you fired Jake Fagin in the end. So when did you start biting the hands that fed you?'

'I didn't fire him. We had an artistic disagreement.'

'I'd better watch my step.'

'You won't even get started.' Colour burns my cheeks, and I lift my chin to yell. 'Pete? There's some freak groupie bothering me. Get him out!'

'You weren't so quick to get rid of me six years ago.'

The groupie comes further into my dressing room. He glances at my rail of identical black sheath dresses. Out on stage I can hear my support act tumbling into their first number. An impressive enough trio, hired a couple of days ago after I took the cutest one to bed. I mean, what's a girl going to do when they call themselves Make Hay and look, and sound, like Jamie Cullum's little brothers? That's just the way I like them these days. Permanently hard and permanently grateful.

I shake my head. 'Six years ago?'

I can tell by the stubble that this Louis is no boy, despite his girlie hair. They're all gorgeous on the jazz circuit. Positively gift wrapped. Next on my wish list is Make Hay's drummer and the double bassist. What was it Cher said about some young stud she wanted? Have him washed and brought to my tent . . .

'A dark alleyway outside Fagin's club in London? You were absolutely wired.' He whistles. 'You couldn't wait till we got to my place, just round the corner. You wanted it hard and fast, right up against the wall.'

'So what? Haven't you heard? Convent girls like a bit of rough.'

Hysteria has been hovering round me since I woke up this morning. Boy, am I spoiling for a fight.

'Yeah, and I was the first. But hey –' he dumps some sheet music on top of Pete's upright, swings a long leg over the piano stool to sit down. '– this time I'm here to do my job. Pete won't be back.'

'Nonsense.' My heart is juddering. No one's ordered me about since I sacked Jake. 'He wouldn't dare leave me.'

'He caught you in the Winnebago screwing the sexy saxophonist when you were supposed to be doing sound-checks. That's more than a gay man can stomach in a lifetime.'

I fling round. 'So? I'm top of the bill here. I can do what I like.' My breasts tingle at the memory of the boy in my trailer, his mouth sucking on my nipples. I pull my kimono tight. My stiff nipples poke against the silk. I'll never be able to watch that saxophonist, any saxophonist, wrap his lips round his mouthpiece again. I urged him to lick and suck till the pain was exquisite. His hair was so soft and curly as I cradled his head against me, burying him there. A well-hung, talented guy suckling me like a lamb – that's the turn-on. His arms virtually crushed me as his own ardour mounted, his cock bumping against my legs. So I opened them to let him in ...

The silk kimono shivers as my heart hammers to get out. 'And if you'd seen the size of his cock, you wouldn't blame me.'

'Cocks aren't my thing. But I know you like them young, Sophie. Cocks, and men.' Louis bites his lower lip. 'I'd like to see you shagging a woman some time. Just think. A fresh menu to choose from.'

I can't see what's going on in his eyes, because he's still wearing those damn glasses. He opens a songbook.

I'm not used to being taunted. I back against the sharp edge of my dressing table and lift one thigh to cross it over the other. Which makes the slip fall right open. I never wear knickers. All the better to relish my arousal when it happens, slicking over my skin. The slow throbbing warmth, the insidious rush, the wetness no one else can see.

'You know nothing about me.' My voice has slipped several octaves down my throat so that only a breathy whisper emerges. These nerves are toxic. I push past him, stare out of the door. Down the rig at the ugly poles of scaffolding supporting the beautiful sparkling backdrop. I can see the drummer's jutting elbows, my saxophonist out front in skin-tight jeans, whipping the crowd into a frenzy like a jazz Jagger . . .

Those swooning girls could never seduce him like I did, his muscled, golden body laid out like a nervous feast, his prick rearing up under my tongue. The pair of us transformed my lonely trailer into a love nest for a whole afternoon. He asked me what I liked best, as I undressed him. I settled myself on him, licked my fingers and pinched my nipples into nuts. I dipped into my snatch and then gave my fingers to him to taste. Always extra naughty, with the young ones, egged on by the half-tried amazement in their eyes. I showed him, and then he did it. Perfectly.

He and his boys, they're totally at home on this open-air stage. They're filling the warm spring air with energetic, quirky covers of the sax greats: Herbie Hancock,

Courtney Pine, masters those young girls won't have heard of. And tonight, Matthew, I'm supposed to be . . .

But I can't do it. Every pluck on the double bass, every brush on the cymbals, every tantalising note held on the sax as he pays tribute drags me closer to the moment when I'm supposed to burst into the limelight and remind them who I am.

But I can't do it.

There are no dark corners to hide in, no smoky, helpful acoustics. No anonymous alleyway where a stranger can push me up against the cool brick wall after a gig to relieve me of my frustration, no crowded street I can run down afterwards to find the comfort of a busy bar. Just a floodlit castle, a sophisticated sound system to cover the cracks and, afterwards, the padded loneliness of my Winnebago.

'Oh, but I know plenty about you. Haven't you heard they call you Sophia the Insatiable?' He silently tickles the ivories. 'And I've been inside you, Sophie. Sorry, Sophia.'

'I'll ask you again.' I'm distracted by the applause erupting outside. 'Who the fuck are you?'

'I was about his age when I came after you. An eager, cute wannabe with a permanent erection.'

Out on stage the boys launch into their penultimate number. They've given it a big band vibe. Normally I'd be dancing behind the scenes, revving myself up, the vodka bottle my prop. But today my legs barely hold me up.

'This is supposed to be my comeback.'

Louis slaps his leg. 'That's why we're going to start with those first songs, the beginning of your career.' .

'Who put you in charge?'

'We're on in five,' he says.

'Tell them not yet. I need an interval.' I totter about

like the drunk I used to be and pick out a dress with sequins all over it.

'An interval? What do you think this is? The bloody opera house?'

I go into autopilot. Let my kimono fall to the floor. My cheeks are hectic spots of pink now, like a child's painted them. The dark glasses watch my naked reflection. His hand is flat against the score, the other resting on the piano keys. I love a man's eyes on me, but the trouble is I can't see his eyes. There's a spark of excitement in my stomach. He has lovely hands, a sexy mouth, superb insolence, but every time I try to think sexy, the stalking fear takes over.

I drop the dress over my head as if it might shield me.

'That dress is too big for you. Everything about you has shrunk. What happened in rehab? You lost your vices, your voice.' He stands up, steps behind me. His hands run down my sides, nudging my breasts together. 'But these are still here. Real? Or silicone now?'

I jab my elbow into him, but he doesn't move. 'Your breasts that night were as mesmerising as your voice. Big, bold, tumbling out of that strapless number Jake squeezed you into. It wasn't your own, was it? But you wore it ever after.'

'Keep your hands for playing scales.' But the spell's working. 'What night?'

His hands fan out over each breast and start to fondle them till they throb. His thumbs rub across my nipples. 'Mmm. Still luscious. Our sexy saxophonist was right. You should have heard him at the catering truck. Not so star-struck that he couldn't give a blow by blow of how you tasted sitting on his face.'

'Fuck off before I call security.' I try to twist away but he catches me closer. He's far stronger than he looks under the showman's outfit.

'Hey. It's meant to be a compliment. So who cares if you've lost your voice when you've still got the body of a goddess?'

'He can quit bragging. I had that boy for breakfast.' I wriggle again, and he lets me go. I ignore the flash of disappointment and start pinning up my hair. 'All that unleashed libido. I love priming them for all those lucky women they'll have in their lives, but they'll never forget me.' I give this Louis my fiercest glare under my eyelashes. 'But you? I've never seen you before.'

'Booze fuddled your brain?' He shrugs. 'The first time you were introduced at La Mome. You sang George Gershwin. And when everyone applauded you looked like you'd just woken up from a wet dream. God, you were like a bitch on heat.'

'Anyone could have told you that. Well, maybe not the bitch bit.' But all these truths are making me light headed. 'So tell me I was sensational.' I lean towards the mirror, pushing my butt into his groin, pick up a lipstick. I open my mouth to spread it on, but my hand is shaking too much.

'Some biographer could interview Jake, or Pete, or you even, and get a version. But I was there.' He runs his finger down my spine, bringing up the little hairs. 'You weren't going to leave the spotlight. Pete had to prance about, make a big show kissing your hand and making you curtsy. Creating his own monster, if he only knew it. He had to drag you off stage.'

'You're saying I was crap?'

'You were sensational, Sophie Smith. Which was your name then.' He leans over my shoulder, pulls me upright again. The lipstick clatters against the mirror. Just a little smear on my mouth. 'Now it's time to sing for your supper.'

'I'm not hungry. And my name is Sophia.' I jerk

backwards, bashing his chin. My eyes in the mirror are black and hollow. 'But I can't do it.'

'Tonight is my big break. Don't fuck it up.' He wipes a speck of blood from where he's cut his lip. 'Tomorrow, you can do what you like. I'll be busy fending off the record companies. But tonight, you sing.'

What's wrong with me? Sophia would have had his smart-ass trousers off by now. There's an inviting enough bulge nudging out of his crotch. I can feel it between my cheeks. He's making me angry, which is good. Anything's better than the paralysing fear. This trembling could be lust as well as terror.

'You're not listening.' I close my eyes. 'I can't sing. I sound like an old crone.'

He shifts away, reaches round me for a glass of water, but his body is still pressed behind me. 'Gargle.'

'You want your moment of glory, Louis? Fine. Go out there and tell them I'm mad. That the rehab finished me.' I push him away, but he grabs my wrists and holds them behind me. 'And then sell your story for thousands, about how you found the jazz queen in her dressing room, gibbering with stage fright.'

'I've already got my story. But it's not about you. It's about a classy flower seller I found dancing alone in the street outside this nightclub in Fulham. She was high on success, so horny with it that when I told her she was sensational she practically begged me to take her right there, up against the wall. Every schoolboy's fantasy.'

'So you keep saying. Loads of guys used to hang around the club. So what?' But I'm listening now. I can smell the rain on the pavement that night, the cigarette smoke from the air vents. The way I burst out of the club looking for satisfaction. 'I didn't care if they were musicians or there to mend the drains, so long as they had a hard-on just for me.'

'This guy was before you became a nymphomaniac. He was your first ever fan, Sophie. No one had heard of you. *You* hadn't heard of you. That was your blossoming.'

There's a knock at the door. 'Two minutes, Sophia.'

'It wasn't you. He had a shaved head. He was big. He told me he was a musician, but he looked more like a bouncer.'

'People change. Lose weight. Grow hair. So let's drop it. I'm going to be famous, even if you're washed up.' Louis points at the pile of music. 'And here's the thing. We're going to wing it. Some old numbers, played my way. Some new, written by me. You can read the music as we go along. And some old-fashioned jamming to make it really intimate. Now gargle, goddamn you.'

'That's not the programme they're expecting.'

'So live dangerously.' He tips the glass, dribbling cold drops of water into my mouth, down my chin, over my throat. It's a relief, and I start to swallow. I've dried up. Lips, tongue, teeth, all like sandpaper.

'Don't drink it. Bubble it at the back of your throat. Keep it there, in a pool. Then be Edith Piaf again. Sing *"Non, Je Ne Regrette Rien"*.'

I hit the first note, and I understand. The pool of gargle ripples at the base of my throat. I'm famous for holding a note. I sound like the Frenchwoman they called the 'little sparrow'. I used to imitate her, busking in Paris. I gargle the first verse, staring at him. He takes his glasses off, and stares right back. He has golden eyelashes framing piercing eyes. I start to choke, and he starts to grin, and more water spurts over me. His eyes get bluer, and I realise that's because the door's open again and the support have finished and the light boys are swinging multicoloured spots all over the stage, ready for my arrival.

'I've rehearsed the band already. We've had all day,

you see, while Sophia's been having her hissy fit.' He's very close, still holding the glass next to my face, ready to pour more down my throat. 'We're going down in history. And then you're going down on me.'

I spit the water out. 'And if I refuse?'

'I tell them the princess is sick. I wipe you off your own map by doing it the way I want it. Solo. Believe me, I'll bring the house down.' He takes his sheet music and starts for the door. 'And then you're going to suck me. For old time's sake.'

'You're full of bullshit. No one orders me around.' I grab my shoes and follow him. 'This is *my* show.'

'Yesss. Right answer. We're gonna rip through it.' He punches the air and I think he's going to run straight onto the stage but he stops so that I fall against his chest and he grabs my arms.

My skin shivers. If he touches me I'll erupt. I risk it, pressing my breasts against him. He looks down and I smile slowly. His hands drop to my hips, round to my butt, and I tilt myself a little. My secret naked pussy is yearning to rub up against his prick.

'Your skin still feels like silk. You wore no knickers then. Just that old dress. It was warm, like it is tonight, and you had sweat trickling down your neck.' I can smell his breath on my face, coffee and mint.

'What happened next?'

'I had a bottle of beer, and you drank it from the neck. You were out of breath, panting, wiped the beer with the back of your hand, and your mouth was open, your tongue kept running across it, you whirled about until you were dizzy and I caught you – pretty much like this.'

He lifts me. God, hands that can play piano as well as lift weights. I wrap my legs round his waist. I want him. I want to drink his mouth. I close my eyes, feel desire churning inside me, my throat loosening as the challenge ahead hits me. His fingers are on my thighs now, spreading my buttocks to work their way into the warm crack and I gasp and strain at the sensations running over my skin. His fingers pause, probing my pussy, discovering my pubes are totally hairless. I keep them that way so that every tiny scrape of clothing, every breath of air can intoxicate me, especially when I'm performing. He runs his finger down the centre of my slit. It twitches to let him in.

My dress rucks up towards my waist and he tugs at it, crumpling the material up into his fist. I can't move. He's wedged me up against the door.

'Do it to me like you did then,' I gasp.

'You wish. No time. I'll have you later.' His fingertip rests just inside me, and my body tries to nip at it. I can feel him getting harder as he tears at the fabric with the other hand. 'First we're going to sort out this stupid dress.'

'I have to wear this dress.' I struggle to get away from him, but I'm helpless. The backing band are twiddling their reeds and pipes and strings. 'I've got scars from a car accident when I was in Paris.'

He drops me to my feet. The dress is in shreds, and I stagger against him. The conductor bustles past. He smiles, thinking I'm jiving with my new pianist.

'Liar. You told me it's because when you sang all those requiems everyone teased you about your knees knocking under your school skirt.'

I tug at the ragged hem of my dress. I have to admit that my legs look better exposed, slim and bare, emphasising my killer heels. The spring breeze insinuates round the backdrop curtain to play under my dress, up my legs to where my pussy purrs. 'So you want me to come on like a humiliated schoolgirl now?'

'Kinky thought! No. I want you to strut and glide like

a real woman, just like you always do. Dance for me, for the crowd, like you're on the brink of having the best sex of your life. They'll be too busy trying to see up your skirt to notice your ruddy knees.'

I have to teeter on those heels to catch up with him, and then we're out in this blaze of light and there's a sea of invisible heads out there. A perfect round moon bowls in the sky above.

I try to grab at him. 'I know you're not my lover from that night,' I shout as the compere announces us and you can feel the night air shifting with anticipation, 'because he had a tattoo.'

He doesn't hear me. He's too busy lapping it all up, waving like he's the main event. I hang back, still time to leg it, but then he turns and bows and reaches for me, and it's too late because they've all seen me and amazingly they rise to their feet and clap and cheer and whistle and whoop and it's bloody brilliant and Louis is beside me, holding my hand up to greet my audience, and just before he leaves me there in the middle of nowhere he puts his mouth to my ear and says, 'Yeah. A treble clef.'

I freeze. The commotion fades, people cough, a quick burst of laughter, then there's deathly quiet. I turn to look at Louis, but he's bent over the piano, and then this music starts winding out from under his fingers, silky and slow. I keep watching him. I need him to look up. Of course I remember. He told me he was a musician that night, but honestly he looked like a bouncer, all mean and thickset. I've turned away from the audience. You should never do that, unless you're thanking your band. The bones of my knees crunch together. All those eyes on my back. I'm still frozen.

He gestures, and the strings murmur up from the band. Warmth seeps from my toes up my legs. I move across the stage, letting the melody settle itself in my ears, in my veins. I glide like an ice skater towards Louis, swinging my hips exaggeratedly so he'll notice me and that's when he slips the tune like changing gear, and an electric charge shoots through me, and we're into my first ever song. 'Summertime'.

Louis beckons me. I come, obediently, then stretch myself like a cat all over the grand piano, very theatrical and showy. My dress rides up. Louis looks up sleepily as if he has no idea who I am, glances past me at the audience as if sharing a joke, then chucks over some sheet music.

Then he presses the pedal, and the music grows louder. The plan is obviously to keep shocking me because now the sexy saxophonist wanders back on like some kind of minstrel, wailing my tune, and I'm expected to echo it. Everyone cheers, and I pick up the sheets that I've failed to catch, toss them up in the air like so many dead leaves, fling myself round, hand on hip, and take the cheering just like I was born to do. The light boys pop a single spot at the front, just like that first night. We could be in that tiny nightclub. The furore dies down, and I start to hum, making my whole body buzz. My mouth opens and out it all comes.

And seconds later it seems we've reached the end. Here's the finale, but I'm not done. I'm drinking in the applause, that sexy triumph building like a wave inside me. Louis has tested me to the limit, playing music I don't know, giving me sheets with no words, standing up to rip his coat off, then his white tie, hair dripping with sweat. During 'Making Whoopee' I kicked my shoes off à la Joss Stone and he lifted me onto the piano, bent me backwards over it, let the band take the slack while he slid his hands up my bare thighs, up under my skirt to dig right into my warm sex. I hooked my leg over his and pulled him in to me and the crowd went wild. I was so hot I wanted to do it for real, right there in front of everybody.

But he jumped away, back to his keyboard, and my saxophonist was back again for a three-way version of 'The Look of Love', the pair of them vying for my attention in a sensuous harmony that made me shiver as I planned the delight to come. Oh yes. Both of them taking me every which way in my Winnebago. I turned my back on them both and yelled to the crowd, 'Ain't you heard? Two's company, honey. But three's a sex romp!'

They're screaming for encores. Louis is rising from his seat but my saxophonist gets to me first, lifts the gold pipe to his lips again, starts to play the kind of throaty John Coltrane melody that's like sleepy syrup dripping off a spoon.

Have him washed and brought to my tent.

I gyrate around him, running my hands all over myself, up and down my legs, my sides, over my breasts like some kind of lap dancer. I don't care if they can tell I'm creaming myself, this is a mating dance, making me randy, making me want to come. Let it vibrate and explode, nearly there, but suddenly Louis vaults over the piano to more hysteria and swings me round. Then he shouts, 'Cut the lights!' and everything's dark. The sax slides on. He doesn't need light to play.

Maybe not, but I need the light to sing.

'You can drop the loved-up act now,' I hiss as Louis drags me to the piano stool. The straps of the dress slip down my shoulders. There's only the moon and the stars punching the sky. 'We've had our night.'

'How is this an act? No one can see.' The leather seat is still warm. 'And I want more than one night, Sophie Smith.'

He pushes my dress up. I nip at his neck.

'Ever been fucked on stage?' He's throwing his shirt off. I was right about him being a rock star. I can feel his smooth torso as he thumps down beside me and pulls me to straddle him.

'Never.'

'They'll keep playing till I strike the next chord, but we have to be quick.' He slides his hand up my legs, squeezes my breasts. 'You're so ready. You've got the whole joint humping.'

I can't wait. My legs are spread over his, and his fingers edge into the juicy softness of my sex. I shift to part my legs a little more, and stifle a moan as his nails graze the hidden clit. My dress slips down. My breasts strain, nipples burning to be bitten. But he's kissing me now. Really kissing, warm and wet, forcing my mouth open as his fingers explore my warm, wet pussy.

I reach down to get at his zip. My pussy sticks to his trousers for a minute as he eases them down, the fabric tugging at the tender skin before letting go. I wriggle about impatiently, less jazz diva, more spoilt brat, but when my fingers land on the thick shape of his waiting prick I nearly crush it.

His penis jumps in my hand. I rise up on my knees and grasp the knob to guide it between my lips, letting it rest just inside me. The band are playing slow funk as if they're falling asleep, the rhythm as regular and deep as a heartbeat. My body pulsates now with music and wanting.

Their eyes must be getting used to the dark. They'll see our shapes, flailing behind the piano.

'So what about that tattoo, Louis?' I whisper, slicking my tongue across his warm mouth. 'Are you my first lover?'

Instead of waiting for his answer, hearing him chuckle, I let myself drop, driving myself on to his cock.

He jerks his mouth away with shock, and his laughing breath is hot on my throat.

'Oh, yes,' he breathes. 'The bitch is back.'

I grip him with my thighs. He slides in further. I let him all the way in, then I back off a little, slide back down, till the shaft is slippery with my juice and I'm aching to buck against him. And then I do it. I start grinding against him, cramming him in, dancing right down to the very base so that I'm filled with glorious inches of rock-hard, thrusting cock.

Each time we pull back and slam against each other it gets more urgent, I want to scream out loud because I can feel that gathering rush inside me, the orgasm a flicker away.

'What about our encore, Sophia?' someone yells.

I can't hold on much longer. I can't stop the flow, and I can tell that the band is faltering just a little, tiring, slowing the tempo. Louis starts to mutter into my neck. His cock stiffens, he yanks me hard and bangs me, carrying me with him, and I ride him, moaning as I start to come. As the climax breaks and his eyes blaze at me and as I bounce on him, I topple and accidentally strike the keyboard and, as he strains up against me, his load shooting in, the lights all come flooding on and the band blasts straight into our encore.

It's a really hard, fast version of 'Ain't Misbehavin' and there we are, arched in ecstasy, blinking at the lights, only just concealed from our public by the keyboard, but our entire band, conductor, supporting trio *et al* can see that their pianist has his cock rammed up inside their singer and is fucking her like crazy. All we can do is pretend we're simulating it, if you see what I mean, necks arching, arms winding, until he can drag himself out and the juices trickle once more onto my thighs.

Louis zips up his trousers with a flourish. I fuss my skirt down. As I kneel up slowly, my knees tremble. So what. I take the mike off the piano, and run my finger over the inky-blue tattoo now visible on his stomach. A treble clef, etched just to the right of his navel, curling into his trousers.

I prance to the front, giving it to the crowd, pulsating, still breathless. They want another encore. My cute saxophonist appears beside me, the boy with the double bass, behind me the black-haired drummer, Louis at the piano, all revving up the sparrow's song which could have been written for me.

I look at my gorgeous musicians and wonder which one I'll have next. I can't wait. I lick my lips at all the pleasure to come. I open my mouth and sing it:

'Non, je ne regrette rien . . .'

Out of Time Maddie Mackeown

Rock 'n' roll has been around for a long time but only recently did I make its acquaintance. A couple of years ago I decided to dip my toes into the frothy waters of jive and, from the first bar that slid into my ears and the first bop that my feet tapped, I loved it. Still do. Even now since it all happened. Maybe even more so. I love the dance, the music and the people who inhabit its circuit.

Energy. That's what it is. Raw energy. That's what I like about it.

Music and I have an elusive relationship. It has to move me, either physically or emotionally. The style doesn't matter so long as it stirs my soul or makes me want to dance.

Rock 'n' roll had never been a part of my appreciation until tried at first hand. But suddenly there it was, bursting with life that stamped out apathy and pulsed through my body with an insistence that was not to be ignored. I was hooked and taken, hopping and bopping, into the vibrant, exuberant world of band nights, halls and jamborees.

Sometimes I stand outside the thrall and watch the magic play itself as the beat sparks like a multiple explosion and draws the jivers onto the floor. I watch and wait as the excitement builds within me and my eyes scan the hall for available partners.

It was on one of these nights that it all began.

I had left the hall to cool down for a while. Jive can leave you hot, very hot, like, covered in a sheen of sweat.

I leant against a wall that had soaked up heat from the day. The night air was soft and fresh, shifting in a welcome breeze, but the hour too early to have the chill that settles with lateness. The sweat that slicked my hair and skin began to dry and cool me. It felt good but it wasn't long before the repetitive beat called me back.

On re-entering the building I was intoxicated anew by the swirling bodies of couples in vigorous harmony. I knew that when I opened the door to the hall there would be an escape of trapped heat so I looked through the glass for a while to appreciate the buzz, with my foot tapping and body twitching in time to the beat, doing my own 'shake, rattle and roll'.

I like to watch the 50s skirts that swirl on the spin and give a glimpse of territory that is usually hidden: thighs that gleam above stocking tops and the flash of tight knickers. I watch to see what is revealed before the skirt falls again. Not because I fancy other women but because I can check out what will be revealed when I wear such skirts. I manage my skirt well and can make it spin high from a neat flick of the hips. The thought pleases me. It is saucy and cheeky and fun. A tease.

Now, dances vary. They last with the track, a short space of snatched time when you are the centre of someone else's universe. It can turn into a three-minute flirtation that ends with the final bars of the song. Mostly, your partners are there for the straightforward joy of dance but sometimes there are those who sniff around the hem of your skirt. The trick is to decipher the clues and respond accordingly.

The track changed and, as I was about to meander my way through the milling throng, I became aware of a slight coolness behind me as if someone had opened the main door.

I turned and saw him.

He must have just arrived. Quite late. There was a tenuous moment, a trapped stillness that lasted for a heartbeat. He stepped into the light and impressed me at once. He was one cool dude in his Teddy boy gear: midnight-blue suit, waistcoat of blue and gold, thin tie and – yes! – blue suede shoes. A loose strand of hair curled appealingly onto his forehead in escape from the slicked back quiff.

'Good evening. I'm Lennox.'

Lennox. The name rolled smoothly, softly mouthed, in my mind.

He held out his hand and I took it. 'Hi, Lennox.' I wanted to say the name out loud to try its fit on my tongue. Anyway, it was jive etiquette to introduce yourself. It's sort of polite when you're about to invade someone else's personal space and gyrate in close proximity. 'I'm Stella,' I said.

For some obscure reason we both laughed. He held onto my hand, his cool palm a welcome invitation. A disembodied voice from inside the hall was in the final throes of telling us that everybody wants to dance with 'Sweet Sixteen'.

'It's nearly finished,' he said, low pitched. 'Would you like to dance?'

I glanced around us at the limited space of the entrance hall. 'Here?'

He shrugged his shoulders and nodded.

Well, the space was ours and ours alone. I smiled up at him. 'Why not!'

We were well matched, he being a little taller. His arm slid round me and we shifted into the basic hold, facing each other and waiting for the song to end. I could feel the firm but subtle pressure of his hand on my shoulder blade. My fingers rested loosely in his but I was ready as always to feel the lead through his touch.

The sustained introduction of 'Old Black Joe' came to us and we circled slowly before the upbeat rhythm swept us into its energy.

Now, I'm a good dancer and like to be challenged. You always wonder what you're in for when a stranger asks you to dance. I soon found out. He was good. Very good. I'm always happy to be in the power of such a master. We were almost faultless and, as the song came to its finale, we brought the dance to an end with a flourish of turns and an exaggerated pose.

I laughed, almost a girlie giggle of excitement. 'Well, I came out to cool down and now I'm all hot again!' I lifted my hair off my neck in an attempt to release some heat.

He held up both hands in mock surrender. 'My fault,' he said. 'I offer sincere apologies.'

'No. That's fine. I enjoyed it. Thank you.'

It seemed that he was standing very still against the backdrop of bodies that whirled behind the glass of the door, such a contrast of seething movement to his composure. His eyes were direct and steady as they surveyed me. He was also remarkably cool and sweat free. How do some people manage that?

'Anyway, I'd better get back. My friends will be wondering what's happened to me.' I opened the door and a mini blast of heat surged over us. 'Are you coming in?'

'No. I think I'll just stay here for a while and watch.'

There followed one of those pauses that simmer with an expectation that you can't quite quantify.

'OK. Thanks again for the dance.' I let the door close behind me and was swallowed into a mass of heaving bodies that were 'all shook up'.

For the rest of the evening I kept checking to see if he was still there. He was. I could see him through the glass of the door but he didn't come in. I was curious, wondering if he was waiting for someone but no one else appeared to talk to him. Whenever I danced, my eyes kept flicking towards the door and I hoped that it was me whom he watched. I danced for him and I hoped that he knew.

Then suddenly he wasn't there any more.

And so began the strangest and most tenuous but compelling and irresistible relationship of my life. The weeks passed, the months passed, and I realised that the indefinite nature of our meetings had become a fascination.

From time to time, Lennox would turn up at a function but somehow remain always on the periphery. He rarely entered the main halls. Occasionally he would arrive unannounced and slip inconspicuously into a seat nearby. Once, as I sat out between dances, I felt a gentle touch on my shoulder from behind and knew it was him. I reached to touch his fingers before they slid from my skin, feeling an excitement that had nothing to do with the incessant throb of the music.

We would bump into each other as if by chance in the entrance hall or corridor where we would dance together almost secretly. With some partners there is such a rapport that it's almost sex – or at least it could be but a small step away. It was like that with Lennox.

I didn't introduce him to my friends. They made no comment about him. It was understandable. People hovered and moved around the halls all the time so maybe they didn't even realise that he gravitated to me.

We didn't actually ask about each other or exchange phone numbers. The whole thing was an enigma and I was happy for it to be that way. It intrigued me.

I went to many places, at some of which he appeared, at others he did not and when he didn't I was aware of a vague disappointment beneath the pleasure of the evening. Despite the intermittency, I knew that what we shared was leading to something that had to be played out.

He had become my elusive lover. He'd become my obsession.

'Stella.'

My name came as a whisper from the depths of shadow at the edge of the room. My heart missed a beat and my skin prickled but not with fear because I recognised his voice.

Lennox hadn't shown on that night. The evening had been lively and we'd all decided to stay for a last drink at the bar until midnight while the DJ packed up. On leaving the building I'd realised that my scarf must have dropped from my bag.

'I'll go back and get it. You go,' I said to my friend.

'Are you sure?'

'Of course. It'll only take a minute.' I kissed her cheek. 'See you on Thursday.'

'OK. Bye,' she said and she left.

In the darkened room I turned towards the sound and tried to see beyond the pool of shafting moonlight that spread centre floor like a stage spot. There he was: Lennox. The thought of his name washed through my body. He walked over and stopped before me, close enough for my breath to stroke his skin. A shiver disturbed me.

'Why don't you turn up at the normal time like everyone else?'

'Because I'm different,' he said. 'Don't you like our secret times?'

'You know that I do.'

The room held the hollow silence of emptiness. I could hear no noise from beyond the doors. Had everybody gone? I wondered. A chill had entered from the outside but a warmth grew inside me. His unorthodox timing posed no threat. It held the mark of a true romantic.

'So, babe, shall we dance then?' He smiled at me.

I looked at him with a puzzled frown and spread my palms to query the dark silence.

'Oh ye of little faith!' he said. 'Trust me.'

He went over to the lights and switched on a single beam that sent a splash of glowing warmth to mix with moonshine in the middle of the hall. At the DJ's desk he seemed to press a control before returning to stand in the pool of light. He must have set this up in advance, I thought. Sneaky. How did he know I'd come back in? Mm. How did my scarf fall out of my bag?

A frisson sparked through the air between us as the intro to 'Old Black Joe' insinuated into the atmosphere. I let my bag drop and my jacket slip to the floor. He began to step in time to the music, solo, his eyes boring into mine, his eyebrows and smile beckoning. I moved, giving myself to the music, giving myself to him, approaching his pool of light and entering it to navigate around his body, not touching but keeping my eyes focused on his throughout the slow bars, looking at him over my shoulder as I turned.

The chords suddenly filled out on an increase in tempo. I gave in to the beat, absorbing it, the rhythm pulling me into its core. He fired me with his cool control, strong, firm but never rough, providing a momentum to my wildness.

We were alone in our space, gliding across the sound waves, brimming with desire and intent. We gave in to the exuberance, reflecting each other's moves to make one unit of fluid motion. Not a single beat was missed. Every surge, every nuance we followed. We created an electric aura. If anyone had been on the outside of our charmed circle they would have been scorched by the red-hot ripples that emanated and spiralled out into the shadows.

The song flowed smoothly into another and we were encouraged to 'move it' and groove it – although probably not with quite such an explicit interpretation as ours. The rhythm was slower and reached inside, driving us along. He pulled me against his body and we marked time without losing a fraction of a beat as his lips pressed onto mine. We'd known all along that this would happen. We'd been leading up to such a point in time. It was simply a culmination that seemed right.

Nevertheless, it felt good, very good, and pleasure flooded through my body.

With his hand on my hip, he pushed me away from him and turned me into a wrap so my back was against him in a hold much closer than is usual. He put his mouth to my neck and I pressed my body into his hold.

He unwrapped me and spun me behind him. As we stepped and kicked from side to side, I gradually loosened my touch from his fingers. I ran my hand up his arm and across his shoulder, down his back and around his waist, to lay my palm flat on his belly inside his jacket, pulling him against me. His head tilted back, turning to mine, and his fingers trailed through my hair, lifting its curls to his face. My tongue licked a path up his neck until I stopped to nibble his ear. Our hips circled together until he spun me round in a double spin and pulled my back towards him once more.

We were breathing hard but not from the exertions of the dance. We marked time, pacing our passion, as his hand slid under my petticoat. Fingertips stroked upwards until they met the smooth flesh and he slid them beneath the suspender.

He made a sound close to my ear and whispered my

name. The tease of his breath crept through me, tickling like butterfly wings down through my belly to settle between my legs where his fingers had rested and were beginning to rotate in time to the music. I rested my head back onto his shoulder, turning my face into him.

The song was by now more than halfway sung and there was an urgency to reach a climax before it ended. This stirred in me a greater excitement. I circled my hips more strongly, pressing into his thighs as his fingers crept into my knickers and slid into me, thrusting slowly. I came as the song was beginning its final climb. I put my hand over his in its hidden place as I jerked against him but his hold held firm. We settled into a dying sway until the song ended.

There had never been such a silence.

There had never been such a stillness.

We lifted our hands from beneath the skirt and it fell to cover me. He took my hand and pressed it to his lips, tasting me on our fingers.

I could feel his rigid hardness and turned to face him when sudden sounds invaded our privacy. The door opened into it, banishing the magic.

'Oh, I thought everyone had gone!' said a friendly voice.

I blinked myself back to reality and we moved apart.

'We had but I left my scarf in here.' I went over to pick up my things, my legs a bit wobbly. 'Found it.' I held up the scarf and waved it. The man smiled at me. 'Goodnight.' And we left the building.

Lennox walked me to my car. I considered that it still wasn't too late to carry on. I checked my watch. It must have stopped again for it showed seven minutes past midnight. I made a mental note to replace the battery. 'Do you need a lift?' I asked.

He smiled at me. 'No.' Infuriating!

'Lennox, that was sort of unfinished back there and –'

'It's OK.' He knotted the scarf that hung loose around my neck. 'We'll meet again.' He placed a finger on my mouth. 'See ya later, alligator.' How quaint. It made me smile.

I removed a flier from under my windscreen wiper, got into the car and drove off slowly. When I looked in my mirror, he was gone.

The flier from my windscreen read: '50s Night at The Rising Sun Hotel, Dress to impress, Live band, Jive the night away, Sat. 19 October, 8–midnight and a half.' I'd decided to go. My friend couldn't make it but there'd be people I knew.

Lennox arrived at the hotel shortly after me. I wasn't surprised and realised that I had been expecting him to be there. Strangely, we almost ignored each other for most of the evening. Well, no. We didn't actually ignore each other at all. In fact the air probably sizzled between us and anyone in its path must have felt the heat. It was just that we didn't make contact to an outsider's perception. Our eyes kept locking but we didn't approach. I danced a lot. He watched a lot. I began to burn with more than the heat of exertion but still I waited. I knew that at some undesignated point of time we would come together.

Eventually, at a late hour well into the event, he made his move. He nodded once and began to walk towards me. 'Old Black Joe's' call to home seeped across the hall in the slow opening chords, filling the space between us and wiping all the other dancers into oblivion. I remember declining an invitation to dance, quite rudely in fact, but I didn't care. This was to be our moment. I sensed it.

Lennox stopped to stand a breath's distance from me. He placed fingertips in the hollow at the base of my neck and trailed them down through the sweat on my chest until they rested on the swell of my breasts.

He spoke, his voice cutting clearly through the music. 'Are you lonesome tonight?'

'Not any more.'

'Let's go home, Stella.' It made no sense at all but at the same time it made perfect sense. He took my hand and we left the hall.

We rose slowly as the lift carried us upwards to the second floor. Slowly, but not slowly enough for me because as soon as the doors had closed he pulled me against him and I wanted to stay there forever.

He threaded his fingers through my hair then pulled my head backwards so his eyes could look straight into mine. He rubbed my nose with his. I liked that. Softly, he started to sing, telling me that he wanted to be my 'Teddy bear'. Giggles bubbled inside me but it was only a few seconds before we reached floor two and the doors slid open.

In the confines of the lift I could smell, I thought, smoke but it was the last thing on my mind just then. The doors slid open with a hush and he spun me out before they closed silently behind us. He continued to sing along the landing, serenading me while leading in steps and turns that danced us along to our room. It took the whole song to achieve the length of the corridor due to various stops with interesting clinches in which his fingers found many different ways to touch my skin.

We finally reached number seven, at the end where the new annexe turned off to the left. As I leant against the door he told me for the last time of his anthropomorphic wish for the teddy bear.

'How did you know I love teddies?'

He smiled. 'Maybe I don't. Maybe I just like the record.' His face came close and we rubbed noses while he fitted the key into the lock. The corridor was very quiet. The revellers were still revelling, of course, but I could hear no sound from the band or bedrooms. It was almost eerily quiet.

I placed my hand on his chest. 'Lennox, can you smell smoke?'

His eyes looked vaguely startled, alarmed even, then the door opened behind me and as I turned I was stunned by the sight of the candlelit room.

There were candles on every available surface, flickering with warm life and reflecting from the mirrors. He had created an essence of beauty that took any words away. The room appeared to hover in its softness. We stepped quietly into it and the door shut out the world.

The style was pure 50s; a retro look tastefully achieved with clean uncluttered lines, the harsh edges softened by the candlelight. They must have gone to a lot of trouble to provide rooms to suit the event, I thought, or maybe there were different styles all along the corridor. Did I care? No, because while I soaked it all up, his arms slid round my waist. It enhanced the pleasure to feel his body pressed against mine in a stillness that we had not often shared. He buried his nose in my hair and began to hum a song that I recognised – 'I Want You, I Need You, I Love You' – and I wanted to believe it.

It felt glorious but a tiny flicker of unease twanged discordantly inside me. How had he known that I would be there on that night? And the candles. When had he set them up? However, my fleeting thoughts were chased away by the feel of his breath on my ear. 'Dance for me,' he whispered.

It suddenly struck me what this was all about. He wanted to watch me dance in private, to watch my body move in candlelight. The flickering on my skin would be tantalising, full of gliding, sinuous shapes. I felt a responsive warmth smoulder inside me.

I turned within the circle of his arms and his eyes burnt into mine. I put my hands on his and gently released his grip. Stepping away from him, I carefully twirled one complete slow spin. He seemed to take in a deep breath. My glance gestured to the chair and he sat, never taking his eyes from me.

My skirt was stitched with shiny pieces of glass that caught the light when I moved. I turned again, coaxing it to undulate around me a little higher, then stepped towards him and placed one foot on his thigh. A glimpse of stocking top and a gleam of thigh peeped at him. He undid the shoe and slipped it from my foot. When he did the same with the other, I let my foot slide up his thigh. He caught it as it pressed onto his erection.

I pulled from his grasp and went over to the CD player. No, not CD: more like a wireless or transistor radio or cassette player. Whatever, I simply pressed the play button, knowing that music would be ready. I was right. Fresh energy burst into the room, feeding us.

I marked time before him, always in motion, as I undid the clasp at my waist. The skirt fell in a shimmer of falling sparkle and I neatly stepped outside its circle, not missing a beat. My top soon followed and the bright red of my underwear glowed richly in the agitated light. I turned my back on him as I removed my bra, stirred to a provocative sensuality by this personal striptease.

I continued to dance, drawn by the flicker of tiny flames, imagining their play of light and dark on my naked skin. My fingers merged in duet with the dancing shadows as they traced across my body, knowing that candlelight does kind things to skin.

Nearing him, I swayed my hips as my fingers rested

on my knickers. He shifted forwards and took over from me, pulling them down in one smooth action. I circled between his hands that touched in a subtle hold of feathery lightness.

He slipped from the chair to kneel before me. My hands crept down to between my legs and I opened myself to him. He placed his tongue where I wanted it to be, licking and sliding up inside me. I stroked his hair as it moved at the top of my thighs.

The track changed – it was faster, frantic in its demand – and I swung away from him. He sat back while I danced, feeling the music, feeling his eyes, feeling the light and shades, feeling a wetness that trickled on my thigh. My feet were nimble, my body impelled to keep with the rhythm. My hair tumbled around me and I lifted it from my neck.

I finished in front of him, panting and aroused. I began to undo one of my stockings but he stopped me. 'Leave them,' he muttered, reaching up to place his outstretched fingers on my neck. His hand slid across my moist skin in a long caress of shoulder, chest, breast, belly and thigh.

I closed my eyes while he explored my body, expecting the thrill of a new touch on my skin but my body was responding to a familiarity that I didn't understand. I slipped astride his lap, my thumbs stroking the velvet lapels of his drape jacket, my hair falling softly around his face, tickling as I bent to kiss him.

The music changed again to something more sensuous, pulsating with the throb of a slow walking bass. It stirred the desire that thrilled below the surface whenever we danced together.

Lennox stood, lifting me with him. I gripped my legs around him and clung on as he carried me over to the bed. He hardly paused before throwing me onto the eiderdown. I landed on my back, breathing hard, sinking into the softness of feathers. I leant on my elbows, bringing up my knees and opened my legs to him. He stood there looking down at me then knelt between my legs.

He held his hand above me in a fist. On spreading his fingers, a bracelet dangled, swinging over my body and twinkling in the light. He lowered it and trailed it gently from my lips, down my neck, shoulder, arm, to my wrist where he fastened it.

He began to unclip my stockings, not peeling them from me as most men might but rolling them down my legs like an expert. I turned over onto my knees so he could undo the suspender. Then I started to roll over, slowly, lifting my arms, arching my back, running my fingers over my skin as they played with the shadows. And as I moved, his hands travelled all over me, causing dormant nerves to jump.

I looked up at him, breathing fast. 'Make yourself come,' he told me. He rested his hands under my thighs and lifted my legs apart. I lay back on the pillows and my fingers crept through the thatch of pubic hair.

The music slid through my body in search of a pulse and I began to rock my hips, at one with the rhythm. He watched my rubbing fingers. He watched as the momentum built, urging me on with fingertip caresses in secret places that made my excitement leap. How did he know just where to touch me? I rocked in checked tempo until I could hold back no more. I gripped his fingers with my free hand.

'Come on, baby,' he whispered, low pitched.

His words played along the surface of the tension to a vibrating chord deep inside me. The pressure increased as I moved faster, outpacing the music in an on-off beat of rampant pleasure until I let it go to ripple in a falling cadence that was way out of time.

He ran his fingers through my hair, firmly as you do to calm a startled animal. Then he said, 'I'm so sorry, Stella. Forgive me.' For what? I was bemused.

I reached to pull him down onto me. 'It's OK. It's OK.'

As he felt my naked body warm beneath him, his hands began to touch me and I writhed to encourage his exploring fingers. I pulled at his jacket and he shrugged it off. I wanted him inside me. We both tugged frantically at buttons and cloth.

'Wait!' he said. 'There is something I must do.'

He slid off the bed and crossed the room, undressing as he went, scattering clothes onto the floor. He began to blow out the candles one by one until only darkness remained, a darkness I had never felt before, a velvety richness that descended to wrap us in its blanket.

I felt a pressure on the bed beside me and he was there. I reached out and felt him. My arms and legs closed round him. My hips pushed upwards and he slipped inside me. It felt good. Very good.

A creeping beam of sunlight filtered through the curtains and teased my eyes to half wakefulness. I could hear the staccato tick of the water pipes and the trill of songbirds that seemed intrusive after the silence of the night. I sat up suddenly wanting to be awake. But Lennox wasn't there.

I snuggled into the pillows. I remember that I closed my eyes in a satisfying expectation of his return. Return from where? He was playing Mr Elusive again. I smiled a smile that froze, knowing suddenly that he would not be coming back.

I opened my eyes and looked around the room, feeling as though a trickle of cold water was creeping from the nape of my neck and along my spine.

There was no sign of the candles. No drape suit or blue suede shoes. No sign that Lennox had been here with me. The retro magic of the night had vanished and in the muted morning light the room now was different: minimalist in clear 90s style. Gone was that retro chic, dissipated into nothingness with the shades of night. Had I imagined it?

I felt an emptiness that I had never felt before.

My flitting eyes noticed a newspaper on the bedside table along with the information folder. I picked it up. On the front page there were photos of jiving couples and one of me dancing with Lennox. I smoothed the paper fastidiously. When was this taken? What on earth was I wearing? And my hair. I've never worn it in a ponytail. I looked more closely. No. It wasn't me but a very close likeness. The girl in the photo looked younger. The caption read: LUCKY ESCAPE.

A suddenly flaring heat sprung up within me.

On scanning the report it told of deaths during a fire on the night of 19 October. A shiver went through me, immediately quelling the heat.

My fingers trembled slightly as I forced myself to read more carefully and in the list of named people were Lennox Marsden and Estelle Dubois who had been at the jive competition earlier that night. Most people had escaped unhurt, the article told me, but the couple had been trapped in their room and exposed to smoke inhalation.

I pulled the duvet around me in search of warmth for the icy trickle was by then flowing slowly through my veins.

After a while I took a deep breath and went over to the window that overlooked the car park. I opened the curtains, relieved to see neat rows of modern cars.

I lifted the newspaper, daring to check its date: 23 October 1959.

They had died here fifteen years before I was born.

I stared at nothing through the window for long moments of time then focused on my reflection. I just couldn't get my mind around this.

I replaced the paper neatly. As I did so the bracelet slipped down my wrist. I unclasped it, about to leave it on the table but changed my mind. I put it into my bag and began to dress in slow motion. I went down the stairs, got into my car and drove away without a backwards glance.

I thought that had my numbness melted just then, the tears that threatened would have been shed as tiny shards of ice as, by a cruel quirk of fate, my CD began playing 'Heartbreak Hotel'. I sped up into my day.

Musical Chairs Kay Jaybee

Music was thundering out of the doors. The club had been in full swing for several hours when Sean pulled Jess into the entrance hall.

'I'm really not sure about this.' Jess's free hand began to rub around her tethered wrist. 'Take me home.'

Sean looked her straight in the eye. 'Are you really telling me that you don't want a chance to perform? Or are you just saying that you are shit scared you won't match up to the competition?' Jess's face cracked into something that might have been a smile if she hadn't been so apprehensive. ''Cos I can tell you now, honey, you are gonna scare them to death. You certainly frighten me.'

Jess stuck her tongue out playfully, before quickly composing herself. It was the club's exclusive games night, and they were next in the queue.

Sean caught his breath at the sight of her small neat body as he removed the grey duffel coat from her shoulders. Jess could appear very proper at times, but not tonight. Her shoulder-length red hair was swept back behind her neck in a tiny ponytail, showing off her delicate neck to perfection. Only Jess's chest and rounded bum were covered, swathed lightly in gauze cloth. Her wrist lead of worn black leather was clasped firmly in Sean's hand. He had warned her that it was unlikely they would remain together for the duration of the night. It would all depend on the luck of the game and the whim of their host.

The room they were ushered into was lit with candles. The cream walls, supported by beams, ran up into a vaulted ceiling. The wooden floor echoed with the sound of high heels as four couples walked through the arched doorway.

It was easy to spot the other first timers. Huddled closely, another couple were looking around with open curiosity. The remaining four players were obviously old hands at such games nights, and stood proud, watching, sizing up the competition.

Sean pointed to a large pile of cushions at one end of the room and, stacked next to them, a dozen or so wooden chairs. He smiled at Jess, who was looking carefully about her. 'Come on, honey,' he whispered, 'you'll love it.'

Jess didn't reply, but carried on looking, taking in her temporary companions. Two of the women were staring daggers at each other from either side of the doorway. Jess watched them closely. The first was leaving absolutely no doubt in anyone's mind of her personal preferences. Thigh-length leather boots, a PVC bodice that reached just beneath her breasts, pushing them both up and out, and a tight black neck band made her dominatrix role so stereotypical that Jess had to suppress the urge to rush out and buy her a whip. Unlike the other couples, it was the man who was subservient here. On all fours at his mistress's feet, he was a little overweight, his stomach hanging down above his tight leather shorts. Jess had to suppress the desire to gag at the sight of his sweaty body.

The other experienced female contender was far shorter than her black-clad rival, but no less determined judging from the expression in her eyes. Her amber hair was piled up on top of her head, her pale skin perfectly complemented by the coffee-coloured satin basque that encased her slim body, with hold ups to match and the sexiest strappy shoes Jess had ever seen. This woman was truly beautiful and Jess found herself imagining what it might be like to be held by her.

Shaking herself slightly, Jess switched her attention to the amber woman's partner, who was holding onto his slave by a slim lead running off a belt which hung provocatively around her waist. He was taller than Sean and his olive skin shone as if he had oiled it in order to highlight every muscle. Clothed simply in ripped denim shorts and an open white shirt, Jess could almost feel what his skin must taste like. In that one moment she knew that Sean had been right; she was going to enjoy herself. She just hoped he would be able to cope with that.

The muted murmurings of the four couples halted when the compère of the evening's event strode into the room. Dressed in a well-cut suit, his greying hair expertly cut, he looked as if he spent a large amount of his time lounging on a sunbed.

'Ladies and gentlemen,' he announced, rubbing his hands together. 'For those of you who have not been here before, my name is Jacque. I advise you to listen to what I say very carefully. I make the rules and, unless I say otherwise, you will faithfully carry out the tasks allotted to you.'

'As you can see, in the far corner of the room we have a pile of chairs and cushions.' Jess and her counterparts looked to where he pointed. 'Please could each of you take a chair and a cushion and place them in a row across the room. Today we are going to play musical chairs.'

It was only a matter of minutes before there was a line of alternately facing chairs, each adorned with a silk cushion, arranged next to each other.

Jacque came amongst them as music flooded the room. It was certainly not one of the childhood classics she associated with musical chairs. Haunting Celtic vibes oozed out of hidden speakers, and Jess felt her heartbeat quicken and her body chill at the sound. All eyes were on their host. The game was about to begin.

Gesturing for them all to gather round, Jacque addressed the group. 'I trust you were all suitably popular in your youth to be invited to birthday parties. Musical chairs.' He pointed towards the line of chairs. 'The rules are almost as you would remember them. But not quite. I will start you gently however. If those of you in charge of slaves could release them, then each of you may take a seat.'

Jess watched as the dominatrix sternly regarded her mate. He reared up onto his haunches, just as if he were an over-pampered dog, his hands begging, his tongue lolling between his slightly parted lips. His mistress looked at him for a second with a face full of disdain, before nodding her approval for his return to the human world, and giving her permission for him to play the game.

Sean unclipped Jess's wrist lead and fastened it around her waist like a belt, before escorting her to a chair. As they sat next to each other Jess didn't dare look at Sean's face. She knew she had already mentally distanced herself from him. He had wanted her to do this; so he would have to watch and take the consequences. Jess jutted out her chin, pulled in her already flat stomach and waited.

The music stopped. The silence it left behind seemed almost as loud as the music had been. 'In just a couple of seconds the music will start again. You will all rise and walk around the chairs in an anti-clockwise circuit. On this occasion –' he paused and the place seemed alive with electricity '– you will all be able to return to your seats.'

The cold tones of a female voice filled the room and, almost as if they were a pack of wolves sizing each other up, the players circled the chairs, each stepping slowly in time to the tune. Jess followed Sean, admiring his tight denim-clad bum. She was concentrating so hard on the moment the music would stop that she almost didn't notice when it did. With an amazing turn of speed, everyone darted to the nearest chair. It was clear that if she didn't want to be the first out of this game she'd have to move a hell of a lot faster next time.

Jacque was surveying the players. 'This time' he said 'we are playing for real. Each chair will be a refuge for two people. The couple who have no seat when the music stops will stand exactly where they are and await my instruction. While you are seated you have my licence to do whatever you like, but as soon as the music restarts you will rise and continue the game. Is that understood?'

The group nodded in silence.

It wasn't until Jacque moved away five of the chairs that Jess fully realised how important it was going to be to stay as close as possible to either Sean in front of her, or the amber woman behind her. She could feel her heartbeat quicken and knew that despite her apprehension the situation had turned her on, and she already longed for some sort of physical contact to break the tension. I'm as bad as the others, she thought to herself.

Jacque nodded to the unseen music controller at the far end of the room, and once again the ghostly strains of an Irish voice filled the room. Jess rose and began a steady, almost stilted walk around the chairs. Sean was walking far quicker, ready to spring towards a chair, and Jess hastened after him. She felt the music run through her; it seemed to vibrate around her brain as she moved. Surely it would stop soon? As the seconds ticked by the tension in the hall increased ten-fold. The walkers were almost jogging now, each increasing their stride.

It stopped. Jess felt her legs move even before her brain engaged the fact that she needed to sit on a chair very, very quickly. Almost throwing herself on top of Sean as he landed on the chair a split second before her, she giggled with relief at finding herself safe this time.

Sean swept a stray hair back behind her ears and kissed her, deeply probing her mouth with his tongue. It was a consuming, melting kiss, which in normal surroundings would have led to much more activity, but Jess wanted to see who had failed to find a seat, and pulled away hastily.

Jess was surprised to see that the olive-skinned man was still standing. He didn't look bothered, in fact quite the opposite and Jess wondered if he'd done it on purpose. The amber woman, who was currently having her neck licked by the dog man as she sat beneath him, was looking knowingly at him. Jess was less surprised to see the other first-time female still upright. The black-haired girl stood, waiting. Jess could guess at the struggle she had not to look scared, as she attempted to stand tall and keep her head high.

The activity on each chair was half hearted, each player being more interested to see what Jacque would choose as a forfeit for those knocked out of the game. He strode back across the floor, his shoes pounding against the wood. 'As you can see we have two willing volunteers to create a spectacle for rest of us.' He beckoned to them to come before him. 'This is my game, and you are just pawns at my beck and call.'

Jess shivered; how had she become an object for his voyeuristic amusement? The idea should have sickened her, but she felt the heat rise within her and her nipples tighten beneath the slightly scratchy material that bound them.

Jacque announced that the olive-skinned man was called Jake and the girl was called Sara. He whispered into Jake's ear, causing him to smile and nod in agreement. Jess shifted against Sean's obvious arousal beneath her, as she saw Jake reach forward and slip Sara's black silk camisole straps off her shoulders, revealing her bare breasts to the room. Jess only had a second to take in their beauty before Jake pushed her roughly to her knees and, freeing his cock, started to rub its tip against her swollen breasts. There was just time to hear Sara sigh as he polished her nipples with his dick's shiny head, before the music refilled the hall and the remaining players took up their march once more.

There were only two chairs left now and there was hardly a gap between them and the six contenders. Jess was trying very hard to focus on the music, on her goal of landing on a chair, but even the sounds of their feet moving faster and faster in a dizzy circle couldn't take her mind off the occasional self-satisfied moan that issued from Jake's mouth, and the soft groans of frustration from Sara as the unfulfilling attention her chest was receiving built up.

The music stopped. If the amber woman hadn't grabbed her around the waist and hoisted her onto her lap, then Jess would now be standing where Sean was: chairless and looking into the eyes of the dog man. Jess was aware of Sean losing his composure for just a split second, before she was distracted by the feel of a woman's long fingernails dancing up and down her spine. Jess sat very still. She wasn't sure if she was enjoying that specifically or if it was the whole occasion that was making the dampness between her legs become a slow seeping wetness, which in turn was producing goose pimples over her bare flesh.

The attention she was receiving from the amber woman, who was now skilfully licking Jess's ear, caused her to miss Jacque issuing instructions to the three men and one woman, who had now taken up new positions.

The dog man, who Jacque was referring to as Slave, was lying flat on his back on the floor. Sara was on all fours, her arms each side of his face, one small breast smothered by his vast mouth, while the other shook slightly as Sean pushed his penis into her from behind and Jake teased Sean's bum with his own dick. Jess wondered how badly he wanted Jake to push inside him like she had done with her beloved dildo on so many occasions. Despite the possibilities of their position, they were hardly moving at all, and Jess suspected that Jacque had forbidden them from coming.

The effect of seeing this erotic tableau, combined with the gentle caress of the amber woman, was more acute than Jess could have imagined. She tried again to focus on Sean; tried to feel jealous at seeing his penis slip in and out of another girl's pussy. Instead she just felt jealous of the attention. Jess knew that the stimulation she herself was receiving was already not enough, and she longed to feel a pair of lips against her pussy, kissing the juices out of her.

Jess glanced at the dominatrix as she reluctantly left the seat; her eyes were full of disgust as her slave slobbered against the globes of another woman.

This wasn't the time to watch the action behind her, she needed to concentrate. But did she want to find a chair, or did she want to be 'out' and join the others? There was always the danger that she would be asked to do something she didn't want to; although at that moment in time Jess wasn't sure that there was much she wouldn't do. The amber woman hadn't relinquished her hold on Jess, even though they were moving. She could feel her hot breath on her neck, and a firm hand pushed against the gauze, which sweat had now moulded to the contours of her bottom.

The song stopped; Jess tried to move to the one remaining chair, but she found herself being pulled back into the amber woman's arms. 'It will be better if we get out now,' she whispered, as Jess realised it was too late to protest anyway. The PVC-clad woman was already sat astride Sara's partner, and was not so gently biting his neck.

Jess's attention snapped back to Jacque. He had halted the foursome where they were. Jess could hear Sara sigh, and judged by the look in her eyes that she was biting back frustrated tears. Had she been just about to come? Jess suspected so, and the added tension of the young woman's predicament served to turn her on further. She feared that if the woman who seemed to have claimed her actually attempted to do any of the things that she longed for her to do, then she would come at the first touch.

'A change of position to incorporate our newcomers,' Jacque declared.

Sean looked slightly shame faced as he glanced at Jess. So now you want reassurance, Jess thought; she smiled and nodded. 'It's all right,' she wanted to say, 'I am enjoying this too. You were right,' but instead she listened to the instructions that Jacque was issuing.

'On your knees, please, gentlemen.' Sean, Jake and Slave dropped onto their knees in a row, their erections standing to attention. 'Ladies, you will please crawl towards your appointed man. Jess, you will pair up with Jake, Sara with Slave and Louisa with Sean.' Jess's eyes flickered to the amber woman. The name Louisa didn't seem to fit her somehow; Amber would have been much better. 'A competition, ladies,' Jacque declared. 'Whoever can make their appointed man come first will win a prize.' Jess wondered if it would be a prize she wanted to win as she caught Louisa's eye just as she enveloped Jess's boyfriend's penis in her beautiful mouth.

Jess was wondering if you could come simply from a lack of stimulation when she heard Jacque declare that the final two people in the musical chairs competition were about to complete the game. The haunting music now felt like the most erotic sound in the world. It filled her mind as she slowly began to probe Jake's tip with delicate strokes of her tongue. It was not lost on her that she and Louisa had swapped partners. She wondered if Jacque had done it on purpose.

Jess kept up the careful teasing until Jake gave the gentle moan she'd been waiting for. Then, very slowly, she enveloped his mass into her mouth. Don't rush, she told herself. The music was still playing, and whilst she manoeuvred him around her mouth, sucking with different degrees of pressure, she could see the two players circling the chair. Louisa had been right, this was better. She wouldn't have relished competing with the dominatrix.

Jess wondered what Sean felt like to someone else. Jake certainly had a cock worth sucking. It seemed to fill every inch of her mouth, and, as she slowly eased him further down her throat, she was suddenly aware that the music had stopped, that there was activity next to her, but she couldn't stop. Jake's breathing had changed, he was nearly there, and she knew it.

The dominatrix was now standing on the chair, and Jess realised that she must have won, and that this wasn't necessarily good news. She risked a glance to the right, where she could see Louisa busily licking Sean's balls. She could hear Sean's familiar deep-throated moans. She must hurry. She wanted to win this one.

Jake's cream filled her throat just as she began to think he'd never break. Gobbling him greedily, Jess pulled away as the last trickles of liquid ran down the corners of her mouth, taking some of her lipstick with it.

'We have a winner.' Jacque's imperial tones filled the room, as both Sara and Louisa pulled away in frustration, while Sean and Slave looked stricken to be so close with no instant relief forthcoming.

Jess looked at Louisa. She thought she might be angry for losing, but in fact the look of lust on her face was even more obvious than before. Jess felt her legs begin to quiver. My God I want her, she thought. It didn't occur to her that she'd never had a woman before. Right now it seemed not only the most obvious thing in the world, but absolutely essential for both her body and her sanity.

Jake swayed slightly as he rose to his feet. Jess could feel his eyes appraising her as they waited to see what would happen next. The frisson in the room was almost palpable. All it would take for a full-blown orgy was a single word from Jacque. It was amazing how his presence alone held them all in check.

Sean was panting hard, trying to get himself back under control. Jess glanced at the others and found them all to be as keen for the next event as she was. She didn't even care who had her any more, but someone had to, and soon.

While she had been occupied with Jake, Jacque had obviously been thinking ahead to the next stage of the evening. Jess noticed that the dominatrix, who Jacque had started referring to as Madame, had developed a half smile. This was far more unnerving than her previous expression of derision, and seemed to be directly connected to the large box that Jacque now placed on the floor in front of her.

'The prize for winning musical chairs,' Jacque declared, 'is to take one trinket from this box. Only one, and use it however you please on whoever you desire for up to ten minutes.' Madame opened the lid and began to rifle through the unseen contents. Jess suppressed a shudder; she had no doubt that this woman could inflict serious pain with the aid of the right weapon.

'Those of you not involved in what follows,' Jacque continued, 'will watch. You will not be touched. You will not touch yourselves. You must simply observe. You may find this more difficult than you think.' He smiled. 'I doubt whether any of you could deny how much you are in need of a good seeing to; some more than others perhaps.'

Jess jumped. Had he directed that final comment at her? He'd certainly looked at her as he had spoken. Anyway, she knew he was right, and her cheeks flushed in a totally uncharacteristic moment of embarrassment.

Madame took Jacque to one side and described what she required. He smiled, nodded and returned to the group. 'You will all remove what garments remain on your person.'

Jess didn't hesitate. The gauze material had begun to rub her already distended nubs and was so sweat sodden that it was leaving nothing to the imagination anyway. Once she had stripped she looked up into the eyes of Sean, who stood before her, naked, beautiful and deliciously desperate. Louisa was next to him. One touch, she thought, that is all it's gonna take.

Sara and Jake were eyeing each other provocatively, and even Slave didn't look too bad now that his constricting clothing had been removed. Now I really am in trouble, Jess thought, if I'd cheerfully screw him, which she had to admit, right now, she would.

Madame was issuing further details of her intentions to Jacque. 'Just one touch.' Jess was aware that obsession was setting in, but she could virtually feel Louisa's breasts, and her tongue still tasted of Jake's saltiness. She was brought back to reality when Jacque called her name.

The PVC suit had gone. Madame stood tall in her killer heels, her incredible body poised and ready; and she was looking straight at Jess. Louisa had also been summoned, and was currently bent over one of the chairs, her bottom ruthlessly exposed, her legs planted on the floor, and her hands gripping the chair's legs.

Jess walked forwards, shaking slightly. Madame was holding a black, nodule-covered, rubber paddle. A smack with that was going to hurt. She was just about to stretch her body over the adjacent chair, when Madame put her arm out to restrain her. 'No. Your prize for winning the sucking contest is to help me. You will follow my instructions very carefully.' Jess hesitated, comprehension dawning; she was about to administer the punishment herself.

Music filled the silent hall. The Celtic sound had its own strange beat, and Jess felt herself compelled to move with it. Smoothing the shape of Louisa's luscious bottom with her free had, she whispered, 'Sorry,' just as she made the first blow.

However practised the amber woman obviously was it didn't prevent her from crying out in shock at that first hit. Swinging her arm in time to the music, Jess slapped one buttock and then the next, building up a pretty pattern of red marks across the perfect skin. Glancing at Madame for reassurance that she was doing the right thing, Jess saw her face glowing with satisfaction at the discomfort of her rival. Jess realised that she too was gaining pleasure from wielding the paddle. She had punished Sean on many occasions, but she was unsure that he would have withstood such a public humiliation with such little fuss. The cries were small now, mostly drowned out by the mystic thud of the music. Jess was listening carefully; surely she would soon hear the moment when pain became that bizarre brand of pleasure which burnt through the body with each strike, making the need for it to continue as essential as the need for it to stop.

Jess stole a look at the others. They were all stood with their hands on their heads, their legs wide apart, and all eyes were fixed on the trio in front of them.

Madame heard the change in Louisa's breathing before Jess did, and was obviously ready for it. 'Stop.' The command was softly spoken, but was not one that any-one would have dared contradict. Jess lowered her arm. Madame's face as she regarded Louisa's chequered bum was both lust filled and revenge fuelled. Jess wondered what old scores were being settled here.

Jess helped Louisa to stand up. Supporting her, as the blood rushed back to her head, she placed her hand on the burning buttocks, admiring the pretty criss-cross pattern of welts she had so recently created. Nothing was said as the two women regarded each other, but Jess knew that whatever happened next, this was one woman she wanted to meet again.

Jacque strode forwards. He looked slightly more dishevelled than before, and Jess couldn't help but notice the prominent bulge in his trousers, illustrating just how much he too had enjoyed the spanking spectacle he had just witnessed. 'Time for the climax of the evening, if you will excuse the pun,' he smirked.

Jess would have forgiven him anything if he would just allow her to get screwed. Jacque dipped his hand back into the wooden box, and pulled out four strap-on dildos, which he silently passed to each woman, before manoeuvring the group into a circle, one behind another, in strict boy–girl rotation. As they waited, Jess could feel Slave's hot breath on her back as she inspected Jake's back view at close quarters. She struggled to keep her arms at her sides. It would have been so easy just to smooth her hands over Jake's bum. Jess could feel the pressure of the false cock as it hung from her, and felt a surge of power course through her body.

'When the music starts,' Jacque said, his voice showing signs of his own struggle to remain in control as he observed the naked ring before him, 'you will each wrap your arms around the person in front of you. Then, on my word, the men will all penetrate the woman ahead of them, and the girls will pierce the butts of the boys before them.' He strode around as they each eased forwards. Jess had to prevent herself from yelping at the sheer relief of Slave's fingers scrapping over her nipples, as his huge hands kneaded her breasts. The frisson between her legs, beneath the strap-on, was intoxicating, and the wait for the music to restart seemed longer than ever.

At last Jacque signalled and the music began again, this time with a stronger beat, perfect for pumping the hell out of the person in front of you. 'Now,' cried Jacque.

Jess screamed as Slave spent no time in pushing himself into her slippery wetness, whilst she positioned her fake dick between Jake's waiting buttocks. Sandwiched between these two hard men was like nothing she had ever known. Her head swam with the overwhelming sensations that she was at last experiencing, after an incredible evening of watching, teasing and wanting.

Their circle, linked at the crotch and bum, shuddered and cried out in release as breasts were kneaded, ears were bitten, backs were scratched and balls were crushed.

Jess wasn't sure how long it had lasted. Real time seemed to be suspended, replaced instead by the relentless beat of the strange music and the moans from her and her compatriots. She might have passed out, she didn't know. She wasn't even sure how the circle had broken down and how she'd reached the chair on which she was now sat, Louisa astride her lap, their tongues dancing together and their hands exploring.

Jess was briefly aware of Jacque lying across Slave's lap, as Madame whipped the back of his legs, of Sean taking Sara from behind, whilst Jake knelt before Sara's partner, whose name Jess had already forgotten, sucking on his balls.

This could go on a while, she thought to herself, as she slid off the chair and finally brought her lips down between the amber woman's beautifully spread legs.

Duet for Three Portia Da Costa

What the fuck?

What is this? I wasn't expecting this. When the woman on reception said there was a bit of a 'do' on, and I was welcome to join in, I didn't expect it to be the bastard child of a fetish party, a rave and Northern wedding reception.

Too weird.

It's a biggish room, an old ballroom or something, I suppose, but tonight it's decked out like a rough approximation of clubland. The music's a solid wall of complex, juddering sound, and there's flashing, strobing light bouncing off the walls and the mass of gyrating bodies.

God, it's all completely mad. But I like it. I haven't felt this psyched up in ages. My ears and my toes, and everything else between, are vibrating in time to the hard, thudding base beats, and my groin is suddenly tight with anticipation.

I suddenly feel an intense desire to get laid.

Smiling, I stroll towards the small, paid-for bar. I was expecting *Strictly Come Dancing* in a place like this – a discreet, out-of-the-way country hotel that I stumbled into by mistake when I got fed up of the motorway – but there's no poncy foxtrotting around here, no way. They're all throwing themselves around like maniacs, lost in the music, and the sweaty smell of adrenaline is almost solid.

Yeah, Jason, you could have some fun here ... My prick kicks again inside my shorts.

At the bar, Mr Jack Daniels calls plaintively to me, but I ignore him. The fact I've been to a health farm – aka celebrity rehab – is the reason I've ended up in this godforsaken place. And I'm not going to undo all the shit from hell I've just gone through to get clean. Which means no booze for me. And no fags. And none of that other stuff either . . .

But I will allow myself a woman, if I get lucky.

I say, *if* . . .

At one time, it would have been a piece of cake. I could have had a dozen bimbettes a night if I could've coped with them . . . and sometimes, high as a kite, I did. But I'm not part of a headlining boy band any more. I'm not even recognisable – I hope – as a washed-up ex-member of a washed-up ex-boy band. I'm just Jason Ripley, an average guy who'd maybe like to start again as a real singer . . .

So, no JD. I order a mineral water and, as the young chap behind the bar hands it me, he gives me a strange, almost knowing look.

Hmmm . . . Well, maybe I'm not as unrecognisable as I thought. I thought I'd be safe now my long, trademark blond locks are gone, along with my shades and/or my bright-green contact lenses. I'm just Mr Man in the Street with short, nondescript brown hair and an unremarkable pair of glasses. And no designer gear any more either, just a plain shirt, off-the-peg jeans and running shoes.

No, I'm pretty sure the barman hasn't recognised J-Boy Jones of the Forever Boys from Adam. He's serving someone else now and has completely lost interest.

As I sip, I turn my attention to the dance floor. There's plenty to see, once my eyes adjust to the light and the movement.

I was right about the fetish party thing. Although there are plenty of folk in ordinary clothes – jeans, smart casual, some quite dressed up – there's also quite a lot of rubber and leather and all the rest of it.

A man in arseless leather trousers. A woman in a rubber catsuit. A full on gimp. It's all a bit clichéd. But then I think about some of the stupid stage costumes that I wore, which played around with fetish looks. I must have looked a complete berk. Especially as I hadn't the faintest idea in the beginning what it all meant. These people aren't famous, or particularly glamorous, but at least I get the feeling that they understand kinkiness and perversity in a way that I never did. I was just playing. These dancers are for real.

I'm just about dragging my jaw up off the dance floor at the sight of a truly gorgeous drag queen – who, disturbingly, also makes my prick twitch a bit – when a female voice pierces the cocoon of booming sound.

'Do you come here often?'

My heart jerks. It's a voice I recognise, despite the music.

I turn, and it feels like slo-mo. Surely it can't be her? Why would she be here?

But it *is* her. She's here. And I feel kind of sick inside from a mix of shock jumbled up with guilt . . . and regret.

'Do you come here often?' repeats Maria Lewis, a woman I once dated in London. A lovely girl who I really didn't treat well.

'Maria?'

An oblique smile, not unlike that of the barman, curves her soft pink mouth and, before I can say anything else, she reaches out and places her fingertips over my lips, to shush me.

I'm semi-speechless anyway, so it doesn't really matter. But the warm contact of her skin almost makes my heart stop.

Fucking hell, she looks amazing.

I didn't know her for long, but she was always pretty, and in a far more refined way than a lot of the Z-list slappers that I went through.

But now, oh hell, she's just beautiful.

Blue eyes brighter. Hair shorter, but blonder and wilder in a sort of sexy shag cut. Her perfect heart-shaped face has an inner glow of mystery, of life, of supreme confidence.

And her body?

Dear God Almighty, her body is just perfection – the stuff of every wet or waking dream I've ever had.

She's become every inch the superstar that I aspired to be and never was.

'Let's dance,' she purrs, the tip of her forefinger pressing heavily on my lower lip for a second, dragging it down.

I feel as if I've just been struck by lightning.

And my cock, which was formerly just perky, has turned to iron.

It's a wonder I don't fall arse over tit into the mass of dancing people. I just can't take my eyes off her delicious bottom as she walks ahead of me, parting the swaying, gesticulating throng like a queen on a progress. Like I said, her body is perfect. And her bottom is more than perfect, if that's possible. It moves and sways and lilts as if she's dancing before we've even found our spot. As if she hears the music in her bones and in her heart.

Was she always this gorgeous? I suppose she must have been, but I was either just too wasted or too full of my own self-importance to appreciate her.

But I'm appreciating her now. Bloody hell, am I appreciating her.

Appreciating that marvellous firm arse, those long, long legs in a sleek, short, but elegant little black dress, and her superb breasts, as she turns towards me and gives me that narrow, cryptic little smile again. A smile that seems to combine with the staccato beat of the heavy, Latin-influenced track that's playing and wind itself around my dick like a serpent.

Shit, I'm in trouble.

And then we're dancing and I feel like a terpsichoreally challenged farmhand with seven left feet, instead of the pretty slick mover I once was. Seeing Maria again has rendered me helpless, almost infantile.

But she moves like a goddess. A wild, uninhibited poem of graceful syncopation. I can't remember if we ever danced together when we clubbed in the old days, but if we ever did, I'm sure she never danced like this.

She commands the space we've found ourselves in, carving out more and more with the sheer force of her personality and the energy with which she twists and turns and sways. Her sinuous body seems to interpret subtle rhythms and embedded harmonies that lesser mortals just aren't equipped to hear. I can hear them, because I was a musician of sorts before I pissed most of it away, but I can't do with this music what Maria does.

Fuck, I want her so much.

Maybe that's why my own feet and limbs just won't work properly. Because my hard-on is so ironclad it's almost agony. It's as if I've been disconnected from all rhythm and co-ordination.

She doesn't look at me. Which is probably a good thing. She seems ensorcelled by the beats, her white arms lifted to heaven and her eyes closed.

And yet, from time to time, when her eyes do open, she does look at somebody.

We're close to the edge of the dance floor, and when – with enormous difficulty – I can shake my eyes away from her for a few seconds, and follow her eye line, I see that I'm not the only one who's watching her swirl and shimmy.

Lounging at a table, alone, is a large, stocky man with darkish, greying hair, a broad, stubble-shadowed face and intense, gleaming eyes. For a fraction of a second his attention strays from Maria and fixes on me ... and I feel almost the same sense of shock I get from her.

I'm not gay.

Really I'm not.

OK, so maybe once ... or twice ... when I was pissed or high, I had a fumble around with Christian, the guy in the band who was bent. But that doesn't mean I'm homosexual or even bi.

Yet there's something about this guy who's watching us that seems to grab me somehow. Makes me want to shudder and look away, and yet look again. I miss yet another beat and stumble in my pathetic attempt to match Maria's moves. Torn between her and him, I get strange flash visions of being in a room somewhere, doing dark and dangerous things. With her, and also with him.

As my dick gets harder, I feel scared, yet infinitely excited. It's like I'm filled with a sense of anticipation of I know not what. I glance at the happy fetish crowd around me, who all seem to know what they want and why – and I envy them.

Maybe I want what they want? I wish I knew ... I'm just feeling more and more confused. Like a disenfranchised stranger in a very strange land indeed.

And it's right at that moment – as if she's read my mind – that Maria suddenly halts, mid-gyration, and fixes me with a steady blue stare.

'Come on. Let's get out of here.'

With that she walks from the floor, not looking back,

just leading me with her lithe, silky stride in her perfect black heels, and the muscular undulation of her gently swaying buttocks.

I couldn't not follow if my next breath depended on it.

Like an eager, panting puppy, I almost trot after her, out of the function room, across the lobby and to the lift. She doesn't check if I'm following, not once, and I have to run and almost fall into the lift carriage behind her in order to avoid it closing in my face.

'Maria. What on earth are you doing here?' I babble, still to her straight, smooth back and shoulders, 'Look, I'm sorry –'

Whirling like a ballet dancer, she cuts me off, mid-grovel, by the simple expedient of pushing hard on my chest, backing me up against the lift wall, and kissing me. Hard.

And as her tongue pushes imperiously into my mouth, her hand unzips my jeans with astonishing deftness, negotiates my underwear, and takes hold of my cock.

I'm so shocked I almost come all over her fingers.

Yet still, inanely, I try to speak and apologise … or something. She allows me my mouth for a moment, even while her fingertips do something infernal to the head of my penis, but her eyes utterly quell me. I can't utter a word. Somewhere in those periwinkle blue depths there could well be the answer to the meaning of the universe, but all I see is a blend of amusement and disdain, coupled with a disquieting foreknowledge of something I daren't even think about.

Then she's kissing me again, and almost dispassion-ately handling my equipment as if it's some mildly amusing curiosity she's passing a minute or two with while listening to the piped lift music.

There's barely time for a couple of bars of 'The Girl

From Ipanema' before the lift door slides open and she drops me like the proverbial hot potato and just walks away, leaving me standing there with my erection poking out of my flies.

Thank Christ there's no one on the landing.

Shoving myself ignominiously and uncomfortably back into my jeans, I scuttle after Maria. That beautiful bottom of hers wafts from side to side as if she's still dancing, still hearing the samba rhythm of Astrud Gilberto. I can't take my eyes off it, and nearly trip on the edge of the carpet runner in my haste to catch up.

Which means that I nearly cannon right into her when she stops abruptly in front of one of the room doors.

The brass numerals read '17', and my eyes bug when Maria reaches into the front of her dress and pulls out a key card, which has presumably been tucked cosily inside her bra.

Lucky card.

The polished door swings open, and I follow her inside to a softly lit room, where astonishingly, it isn't Astrud Gilberto singing, but *me*.

Ack, how I hate some of those songs now. And 'You're My Fire, Baby' is a prime example. Poppy, bouncy, over-produced, conveyor-belt chart drivel. I cringe. Even with all the vocal enhancements at the studio engineer's disposal, I'm barely even carrying the tune. I *can* sing, but this wasn't one of my finest moments.

Maria turns to me and gives me a look of almost pitying amusement.

She obviously doesn't think it's much cop either.

What bothers me even more than my former lack of glory is the fact that the loathsome doggerel is playing at all.

How has that happened? Even I'm not stupid or

bemused enough to believe that it's a coincidence. I start to ask, but she silences me again with her fingers across my open lips.

The scent of my cock is still on her skin.

A second later she's kissing me again. Dominating me again with her lips and her hands. Her tongue is dainty and mobile but it seems to fill my mouth, and her fingers move efficiently on the fastenings of my jeans. Loosening them so she can slide a hand inside the back of them – and my shorts – and caress my backside.

It feels so sensational that I groan, muffled by her lips, and my dick hardens anew against her belly. I try to caress her in return, but she presses her curved fingers so firmly and so suddenly against my arsehole that I yelp against her mouth, and I can barely remember my own name.

And then she abandons me again, and whirls away. With a casual, uncaring grace, she throws herself down into a big, deep, chintz-covered armchair, and I'm left standing around like a dolt, my eyes skittering between the overdecorated bed with its elaborate, also chintz-patterned hangings, and the perfection of Maria's relaxed body and long, sleek legs.

'Look, Maria ... I ... um ... I'm sorry I never called you,' I bluster, then dry up when she raises an imperious hand to stop my babble.

'Shut the fuck up, Jason,' she says in a quiet, unperturbed, almost affable voice, 'and take your shirt off.'

What?

I feel confused and excited again, but I obey her. I've started working out again now I've cleaned up my act, but I'm painfully aware of the fact that I'm not as buff as I once was. Her all-seeing eyes seem to notice it too, and narrow slightly.

Fucking hell, I wish she'd turn off that music. My own

trilling voice mocks me as I stand there shivering despite the gentle warmth from the central heating.

I wait, but she doesn't speak again, and I feel nullified, unable to act or move until she does.

Slowly, she licks her pink-painted lips.

She uncrosses and recrosses her peerless legs, careful not to allow me even the slightest glimpse of what lies between her thighs.

Barely seeming to pay the slightest attention to what she's doing, she reaches back into the low neckline of her black dress and slowly and idly begins to play with her nipple. Her fingertips move like some tiny animal burrowing about beneath the dark fabric and, after a moment, she closes her eyes and gives a little gasp of pleasure.

It's the most erotic thing I've ever seen in my entire life.

I'm in agony. My cock is tenting my jeans, and it's aching for me to wank it. But I know I can't touch it until she gives permission.

I've never done the submission and domination thing. And I've seen no more than odd bits of scenes in films and half-watched documentaries. But suddenly I seem to understand ... or at least begin to.

It's something I never wanted until now.

I watch and watch as she rubs her long, silky thighs together and continues to fondle her breast. I'm still immobilised, like a pillar of burning salt.

Eventually she gives a little gasp, and a little sigh, and relaxes back into her seat.

Has she come? I didn't think women could do that ... just orgasm from rubbing their own nipples. Maybe she hasn't ... I get the feeling she's just teasing me, and that's strengthened when she opens her limpid blue eyes, and they mock me.

Men are such idiots, she seems to say, without speaking.

I don't speak either, but while my voice burbles on and on from the sound system, a thousand questions jostle behind my lips.

Chief amongst which is ... why did I ever, in my right or addled mind, let this glorious woman go?

I nearly fall over when she springs lightly to her feet and sashays towards me and, as I fight for composure, she looks me up and down as if I'm some kind of stud animal or piece of meat she's assessing.

'Unzip your jeans. Drop them to your ankles. Don't step out of them,' she instructs, her voice strangely neutral. As if she doesn't really care if I obey her or not.

I do though. I really care.

'Pants now. The same.'

I obey again. My mouth is dry. My heart is bashing against my chest. My cock bounces up against my belly as it's released, tip moist and sticky.

She does that stockwoman looking at the beast thing again, and I have a horrible feeling I've been judged lacking. I feel like a complete idiot standing here buck naked, with my jeans and underpants round my ankles, yet in a slightly sick but overpowering way, I like it. I like it a lot.

There's a knock at the door and I sway, nearly toppling over. Our eyes lock.

'If you so much as move a muscle, you can put your clothes on, get out of here and I never want to see you again.'

I've never fainted in my life, but I feel as if I want to now.

But no way on earth am I going to move. Not a millimetre.

'Come!' she calls out and, as the door handle turns, I realise the door was never locked.

I close my eyes for a moment, and I feel sweat trickling from my armpits and from between my thighs. I imagine if I could stand outside myself, and look at my skin, every inch of it would be blushing, especially my rigid, seeping cock.

'Robert,' she breathes, her voice soft, loving and happy. As she walks right past me the air she displaces feels almost blissfully cool, and a moment later I hear the small, feverish sounds of an intensely passionate kiss.

Fight or flight instinct screams at me to grab up my clothing, bolt for the door and run for my room, then check out as soon as is possible. But another force, a greater force, keeps me in place. Rigid in muscle and in cock. Eyes wide open now and wondering what's going on behind my back. I glance at the mirror on the dressing table, but frustratingly, the angle doesn't show them.

The kiss goes on and on, and not only does Maria purr and murmur, but her mysterious companion – Robert – does too. I remember her kiss and I can't blame him.

'So, my dear, aren't you going to introduce me to your friend?' he says at length, when they disengage and, as he walks forwards into the room, I see that the look of wry, mocking amusement on his face matches the tone in his voice.

It's the big man from the 'do', of course. The one who watched us both so assiduously and made me feel so freaked. He's very tall, and a bit heavy set, and has a vague look of a younger Orson Welles before he went to fat. That, and a character I might have seen on the telly recently, but I don't know what in.

I'm fighting the reflex to shake violently, and I don't know what's the most mortifying to me – my nakedness and my erection, or the fact that my own voice is still issuing interminably from the sound system. I'd give anything if one of them would turn the fucking thing off.

I can, I think, take anything sexual that this pair choose to dish out to me, but I wish to God that all trace of J-Boy Jones and the Forever Boys could be wiped off the face of the earth now and forever . . .

'This is Jason, darling,' declares Maria, her voice arch and her face beautiful in quiet triumph. 'The one I told you about. Don't you recognise him from the magazines? He's changed a little, of course, but when it comes down to it, it's easy to see who he is.'

Robert subjects me to a long, considered scrutiny, his dark gaze returning again and again to my cock.

Hell, this guy is most definitely bisexual. There's hunger in that slow, sly look of his. I find myself glancing towards Maria, wondering what her reaction to this is, and I find her grinning with delight and high approval.

Oh God. Oh God. Oh God. I thought I was worldly and experienced, living large on booze and drugs and faux celebrity. But I know nothing. Nothing at all. Not a thing.

Suddenly Robert frowns. 'Do we have to listen to this?' He cocks his large head, grimacing.

'I don't know. Do we?' Maria sidles towards me, touches first my face and then my cock, and I nearly come. Dragging in air, fighting for control, I shake my head.

Her companion moves to a small console beside the bed and depresses a button, once, twice, three times, cycling through a couple of radio stations until a very different kind of music issues from the hidden speakers.

The delicate melody of what sounds like a piano trio fills the room, stately and elegant and a balm to my overheated soul.

'Excellent,' proclaims Robert roundly, smile widening. 'Mozart . . . a well-known fetishist in his day. Couldn't be more appropriate, could it, my love?' He strides across the room, a looming imposing presence, and suddenly they're both deep in my personal space and owning it completely.

I clench every muscle, every sinew, anticipating his touch as well as Maria's.

But it doesn't come. He gently fondles Maria's breast as she pinches the tip of my cock, expertly containing my hair-trigger urge to shoot my load all over her beautiful black dress.

The couple exchange a look while the fondling and handling continues. A glance that's quick, yet deep and full of transferred intelligence. A decision's just been made, I realise, and whatever my wishes are simply doesn't factor into the equation.

I should be horrified. I should be scared. And yet a sense of rightness, almost of calm settles over me. Everything is exactly as it should be, just like the rippling, swooping phrases of the piano and the strings, every note perfect, precise and virtuouso.

'Shall we begin, my love?' says Maria at length, sounding pleased with herself. She's loving this, but there's no malice in her, I realise. Her happiness is purely from the anticipation of pleasure and entertainment.

'Why not?' concurs Robert, and for just a second his hand curves around hers, cradling my cock.

The touch of a man's hand on my flesh makes my head go light, and something inside me soars and lifts like the rising, dancing notes around us.

But just as I'm accepting and enjoying it, the touch is gone and they both whirl away as if dancing a secret tango. Robert crosses to the dressing table and picks up a small remote, and Maria opens a drawer in a tallboy at the other side of the room, and starts removing a selection of objects. My eyes bug at the sight of them, and then bulge even more when Robert presses a button on the remote, and a whirring and a light tinkling and jingling sound overlays Mozart's exquisite precision phrasing.

To my astonishment, when I look up, I see a set of shackles descending from the ceiling. A couple of tiny, concealed panels have slid aside to release them. Robert tilts his large head on one side, as if calculating, and the cuffs and chains halt in their downward progress and swing slowly in the air.

Real fear now overcomes me, but before I've a chance to voice it, he's beside me, lifting my arms one by one, and snapping me into the restraints. They're padded and surprisingly comfortable around my wrists.

That is until he presses the remote again, causing the chains to retract a little, and me to rise on my toes to ameliorate the sudden strain in my arms.

I can't help it. I whimper out loud. I'm so out of my depth. I'm in a different world to the one I've always known until now.

'Hush, baby,' murmurs Maria, instantly at my side. She smoothes my brow with her fingers, then kisses the side of my face while Robert looks on with approval. I start to feel calm again, despite the grinding, agonising ache of frustrated desire that grips my genitals as if they were trapped in a vice.

She peppers my jaw and the side of my neck with little kisses. Her fingers move lightly over me, touching my chest, then my flanks. I hear jingling again, but this time it's tiny, barely audible. I'm not sure what it is, but in a second or two I find out.

With a dexterity that suggests she's done it a score of times before – possibly to her beloved Robert – Maria straps a neat, carefully crafted little leather harness around my equipment, securing my cock and balls so I remain erect but probably can't get the blessed relief of orgasm. The constriction makes me harder than ever, and my rigid flesh flushes a brilliant crimson. Clear fluid trickles copiously from my tip.

I groan again and she swiftly inserts a gag in my mouth. It's a small rubber sphere that presses down on my tongue, and is buckled into place. I start to salivate around it, drooling above as I do below.

How perfect is this subjugation? How much do I realise that I've always wanted it, even though I didn't know it? Maria understands it completely, although I'm sure she never did when we were together in London.

My eyes are wet too, and it dawns on me that there are tears streaming across my cheeks. I gaze at Maria imploringly, begging her silently to take me down and down and further down into a peaceful, if not exactly comfortable, submissive place. I glance too at the man who I now understand is her mentor. The one who gave her all the knowledge she now possesses.

He comes to me too, and also kisses my face, running his tongue around the corners of my lips where they're stretched around the gag.

'Delicious,' he whispers, kissing me one last time, then kissing Maria deeply and voraciously. 'Thank you, my love,' he whispers to her. 'You always know how to give me the nicest presents.'

'Well, it's a bit impromptu, sweetheart,' she murmurs back to him, her hands dropping to cup his clearly rampant erection through his trousers. 'But I knew you'd enjoy it. Happy birthday.'

Somewhere in the back of my drifting mind, I hear the receptionist saying, 'There's a bit of a do on ... somebody's birthday ... but you're welcome to join in.'

'Come on, let's play with our toy, shall we?' she says brightly, her expert fingers administering just the delicious, detailed and delightful handling to Robert's equipment that I'm currently denied.

'You play with him, my dear,' says Robert, clearly appreciating her attentions. His even teeth look very white in his broad face as he smiles a dreamy smile. Giving her one last kiss, he retreats to the large chintz chair, from which he has a perfect view of my dangling, exhibited body.

As he spreads his long, solid legs and gets comfortable, he unzips his flies to reveal a truly enormous tool. Strapped up the way I am, I feel as if I'm more huge than I've ever been in my life, but next to that rosy, gleaming colossus, my own cock seems almost rudimentary.

He gives me that age-old macho smile of 'mine's the biggest' and promptly begins to stroke it to make it bigger.

My own cock feels like lead.

Mozart plays on.

'So, Jason,' breathes Maria, suddenly in my face again, all glorious breasts, long sinuous legs and miraculous, confident femininity. I remember sleeping with her more than once, and enjoying that fabulous body. But right now I'd be in heaven if she'd just let me kiss her shoes.

'So, Jason,' she repeats, tilting her golden head, almost Medusa-like as she prowls around me, 'I guess you're wondering how we find ourselves together again like this?'

I nod. Even though I don't care what's brought me to this place and this strange condition.

'Pure chance, in the beginning. I would never have expected you to turn up here,' she admits, taking one of my nipples between her prettily manicured fingers. She pinches me – hard – and, as I writhe, I watch the blood turn my teat to exactly the same colour as her nail polish. 'But after that ... design, my dear. Design. And desire.' She tweaks both nipples now and twists them this way and that, dragging them away from the wall of my chest and making me gobble and bubble behind my gag in a suppressed howl of anguish. I toss my head from side to side, and my cock tries to leap in its bonds, to no avail.

She smiles, both beauty and cruelty personified.

'The people who work here at the Waverley are our friends –' she nods towards her lover, who's still cheerfully masturbating '– and they know my history. You were recognised when you checked in, despite your "new look" and that's why you were invited to Robert's party.'

As she speaks her man's name, she releases me, and reaches down to cup her crotch as if just the word 'Robert' induces an *arpeggio* of pleasure.

Maybe it does? As she massages herself, her lips part and she gasps. She must be as excited as I am in her own way.

'I'm not angry with you, Jason. I never was.' She's circling again, moving behind me now. I try to swing round but she gives me a light slap on the bottom, which doesn't hurt, but still makes my shackled cock lurch and jump. 'It didn't matter about you not calling me. I'd already made my mind up to leave London and come home –' she favours Robert – who's now shifting himself around voluptuously in the plump, padded chair – with an angelic smile '– where the heart is ... although I didn't realise that at the time.'

I should feel disappointed. Broken. Like nothing. But somehow, I'm almost happy. There's a sense of benediction in my diminishment. A correctness that thrills me and induces a high that's far more potent than any stupid thing I've ever ingested or smoked. I realise now that I've always felt bad about the way I treated Maria. It's bugged me and troubled me and screwed me up. But at last, here in this room, swinging in bondage, I have my chance to put things right with her.

I feel as if I'm floating. Borne aloft by adrenaline, a sense of my new-found identity, and the delicate bubbling music that plays around us. As Maria's hands travel skilfully over me, touching, pinching, probing, I almost weep from the intensity of the torment.

And from the scrutiny of her ever-watching lover ...

Maria works on me. Like the Mistress she most assuredly is ...

I hang like a cur in chains as she puts clamps on my nipples, weights on my balls and plagues my ever-reddening arse with fierce pinches and a fusillade of slaps.

Eventually, when she can see that I'm half off my head, she kisses me tenderly, then abandons me in favour of her beloved Robert.

Still facing me, and making me look at her despite my pathetic state, she sits in his lap, hitching up her skirt, pulling aside her knickers, and lowering herself slowly and with great deliberation onto his cock. Her big blue eyes nearly start out of her head as she seems to sink and sink and sink onto that massive edifice, then they close as she leans back and his hands slide around her body to caress her. I moan again, behind my gag, at the sight of his long, flexing forefinger working industriously where I'm no longer deemed worthy to touch. Amongst the sweet, silky curls of Maria's pussy.

It doesn't take long. After just a few moments, her spine stiffens, her legs kick, and she arches back against the substantial, supporting form of her lover, then cries, 'Bobby! Oh, my Bobby!' as she contorts and climaxes.

My eyes swim again, but not with sorrow. I'm excluded, but at the same time included. They won't let me come, yet I'm still part of their pleasure ...

And even more so, a short while later, when a glowing, dishevelled Maria rises like a debauched empress from Robert's lap, and reveals him to be still erect. While she releases me from my bonds – both greater and more intimate – it slowly dawns on me what my next function is to be.

I'm elevated from inert toy to active participant as I crawl on hands and knees towards the big man in the fussy, chintzy chair, crouch before him, and open my mouth as he sinks his hands into my hair and directs my face towards his crotch.

He guides my head. He makes me take him deep and I almost gag. But there's a special sweetness in the taste of her upon him, and an even greater joy as gentle fingers reach beneath me and play a delicate, loving tune upon my own cock.

Somewhere in the background, a lilting, precisely bowed violin is playing too. A stately yet cheerful air, composed by Wolfgang Amadeus Mozart, the well-known fetishist and brilliant musical prodigy.

With a happy, muffled, gulping groan, I both come and am copiously come into.

Are You Ready For Me?
Sarah Dale

A lot could happen in two weeks. Your whole life could change.

Hannah fingered the laminated plastic of the backstage pass that hung from around her neck, and peered out from the side of stage at the audience. The concert theatre was at full capacity.

Nine years ago, as a gawky teenager, she'd fallen down the stairs into the arms of her favourite rock star, Nate Fox. A brief kiss, and then he'd let her go – throwing her back in the pond for being too young.

Two weeks ago, Nate and his manager, Sam, had hired her as Nate's publicist.

Two weeks ago, she and Nate had agreed to get their mutual attraction out of their systems so they could work effectively and professionally together.

They'd failed.

So far, they were still able to work effectively and professionally together. It was just that they hadn't been able to take their hands off one another. The one night of 'getting it out of their systems' had blown completely out of control.

Tonight, Hannah knew, her heartbeat already quickening in anticipation, would be no different.

Excitement thrummed through the air, thick and palpable and crackling with electricity. From her vantage point at the side of the stage, Hannah surveyed the audience. Most of the concert goers – the ones in front, anyway – couldn't seem to stay in their seats. They stood, chatted with each other, fidgeted and stared at the stage. Many wore T-shirts from Nate's past shows, and some wore the commemorative shirts from this tour, newly purchased in the lobby.

A golden-haired beauty standing towards stage left wore a strappy, form-fitting red lace tank top. Hannah remembered how Nate had ignored the busty blonde at a recent Hollywood autograph signing, and grinned evilly.

She thought she recognised another woman from the signing as well. That wasn't surprising. Hannah herself had done the follow-the-tour thing more than once in her life, going to as many concerts within a certain radius of Los Angeles as her budget had permitted. She'd heard of fans who flew back and forth across the country, going to thirty or fifty shows a year. She didn't know how they managed the time or money.

The smooth plastic of the pass was growing warm beneath her touch, and Hannah realised that she'd been rubbing it slowly between her finger and thumb. There was something else she'd like to be rubbing, stroking . . .

She caught her bottom lip between her teeth. Forcing herself to drop the pass, she took one last look at the crowd. It looked as though they were barely containing their excitement. Nate Fox hadn't toured in two years. In a few minutes, they'd see him, whether again or for the first time, in the flesh.

Hannah's excitement was for a different reason. Nestled between her legs, in an area already growing moist, was Nate's gift to her. The hard bullet of the vibrator pressed against her clit, stimulating her even though it wasn't turned on. The tight jeans she wore kept it tucked close, and she was aware of it every time she moved, shifted, walked.

She wondered where Nate had put the remote.

She wondered, for the millionth time, when he would choose to use it. And she shivered.

Sam had been stalking around the stage, barking at roadies and ensuring everything was nothing less than perfect. Now he turned his attention on her.

'If you want to watch the concert from down there, you'd better get going,' he said.

'Everything on schedule?' she asked.

He squinted and surveyed the stage. 'Yeah,' he said in a tone that implied that it probably wasn't, but he couldn't find the flaw, and just had to live with it.

She grinned. 'Glad to hear it.'

Hannah threaded her way further backstage, stepping over the taped-down electrical cords, past the racks of guitars and basses, the monitors, the soundboards, and the small army of technicians whose job it was to ensure every single piece of electronics worked without a glitch. One woman, wearing earphones, tuned a spangly red guitar. Hannah gave her a thumbs-up as she went by, and the woman grinned.

As she passed by Nate's dressing room, she paused, wondering if she should tell him to break a leg. She blew a strand of red hair back from her forehead, acknowledging to herself that she was just looking for an excuse to see him again. She reached up a hand to knock ... and the door opened before she could make contact.

Nate. All six feet of taut muscle, raven-black hair, and striking blue eyes that she, rare among fans, knew darkened into indigo when he was about to come.

Now, he smiled. 'I was hoping to see you before we got started,' he said. His low smoky voice curled around her, promising that she would enjoy everything that he had planned.

'I wanted to wish you good luck,' Hannah said.

He looked incredibly sexy in his black leather pants. The fabric clung to the hard muscles of his thighs, cupping the heavy bulge of his groin. She wanted to touch, wanted to run her hands over his flat stomach hidden behind his tight T-shirt. Past concert experience told her that he would tear the shirt off towards the end of the concert, sending much of the audience into paroxysms of lust at the sight of his ripped body.

'I wanted to kiss you until you couldn't breathe,' Nate said. Taking her by the arm, he pulled her down a short hallway into a darkened alcove, crowding her body with his as he pressed her against the wall. His hands penned her in, resting on each side of her shoulders. He teased her, leaning in just far enough to let his chest rub lightly against her sensitised breasts. Warm breath heated her skin, his mouth only a sigh away from her throat. His dark hair tickled her cheek as he breathed in her scent.

'Are you ready for me?' he whispered. His hips brushed suggestively against her own.

Hannah couldn't have been more ready if he'd laid her down and licked every inch of her skin.

She tangled her fingers in his hair and pulled him in closer. Nate nipped her lower lip and she responded in kind. Their mouths met, lips against lips, tongue sliding against tongue. His kiss was a wonder, all wet heat and maddening friction.

'Are you wearing it?' Nate asked, his teeth nipping her jaw lightly. His breath blew across her ear, and Hannah shivered. Her mouth went dry, in contradiction to the wetness between her legs.

'Yes.' Her voice came out in a shaky whisper.

'Good.' He ran his tongue along her neck. Hannah gripped his shoulders to keep from sagging to the floor. She could smell his shampoo, a memory of the shower they'd taken together earlier. He rubbed one thigh between hers, lightly, not nearly enough pressure to satisfy.

'Good,' he repeated. 'Because I can't tell you how much I'm looking forward to watching your face when ...'

Hannah moaned.

'Yeah, you'll sound like that. Or maybe you'll be screaming. You'll have to tell me afterwards.' His hands slid from her hips, up her sides. She wore a dark-plum satin bra and a semi-sheer purple flowered camisole top over it. His thumbs caressed the underside of her breasts, the motion erotic against the satin. She felt her nipples harden beneath his ministrations, aching for more pressure.

'The hardest part –'

'I think I've found the hardest part,' Hannah said, cupping her hand around the steely bulge beneath the leather of his pants. He caught his breath. The sound, and the knowledge that she caused it, sent a fresh thrill of arousal through her.

'Keep that up, and the concert will have to be delayed,' he warned. The way he looked at her made her wish she could make the concert disappear, keep him entirely to herself.

'What's sauce for the goose ...' she teased.

'The goose's arousal,' Nate said, 'is not as obvious as the gander's. Nor will the goose be standing on stage before thousands of people.'

'True,' she agreed, sliding her hand back to cup his tight ass and pull him closer against her. It was her turn to move against him, knowing by his ragged breathing that she had his complete attention. 'But I'll be the one making the scene, given your intentions with that remote control.'

He made a low rough noise in his throat. Taking her hand, he brought it to his waist. She could feel the remote clipped to his waistband. To someone who didn't know what it was, it would look like part of his stage gear. 'I don't know how I'm going to stand it, watching you come,' he admitted. 'It may be difficult for me not to join you.'

The fact that her arousal turned him on so much thrilled Hannah. It was as if they fed off of each other, bringing each other to new heights and getting dragged along at the same time, higher and higher until they went supernova.

'You deserve a little torture, given what you're putting me through,' she said.

'Is it really torture?' he asked softly, sliding his hand beneath her camisole and lightly pinching her nipple.

'Yes. Exquisite torture,' she managed between gasps.

'Good.' He pulled away, although even in the dim light she could see the reluctance on his face. 'I'll see you after the show.' He cupped her face with one hand. 'I'll be thinking about you.'

He disappeared back into the dressing room, no doubt to adjust himself before he had to appear onstage. Hannah took a deep breath, willing her heartbeat to slow. The aching between her legs wasn't going anywhere, however. She forced her trembling legs to move, always aware of the vibrator nestled between her lips. She knew she was flushed, trembling, her mouth swollen from kissing Nate. She probably looked like sex incarnate.

Hannah made her way to an exit that deposited her just outside the floor seats. The pass around her neck meant she had no problem getting to her front-row VIP seat. The woman in the red lace tank top glared at her. Hannah smiled sweetly as she passed.

Her seat was dead centre, the place where Nate would be able to see every reaction she had when he played her body. She didn't have time to sit before the lights went down and the crowd was on its feet, already roaring its approval. She added her voice to the cheers.

A bass beat began. Drums pounded the rhythm.

An electric guitar wailed a melody.

An explosion of light in the background revealed the silhouette of Nate standing on a riser behind the drums. The screams of the audience intensified. Over them, into a headset microphone, he sang the first line of 'Luck Dried Up'.

The stage fell dark again, but the music pounded, giving the audience a lifeline. When the full lights came on, Nate stood at the front of the stage. His guitar was slung on a strap over his shoulder, his talented fingers drawing music from the metal strings. He launched into the song, the band chiming in on harmonies. Hannah could have sworn he winked at her.

Then she realised that she wasn't some anonymous audience member any more. He *had* winked at her.

With a grin she couldn't have stopped even if she'd tried, she sang along with the chorus, dancing in place at the barrier a few feet from the stage. Seats had been abandoned, the fans energised and on their feet.

Over the years, she'd tried as a professional, as a publicist, to disassociate herself from her feelings about Nate and view his stage performance dispassionately. She hadn't entirely succeeded, but she'd managed to make some analyses. Seeing some of the rehearsals for this tour had solidified her theories. Every movement he made was calculated, planned. Of course, it didn't mean he couldn't be spontaneous. Certainly his between-song banter wasn't memorised, and he'd told her horror stories about the various things that had gone wrong on stage – earphones cutting out, guitar strings breaking, his pants splitting a seam right up the back . . .

But overall, he was in control. When he and the bassist ran over and circled the keyboard, they were all in sync, because they'd gone over it until they had it down to the second. When Nate ran across the stage and smacked one of the drum kit's cymbals, it didn't look like he'd make it back to his mark at the front of the stage on time – but he always did.

And he was in control, all right. During the third song (a heart-wrenching but otherwise innocuous ballad), he slipped long talented fingers over the remote control. Hannah hadn't even seen him do it. One minute she was singing along, lustfully admiring the trickle of sweat that ran down the side of his face, and the next, she was nearly leaping out of her skin when a subtle buzzing began between her legs.

The vibration wasn't strong enough to send her over the edge, but it was more than enough to make her voice falter even as her body lurched in anticipation.

And tremendous arousal.

Hannah felt her nipples snap into hardness again, pressing against the smooth satin of her bra. She knew the angle wasn't right and he couldn't see her reaction, but her expression had changed as well. Nate danced by, and shared with her a wicked grin. Her fingers closed over the edge of the barrier for support. She pressed her hips against the hard wood in front of her, both for support and because it intensified the pleasure.

Hannah tried to pay attention to the concert, she really did. But the world narrowed, her focus tunnelled, until all she could see was Nate, and all she knew was that whenever he was standing near her, at some point his hand would drift to the remote control.

He turned the control down, and she nearly sobbed with frustration. The music pulsed inside of her, her clit throbbing with every heartbeat.

Nate positioned himself in front of her, his legs spread. She looked up, knowing that he could see her arousal. She wondered how hard he was behind the guitar. His hips began to rock. Each thrust timed to the song, to the chord changes that flowed from his fingers. Hannah imagined she could feel him inside of her, each rocking movement sending her higher.

Lifting her hands, she gathered her hair up, a stray breeze cooling the back of her neck. A wicked smile curved his sensual mouth. His hand stole to his waist. The buzzing, vibrating pleasure sped up just a little.

Hannah let out a moan. The crowd noise swallowed it up. Someone jostled her from behind. She barely noticed. He turned the control up again, just a tiny shift of intensity, and Hannah caught her breath, hanging on the edge of orgasm.

Lips parted, low breathy moans came from her throat. She was torn between desperately needing to come and the embarrassment of knowing it would be in front of thousands of people. They pressed against her from behind, from the sides, intimately close, yet none of them knowing what he was doing to her.

But to climax in public, like this, surrounded by people ... He would be able to make her come whenever he wanted to, and she'd be able to do nothing about it.

Nate spun away. The intoxicating buzz between her legs diminished, leaving her moaning with frustration. Her inhibitions were being whittled away with every tiny vibration. She'd never thought that she could ache so badly, be so close, so wet, and still cling to the edge.

The closeness of the crowd added to the thrill, the collective energy stroking over her skin. The fact that everyone was riveted, watching Nate on stage, meant that she could conceivably have a screaming orgasm and nobody would really notice.

Hannah had never considered herself an exhibitionist, wasn't sure if this counted, really. She was fully clothed. Nate wasn't even going to touch her.

But he did. With his eyes, as he ran by. With his fingers, as he stroked music from the guitar strings. With the titillating buzz that surged again and again. The world narrowed to just the two of them. The audience faded away.

The concert was nearing an end. Hannah knew that, because she was enough of a fan and had been to enough concerts to know the pattern of songs. The encore would be coming soon. Once she'd figured out the pattern, it had always caused her a brief moment of grief whenever she heard 'Dragons of Winter' live because it was a signal that all good things must come to an end, that the concert was nearly over, that she'd go home alone, to her empty bed, and relive the magic of the concert and dream of Nathaniel Fox.

But now he wasn't a dream any more, and even though the song still sent a pang of despair straight to the pit of her stomach, it was coupled with heart-fluttering excitement.

The concert was almost over. Soon it would reach its climax, and hopefully so would she.

The time for him to wield the vibrator's control was rapidly declining. Hannah couldn't remember having been kept on the brink of arousal for so long. Oh, she'd always been horny at his concerts, but this was very, very different. She could feel the hard egg of the vibrator against her vulva, pressing the lips open, leaving her ready and willing.

'Dragons of Winter' ended. Hannah hadn't been entirely aware of singing along, but she knew she had. The crowd around her screamed and cheered, and her own arms were in the air as she clapped and pumped her fist.

Kenny started a throbbing beat on his bass. Hannah stared at him, shocked at how well the rhythm was timed with the vibrations. Oh God, had Nate planned this that carefully? But no, it was the heavy bass making her sternum pulse, and her whole body was tuning into the hard-driving pound of the song.

She watched as Nate jumped up onto the keyboard. His hips rocked, the guitar an extension of his body. His head was thrown back, sweat trickling over his chest. His shirt was gone, and she imagined trailing her tongue along his taut flesh, chasing the sweat down his body. He howled the lyrics, and Hannah again pressed her hips against the wooden barrier separating her from the stage.

She hadn't seen his hand move, but she could swear that the teasing egg nestled against her aroused flesh had sped up. Heat pooled low inside of her, tightening, drawing her awareness to it.

The song was close to its finale, and her body echoed it. She didn't know if she could hold back for him. The cliff was waiting, and she was ready to leap.

Looking down into her eyes, Nate sang the final words, 'your strange desires'.

He pulled his head up and gathered himself.

His fingers turned the remote control dial to maximum.

He leapt into the air off the keyboard.

The world exploded into a million shades of red. Hannah heard herself scream, her hips bucking uncontrollably as spasm after spasm consumed her. Heat pulsed outwards from her clit, rolling along her skin, the buzzing egg sustaining the sensations. She came in waves that shattered her, wringing every last drop of pleasure from her aching body.

Looking up, Hannah saw Nate close, kneeling at the edge of the stage where he'd landed. His eyes glittered with dark satisfaction. The look was for her alone. He unclipped the remote, pressing it to his lips before tossing it to her.

A souvenir.

A promise.

Siren Song of Birchwood Gardens Heather Towne

My mother started sniffling as I was packing up the last of my books and CDs.

'Mom,' I said, standing up and taking her hand. 'Please. You knew I had to move out eventually.'

The logic was lost on her. Tears began streaming down her face. 'B-but ... you're only twenty years old,' she whimpered. 'My baby.'

She threw her arms around me, cried all over my shoulder. My father rolled his eyes and patted her on the back, mumbling soothing words about how much money they could make by renting my room out. But Mom's throbbing body got through to the no-nonsense account-ant, and he hugged the both of us, blinking back tears of his own.

Somehow, I wriggled out of my parents' clutches, and they watched me through their watery veils as I hur-riedly tossed things into the last box, hauled it and myself out of the familial home, my own eyes gone misty as the song.

The apartment complex was called Birchwood Gardens; three two-storey, Tudor-style buildings with sixteen one- and two-bedroom apartments in each. There wasn't a birch tree in sight, and the only garden was a few wilted marigolds around the RENTING sign.

My first home away from home was number 17, 201

Clarence Road, a first-floor one-bedroom measuring 650 square feet with a view of the parking lot. It also featured an in-suite washer and dryer, a window air conditioner and all utilities payable by me. It wasn't exactly a Park Avenue penthouse, but it was mine and mine alone.

My girlfriend, Janet, helped me unload the rented van. It didn't take long, because I didn't have much stuff. I'd always lived with my parents, so my first shopping trip was going to be to a second-hand furniture store.

'Well, kiddo,' Janet said, throwing an arm around my shoulders. 'Whaddya think?'

We stared at the bare white walls, the box-scattered, brown shag carpet. 'I love it!' I sang out. 'Not a parent in sight.'

We dissolved in giggles, then got down to the seriously boring job of unpacking my stuff. I set up the stereo system first, so we had Alicia Keys to ease our toil. And after unpacking almost everything by nightfall, we went out for pizza – my treat.

When I came back to the apartment, I was all alone, and I stood in the middle of that wooden and stucco living cubicle all by myself, the silence suddenly deafening. I was already missing the sound of Dad crashing the newspaper around, complaining about the goings-on in the Middle East; Mom clattering around in the kitchen, washing dishes or baking something for church. I could hear my heart beating in the eerie silence.

Thank God my parents were only three blocks away.

I hugged myself and grinned. Then I slid Gwen Stefani's latest into the stereo, and was about to start dancing around to celebrate my new-found privacy, when I heard it. Loud and clear. Coming from upstairs. Music thumping. Bass pounding away loud enough to be heard three blocks over. The ceiling and my eardrums vibrated with the noise.

I couldn't hear my heart any more. I couldn't hear a damn thing but the thunder of someone else's music!

The 'jam' pumped up around six o'clock every night – rap and hip-hop, at top volume – and thumped on and on until eight or so, drowning out my dinner and the daily news. My framed watercolours rattled on the living-room walls and my beanie babies jumped up and down on their bookshelves in my bedroom.

I couldn't think straight, my head throbbing with the racket, my fists balling in impotent rage. And accompanying the earthquake beat was the creaking and cracking of the thin wooden floorboards, as someone or something danced around upstairs in time to the raucous ruckus.

After three straight nights of musical mayhem, my ears blasted red by the ceiling of sound, I'd had it. I considered complaining to the caretaker, but the whisky I'd smelt on his breath and the leer I'd seen in his bloodshot eyes on the couple of occasions that I'd met him, put me off. I considered phoning the property managers, but I really didn't want to get a reputation as a whiner so early in my tenancy; apartments were hard to come by, after all. I considered calling the police, but with car thefts and grow-ops skyrocketing, I suspected that clamping down on noisy neighbours was probably the last thing on their docket.

Some form of retaliation seemed in order, but, unfortunately, my own sound system maxed out at a measly 100 watts, sans subwoofer. I was hopelessly outgunned. And I didn't want to risk my damage deposit by pounding on the plaster.

So, I listened to my inner voice, a furious, cursing voice yelling at the top if its lungs to be heard. It told me to get up some gumption and go, girl, climb the stairway to hell and confront my tormentor with the full force of my feminine fury; demand that he or she or they shut down the show, get their goddamn groove off!

I tore the door open, stomped across the patio, teeth clenched and body rigid with righteous rage, mouth set in a ferocious scowl. But when I reached the stairs, gripped the cool metal railing and felt the cool night air wash over me, I started losing some serious steam.

Frightening images of what lay behind door number eighteen flash-flooded my mind. A gang of bikers, one blonde short of their weekly gang-bang quota? A lone, unmedicated crazy, one swatch of tanned girl-flesh shy of completing his lamp shade, a pair of green girl-eyes short of rounding out his marble collection?

My foot hovered over the first concrete step up. I gazed at the glowing, curtained living-room window of apartment eighteen, imagining the resident evil that rented within. I gulped damp air and tapped the railing with jumping fingernails, foot moving down, then back up again.

Then a gust of bass sonic-boomed the evening calm, and I stormed up the stairs.

I pulled the screen door open and pounded on the vibrating inner door, eschewing the formality of the brass knocker. I meant business.

The music stopped. My fist froze in mid-air. All was breathless. The outside light flashed on, spotlighting me like the proverbial deer in the headlights, about to get run over or gunned down. The doorknob turned, and I trembled like an amped-up speaker. The door opened.

'Hi,' the guy living above me said.

He was my height, with short, glossy brown hair combed to the right and a tanned, fine-boned face. His eyes were Frank Sinatra blue, his smile Elvis brilliant, and he was dressed in a red robe, showing well-turned calves, ankles and bare feet. I figured I could take him.

'H-hi,' I stammered. 'I, uh, heard your music.'

He cinched the robe tighter around his narrow waist with a pair of small, delicate-looking hands, his eyes sparkling. 'Kinda loud, huh?'

'Yes, kinda,' I agreed, my anger vaporising.

'Sorry about that.' He stuck out a hand. 'My name's Dave. I should've introduced myself when you first moved in, but I'm a little on the shy side.'

I took his warm brown hand, and we shook. 'That's OK,' I said. 'My name's Vanessa. I live downstairs.'

Dave grinned a boyish grin at that boner and held the door open wider. 'Why don't you come in and have some coffee? We can get better acquainted – neighbour.'

'Uh, sure. Thanks.' I stepped over his threshold, into the strange man's den, ignoring every hysterical warning my mother had ever issued.

And as I was half-listening for the thud of the bolt shooting home, the robe rustling off onto the floor, the sleazy, sweaty words of rape to begin, I stared at the shiny, silver pole that stretched from floor to ceiling in the middle of the guy's living room.

'You noticed my pole,' he said, making me jump.

I looked at him, my eyes drifting south of the equator. 'Huh? No,' I gasped, blushing like a teenager caught with her hand in her panties and a Justin Timberlake MPEG on her computer. 'I mean, yes. Are you, um, a firefighter or something?'

He laughed at stupid comment number two of the evening. 'Nope. An exotic dancer. My stage name's David Goliath.'

My eyebrows rose, along with my temperature.

'I've been working on some new moves,' he explained,

sticking his hands in the pockets of his robe, 'with some new music, the last couple of nights. Sorry again about all the noise.'

'An exotic dancer,' I mouthed. 'David Goliath.' The most interesting neighbour my parents' ever had was the curator of a miniature museum. 'Uh, hey, no problem about the music. I like music.'

'Yeah? What about exotic dancing?'

I couldn't tell if he was joking or not. 'Well ... I've only ever seen one guy in action once before. When my friend Janet turned eighteen and we arranged for this strip-o-gram to show up at her party. He was kind of old, though, and fat, and he didn't dance very well – just sort of stuck his crotch in Janet's face and ...' I was babbling.

'How 'bout that coffee?'

'Wonderful,' I responded.

We sat on Dave's plush, black leather couch and sipped coffee out of fine china cups, Chris Isaak crooning away quietly in the background. Dave's massive surround-sound system consisted of two three-foot speakers, one two-foot subwoofer, and a many inches thick stack of receivers and tuners and balancers, all tastefully mounted in a maple wood entertainment centre.

And as I drank in the hazelnut coffee and the sur-roundings – the abstract prints hanging on the walls, the cherry-wood bookcases brimming with leather-bound volumes, Dave's gleaming leg dangling out of the end of his robe – he told me some stories about his adventures on the male ballet circuit, strutting his stuff and shaking his moneymaker for both women and men. He had his legs crossed, and his shapely foot looked no bigger than mine, though much better cared for. The small amount of leg visible was smooth and tanned – shaved and brown.

'I have to shave all over,' Dave commented, noticing where my attention was. 'Be nice and streamlined, smooth to the touch.'

'Oh ... yes,' I murmured, looking up into the twin blue pools of the man's eyes. The creamy liquid in my cup started sloshing around in rhythm to my quivering hand, as I pictured the calm, quiet, fine-featured man sitting next to me gyrating wildly on stage to an animal beat in front of a lust-crazed crowd.

'Would you like to see some of my – some of David Goliath's routine?'

I gulped coffee the wrong way. Dave patted me on the back, which did absolutely nothing to restore my breathing – his hand feeling so very warm and tender. 'You mean ... right now?' I managed to gasp.

'Sure,' he replied, grinning. 'I promise I won't even turn the music up loud.'

'Well, OK, yes, sure, go right ahead.' I set my cup down on an antique end table and rubbed my damp hands on my jeans. The last man that had danced for me was Shuster the Clown, at my seventh birthday party.

Dave scooped up the stereo remote and thumbed a button, and Harry Connick Jr came panting out of the giant speakers. Dave stood up and glided over to the polished practice pole, pawing the shag like a stallion. Then he took hold of the pole and swung lazily around, so that he was facing me.

I gave him a shaky smile, my face heating up like a stove element. My very own private dancer! This was exactly the last thing I'd expected when I'd come charging up the stairs and crashed my knuckles against door number eighteen.

Harry was throating all the right notes, low and slow and sexy, his voice filling my head and body, the sound and the visuals turning my insides all wet and squishy.

Dave leant back against the pole, and his fingers started doing mischief with the sash on his robe. He slowly untied his robe, let the sash fall down and the robe fall open. I slid to the very edge of the sofa and hung there, fingernails digging into the leather.

The guy was wearing only a hot-pink G-string under the crimson robe, and his whole body glowed brown and hot, thighs smooth and muscled, abs ribbed and rigid, pouch hanging heavy as advertised. He smiled at me, and I almost melted into the leather.

He spun around as Harry hit a high note, jazzing up the tempo of the sultry torch song. The robe came loose at Dave's shoulders, dropped down his shoulders, my wide eyes following its progress like it was the Berlin Wall coming down. His muscles were thick and bunched on his back, writhing in chiselled relief as he suggestively hunched his shoulders. I swallowed dry, and Dave casually turned his head to look at me.

The robe slid lower as Harry warbled faster, hitting Dave's waist just as my jaw hit carpet. There was a buzz in between my legs, a tingling at the tips of my breasts, like I was plugged into that high-powered stereo system, plugged into Dave and the music. He slid his arms free of the terry-cloth material and the bathrobe puddled at his feet, me along with it.

The twin rounded mounds of his golden butt cheeks gripped the thin cord of his G-string, the string splitting those splendidly ripened peaches right down the middle. He wiggled his bum at me, and the flesh jiggled delightfully, the gleaming orbs filling my eyes.

'Yes,' I breathed, clawing at the sofa.

Harry sent his voice soaring, and Dave leapt up and grabbed onto the pole up high, scissoring his legs in between the shining metal. His arms rippled with muscle, the bulge in his G-string kissing the pole ever so softly. Then he hooked his ankles together and let go with his hands and hung upside down, his movements as smooth and graceful and sexy as Harry's voice, his package provocatively on display.

I almost went to my knees, my jeans and panties pressing into my wetness, my nipples all but poking holes in my stretched-tight sweater. Dave executed a wicked ab crunch and regripped the pole, swung his legs free. His toes touched carpet again and he leant out in a full arm extension, his left hand on the pole, his right reaching out and caressing my cheek, his eyes smiling along with the rest of him.

Harry was winding up his ballad of love gone good in a full-throated climax, and Dave swung away from me and around the pole, then jumped up high and easy and clung to the metal with his legs and hands. He slid down, slowly, his groin caressing the metal, his bum touching bottom just as Harry let the melody fade from his piano, leaving me on the wispy edge of a swoon.

'How'd you like it?' Dave asked, climbing to his feet, his compact body glistening with sweat.

I exhaled. 'I loved it.' Then I jumped up and flung my arms around the exotic, erotic dancer, like he was a gymnast just lighted down from the uneven bars after a perfect ten routine.

Dave hugged me back. Then we stared at each other, stars in my eyes, my heart thumping loud as the man's music once had. His body was hot and throbbing against mine, setting me on fire. And before I could even be restrained by any innate shyness, I kissed the practically nude dancer, really thanking him for his performance, busting open the door to another kind of performance that took two to tango.

He grasped me tightly in his arms and kissed me back, his lips soft and warm and wet. We kissed and kissed, our mouths pressing together for what felt like forever, what felt like heaven, my head spinning and my body burning. Dave finally broke the heated lip-lock by pulling his head back. But that was just to get some air into his lungs, because he quickly mashed his mouth against mine again, pushed his tongue in between my lips.

We entwined our tongues together, Harry urging us on with another soulful track. I ran my fingernails up and down Dave's muscular back, over his hard, slick flesh, then slid my hands down onto his plump buttocks and squeezed.

'Mmmm,' he groaned into my mouth, his breath hot and moist in my face.

I kneaded his taut butt cheeks, and he captured my tongue between his teeth and sucked on it. I could feel him pressing hard and yearning into my stomach, growing, becoming the pole that I wanted to dance around. Then his hands were tugging at my sweater, pulling it out of my jeans. I reluctantly released his bum and raised my arms, and he pulled the sweater right over my head.

I shook out my long blonde locks and then gazed into Dave's shining eyes as he unfastened my bra, pushed it off my shoulders and away. He looked at my bared breasts and smiled, softly kissed me. Then he cupped my handful boobs and gently squeezed.

'Yes,' I moaned, my body surging with heat as he worked my breasts with his hands.

Dave bent his head down and tickled one of my outstretched nipples with the tip of his tongue. I was jolted with joy. He pushed my breasts together and licked at first one aching, pink nipple and then the other, swirling his warm, wet tongue all over and around them, sending tingles of delight shooting all through me. I riffled through his glossy hair with my fingers, as he kneaded my breasts and licked at my buds. Then I clutched at his hair as his hands became rougher and his teeth sank into my nipples.

He finally released my breasts, and they shone with his saliva. He gripped my waist and ran his tongue down from between my boobs all the way to my belly button, tracing fire every wet inch of the way. Then he popped my jeans open and pushed them down, helped me wiggle out of them and my sodden panties till I was even more blazingly bare than he was, just my bunny-tail socks still on.

He rose up and kissed me, his slender fingers fluttering in between my legs and caressing my damp mound. I shuddered, and he breathed, 'How would you like a lap dance, Vanessa?'

I was game for just about anything right then, and I said so. I closed my eyes and whimpered as he rubbed my sex and licked at my neck.

A chair appeared from out of nowhere – a sturdy, cushioned, extra-wide chair with padded armrests – and Dave set me down in it. He fiddled with the remote until Foxy Brown came funking on through the speakers, bass-heavy and insistent, but muted. I jumped up and grabbed the remote out of the guy's hand and thumbed up the volume, so that Foxy was wailing out the lyrics, the beat reverberating loud enough to register on seismographs, setting me and Dave and the walls to vibrating.

I sat back down, naked and expectant, waiting for Dave to set his needle down in my groove. But he had other, kinkier ideas, because he suddenly dashed from the room, then dashed back in again, a strap-on dildo now in his hands.

'Your erection, sir!' he yelled, presenting me with the twelve-inch black rubber dong and its leather strap attachments.

I took the outrageous sex toy and smiled uncertainly,

unsure how to proceed, but more than willing to play along. Dave showed me the way, pulling me and his plaything out of the chair and fitting the strap-on around my waist and pussy, cinching me up tight so I was tingly and towering with cock. He lowered me back down into the chair, and I took hold of the hard-on and stroked, as Dave shook his own outlined erection in front of me, in tune with the earth-moving music.

He spun around and backed in between my legs, then gripped his hips and shuddered his all-but-bare booty, bouncing butt flesh with the best of Sir Mix-A-Lot's video ho's. He eased down into my lap, on top of my foot-long erection, the leather dildo-mount pressing into my pussy, against my clit, sending sexual sparks showering through me.

Dave polished my big black dong with his undulating butt cheeks, and I dug my fingernails into the armrests and hung on for the ride, the erotic rubbing on my pussy turning me electric. Then he was up and out of my lap, facing me and my tight-lipped grin. He pushed my legs together and jumped onto the chair, straddling me, the rigid outline of his cock mere inches from my parted lips. Only a thin layer of silk separated me from the meat of the man.

He waved his arms around over his head and swivelled his hips, part of the music now. Then he danced back a bit and reached down and tore away his G-string, his cock finally springing out rock hard and arrow straight, the smooth, mushroomed hood bumping my nose and brushing my lips.

I stared at his bouncing manhood in awe, realising just how accurate the David Goliath moniker really was; he was just about matching my own erection. I swallowed and stuck out my tongue, boldly licked at his creamed-coffee head like any good, horny customer undoubtedly would. Dave jumped at the impact. He stared down at me, his eyes wild, the music at frenzy level. There was no bouncer holding me back, though, and I licked his hood again, spun my tongue around the twitching cap of his incredible appendage.

He groaned – or I think he did, it was hard to hear anything – and started pumping his hips, banging on my lips with his cockhead. I opened up and took him inside, his manhood sliding into my mouth, my lips sealing around his thick veined shaft. I kept my head rigid and my mouth loose, letting Dave bury himself half-deep, then slide almost right out again. He glided back and forth in my mouth, faster and faster.

I stared up at him and cupped his tight, shaven sac, squeezed, his mouth breaking open in another moan that was consumed by the deafening music. I fingered his balls as he fucked my mouth, his muscled body dewy with sweat, his handsome face contorted with erotic joy.

I became dizzy, the musky scent and taste of the man, the spectacular, gyrating sight of him, the wicked things I was doing with my fingers and mouth, setting my head to spinning. But things quickly spun even further out of control.

Dave pulled his hips back and he popped out of my mouth, wet and dripping. Then he jumped off the chair and grabbed a small bottle off a bookshelf, sprayed some of its contents onto my pussy-mounted dildo – lube. He got me all slippery, gliding his hand up and down my daunting erection, before passing the bottle over to me and showing his beautiful backside again.

Girl next door though I was, I could still figure out what the kinkster had in mind. And it blew my mind. Here I was, a young, somewhat innocent girl living out on her own for the first time, spraying lube over her new neighbour's bum so that she could enter him with a strap-on dildo.

There was no time to maul it over, however, the throbbing music and man urging me to just do it. So, I gripped my slickened pole and steered its moulded head in between Dave's trembling butt cheeks. He pushed back, and the tip of my simulated prick found an opening and eased inside.

Dave's whole body shook, but he pushed further back, and back, until he was sitting in my lap again, the monster hard-on now buried in his bum. My breath came in gasps, my breasts shuddering, my pussy aflame with the leather sensation of Dave pumping up and down on my cock. I clutched his chest and fingered his nipples, as he gripped the armrests and impaled himself.

I pushed up with my hips as Dave pushed down, fucking the man's bum, his cheeks rippling as we smacked together, the dildo plunging deep. The heat of his body and the wet, wicked friction on my pussy, the booming bass in my ears, quickly had me flying close to the edge, teetering on the slippery verge of orgasm. Taking Dave along for the ride.

I bit into the man's back and grabbed onto his cock at the front, frantically stroking him as I fucked him, as he rubbed me off, the fire in my loins turning inferno and sweeping all through me. We both cried out. I jerked thick ropes of semen out of his pulsing member, as my own orgasm gushed and Dave's bum danced around on the end of my cock.

Even the triple-digit-decibel music was swallowed up by the blood-rushing thunder of our mutual ecstasy.

Dave became a very kind and considerate and loving neighbour for the rest of my stay at Birchwood Gardens.

He always kept the music down and himself up. Unfortunately, my company transferred me to a city three hundred miles away from Dave about six months after we first connected, and I reluctantly had to sublet my suite to another young woman on the property manager's list.

And on my second night away, I received a phone call from Ella, the girl who'd taken on my lease.

'Why didn't you tell me you had such a loud neighbour living above you?' she complained.

'What'd you mean?' I innocently enquired.

'The jerk's been blasting away with the music for the last two nights in a row.'

I smiled, picturing devious Dave in all his dancing glory. 'Oh, yeah? Well, maybe you should go up and talk to him. He'll probably turn it down if you ask him.' And turn you on, I failed to add.

Dave, apparently, had his own unique way of meeting new neighbours, really getting to know them. I guess I wasn't the first, and wouldn't be the last, to answer the sexy guy's siren song.

Coda Katie Doyce

My eyes watched his hips, thrusting, pounding, swaying. The rest of the world – the rest of the crowded bar – melted away while I watched his hips move. His long fingers strummed the strings of his guitar. *Lucky strings.* I sipped at the bottle of beer in my hand, the music loud in my ears, ignoring everything else but his body in front of me. I wanted him; wanted him to have me.

Every Friday found me on a stool near the stage, my eyes at the level of his groin as he plucked at the strings on his instrument. I wanted those same fingers playing me; wanted to worship him with more than just applause. I yearned to run my fingers along his instrument, to wrap my mouth around him. I wanted him leaning against a wall, his fingers curled in my hair, panting; me, kneeling before him, watching his face as I sucked. Each night I heard him play I'd work my nerve up a little more, say something to him, smile, and hope he'd hear the desperate need that pounded between my legs.

His band usually attracted a good crowd, from older couples who'd sit as far from the enormous speakers as possible, to the college kids who'd push up in front of the stage, only slightly more obvious than me. The band played a raucous blend of traditional folk music and originals with a Celtic flavour, every song pounding with the understated growl of rock and roll. I'd tracked them through three CDs and a few changes in line-up, but I was always, really, following my guitarist. Without him, they wouldn't be the same. After all the time I'd been coming to the bar to hear them play, I'd gotten to know the various bartenders and the waitress, who earned her tips every time she pushed her way through the crowd in front of the stage with a tray of drinks for the back room. I even took home the doorman once, on a night when my rock star left with some other woman and I'd been so turned on that I had to have someone inside me and knew my little vibrator wasn't going to cut it.

But the doorman wasn't my rock star. As I lay beneath him in my bed, I'd imagined a different body above me, different hands caressing my curves, a different tongue licking me, plunging into me, and I cried out a different name when I came. I smiled politely the next time I saw him at the door, and handed him my cover charge with my usual chit-chat, but I didn't invite him home with me again.

Between Fridays, I listened to their music on CD, his whisky voice filling my apartment as I undressed, slipped between the covers – slipped my fingers between my legs. I played with myself and thought of his fingers; moaned, and heard the sweet harsh growl of his voice as he sang. Thrust my vibrator inside me and imagined his hips pushing against mine. It had been ages since my fantasies, as I strummed myself to orgasm, had been anything but him; under me, over me, behind me, standing, kneeling, rigid or writhing – the details changed, but he was always there. I didn't even know if I *could* come if he wasn't somehow with me, and didn't have the least desire to find out. I bit my lips now as I watched him onstage, thinking of the things he'd done to me in my imagination. The things I wanted to do to him: here, at my apartment, at his, in the small side street next to the bar, sometimes – my face flushed hot thinking about it – sometimes up on the stage.

During the show.

The bartender – a short, friendly Irish girl named Annie – caught my attention and came over to chat, drying off a glass as she did. My face grew even warmer in the dim of the bar, as though she somehow knew what I was thinking and was walking over to confront me with it.

'Odd crowd tonight,' I said. The bar was crowded, but the dance floor was empty, most of the patrons content to have their own quiet conversations at the scattered tables around the floor and in cosy nooks against the wall, nodding to the music but nothing more. The band had responded by toning down their set, playing less of their rabble-rousing rebel songs and more of the love songs that had my insides going gooey and my mind wandering to scenes that involved candles and back rubs and long baths.

'Yeah.' She studied the nearest tables, a crease between her brows, then turned her attention back to me. 'What about you? You gonna dance tonight?'

I smiled to myself. I loved dancing, loved to feel the hard floor against my feet, my body moving to the music. Hot and sweaty, I was happy in the midst of a crowd of dancers, other people pressing against me, unseen hands at my hips, grabbing onto me. I wasn't classically trained – far from it – and my style of dancing, though it owed something to repeated viewings of *Riverdance* and *Footloose*, was something else entirely.

Annie interrupted my musings. 'I'll make it easy for you.' She set a new beer on the bar in front of me. 'If you dance, this is free. If not, it's double.'

I laughed.

She quirked a pierced eyebrow at me. 'You think I'm joking?' She gestured at the tables behind her. 'No one's dancing, which means no one's working up a thirst, which means I'm not making any money.' The corner of her cupid's bow mouth curled. 'I figure one beer's worth it – you get the crowd dancing, I get tips, everyone's happy.'

When she put it like that, it made a certain amount of sense, at least for her. And I couldn't help but think of *his* eyes on me while I danced, alone on the floor.

It was enough.

'All right. I'll do it.' I finished off the rest of my old beer, and stood up, tapping my feet. Behind me, Annie motioned to the band, and my guitarist looked at her, then me. I licked my lips, staring at him. He glanced over his shoulder at the drummer and said something – what song he wanted to play next, I guessed.

The music started, and I began to move.

At the end of the night, no one could remember when they'd started dancing, but they all knew it began with the girl.

The first song, she was alone on the floor. Not truly alone, though, not really – the band was with her like a dance partner – everyone remembered that, though they disagreed over who had been leading whom. It had been the kind of song – the kind of dance – that made you think of kissing someone you just met, pressed up against a wall, soaked from falling rain. When the song ended, the clapping was louder than it had been all night.

Because of her.

The band barely paused, and she started to move again – slower, this time, because it was a sad song, and she danced the way it deserved – swaying along a pathway that the guitarist cleared for her from one end of the floor to the other. People started to move towards her, towards the floor: automatic, drawn in, wanting to be what they saw.

With the next song, the small area in front of the stage was full of other dancers. She wasn't alone any more, but she was still the only one that the guitarist was watching. People remembered that. They remembered how she danced, and how she looked at him, and when they talked about it they looked down and away – embarrassed, as though they'd been caught spying on something private and then forced to describe it.

She left the floor sometime during the set.

No one knew exactly when, because by then they were dancing too.

I drank down the cold beer Annie had bought for me and grinned at her as she whisked past to fill another order. The dance floor was packed, and more than one person had come over to tell me I'd been terrific or ask me to come back out and dance with them. I gave them a smile and a shake of my head, and turned back to the stage. What mattered was my rock star, his eyes on me as I danced.

His eyes were still on me, watching me where I sat.

Looking at me. At *me*.

Finally.

I pushed every doubt I had out of the way and focused on the dream-him that had come home with me so many nights before; I asked him a question with only my expression, and pushed it to him with my eyes.

He answered with a jerk of his head, still playing. *Come back to the dance floor. Come back to me.*

I shook my head, slowly, and bit my lip. I needed more than just dancing. I perched on my bar stool and shifted, feeling warm. No, not just warm – hot. My body called for him. In the dark bar, near the crowded dance floor, would anyone notice if I...? My fingers played with the hem of my short black skirt, as I thought about slipping my hand between my legs. I squirmed in my seat, and he watched me.

I could see it.

All I had to do was scoot forwards on the stool, squirming out to the edge in a way that would give me room enough to move and hitch up my skirt just a little further. I needed only a quick hook of my thumb to drag my panties to the side – just enough to let the moving air of the bar brush the damp. Knees spread, just enough to give me room, or enough to make room for him between them, two fingers on one hand half immersed in my mouth, two from the other circling, stroking, eyes fixed on him while he watched from the stage – the only one watching – seeing the challenge in my eyes. *I'm doing something bad. Come spank me.*

I couldn't take it any more. Couldn't wait. I jumped up, intent on heading to the bathroom and taking care of myself in one of the tight stalls, hand braced on the graffiti-covered wall, music still piped in and pounding. Unfortunately, I jumped up right into Annie, who was handing off a full pint of beer to the waitress. In a split second, I was soaked, my shirt dripping with beer.

'Damn it!' I cursed.

Annie grimaced and handed me a towel, apologising. As I tried to soak up some of the beer with the already damp bar mat, she nodded at the stairway behind the bar. 'I've got some extra T-shirts downstairs, why don't you grab one, dry off?'

'Thanks, I think I will.' I slipped behind the bar and heard the band announcing one more song before the break. The sounds of the bar above faded as I headed downstairs. I peeled my wet shirt off with a disgusted sound and wrung it out in my hands as I entered the large keg room, looking for the box of shirts.

In the corner, in a bit of the room made up as an

office, I found the cardboard boxes underneath a peg board of photos, mostly of bands who'd played at the bar. I dropped my sopping T-shirt on the ground as I studied the photos. My rock star was there, of course, I saw that immediately. Most of the photos were older, though, of bands that used to play the bar and had gone on to bigger and better things, or broken up and gone who knows where. Some shots featured local celebrities, some the bar staff, and I smiled as I remembered some of the parties and scenes the pictures captured, fluffing my hair to keep the beer soaked strands off the back off my neck.

I don't know why I didn't hear him; I thought about it later and decided maybe I had, but wanted to see what he'd do if I didn't react.

What he did – I was glad I hadn't moved. No, the moving came soon afterwards, but not before he came up behind me and ran a finger down my back, tracing my bra strap.

A shiver of goosebumps raced across my skin – not cold, just excited. Very excited. He curled his calloused index finger around the thin strap and tugged it gently down off my shoulder – first one, then the other. His lips followed, a gentle kiss on my shoulder, hot breath against my skin as his deft fingers undid the clasp.

I dropped my hands, and let my hair fall down against my neck, wet strands sticking to super-heated flesh. Still silent, I turned around, not trying to cover myself as my bra dropped to the floor. Not wanting to. This was what I wanted. What I'd fantasised about to orgasm God only knows how many times.

His hand was still up, and he ran his fingers gently across my collarbone. 'Hey, dancing girl.'

'Hey, rock star.' I stared up at him, thought for about half a second of what I wanted, and said, 'Fuck it.'

'What's that?' he asked, bemused.

'You.' I dipped one hand in the waist band of his low-slung jeans and pulled him towards me, the other hand wrapping around his sweat-spiked hair, tugging his lips down to meet mine. With a groan that I felt in my belly, his lips crushed mine and he pushed me back against the desk.

His teeth nipped at my lips, hard. I stretched out against him, both arms going around his neck. The heat coming off him burnt through the damp chill on my skin, and his mouth was even hotter, his tongue teasing. I caught it, sucked at it, felt his dick hard against my stomach.

He grabbed my ass, boosting me onto the edge of the desk, lifting my legs to half-wrap his thighs, so I could feel him pressing against my pussy as he rocked against me. I was swollen, wet, and the way the press of his cock dragged my panties back and forth over my clit was torture. On his next thrust against me, my breath hissed and I bit his lip – almost an accident – clawed at his shoulders, and squeezed him with my legs so hard that for a moment I lifted myself completely off the desk.

'Here or somewhere else. Now. I don't care.'

I didn't know which one of us said it. Didn't matter.

His lips along my jaw, throat, his teeth on my earlobe, pulling, his soft-leather voice, growling. 'Here. Right here.'

My face burnt. He thrust against me again, harder.

'Yeah.' It was my voice, barely.

I felt him shove at my skirt, the cool basement air kissing my thighs. One hard yank and my panties were pulled away, damp, slipping down my legs, shoved and discarded. He reached for me, thrust his fingers in me without warning, and I threw my head back at the rush of sensation, back arching. He thumbed my clit and my body quivered, limbs shaking as I fumbled for his fly, fingers clumsy. I fished him out from the worn denim and closed my hand around him, his heat on my fingers. He groaned – growled – thrust against my hand, and I squeezed. Stroked.

Teased.

'Like?'

A groan was my only answer, and it made me smile. I had him, and though the blood raced in my veins, my heartbeat pulsing between my legs, begging for him, I wanted to play out a few of the images in my head. I stood in the small space between his body and the desk and pressed myself against him, then slid down his body, slowly. Kneeling before him, my hand still wrapped around his cock, I licked him. Once, twice, my tongue swirled around him before I stretched my mouth open and took him in, tongue lashing the underside of his shaft, stretching the skin taut with my hand as I slid my lips over him, down him, until he pressed against the back of my throat, in me as far as he could go, the way I always wanted. The way I wanted, always. I played his instrument, and his moans were like music.

I pulled back, teasing once more, but only for a few seconds. I'd waited, already, long enough – too long. I stood and nipped at his ear, whispering against it, 'Now.' He reached behind me, swept the desk blotter and a pint glass full of pens to the floor, and dropped his hands to my hips as he sat me in front of him again. His voice shook. 'Legs. Around me. Lean back.'

I held onto his shoulders and strained upwards; managed to lock my ankles, barely, before the feel of his cock sliding against me drove every other thought out of my head. He watched me – memorised me – with those gorgeous eyes before his mouth dropped to mine again, then to my throat.

I said things then; I don't know what, but he liked them.

He gripped my hips and pushed, sliding into me, slow and solid. Perfect. Stung, but in a good way. I squeezed him with my legs – with me – and he groaned. Panted. *I'm doing that to you. Me. You. Mine.* I started to roll my hips against him, tight circles that worked him in further. It felt good, so fucking good.

I slipped my arms around his neck. Dropped my mouth to his throat; his skin sweat-salty from the set and from us, right now – here. I licked. Sucked.

Bit. Made him shake. Made him let go, and I didn't even know he'd been holding back. He hammered with his hips, forcing himself deep while I ground my clit against the base of his cock, and then he was pumping, hard, fast, hands gripping me, pulling me against him with each thrust, the shock of the impact shaking both of us.

I couldn't affect the rhythm, and that was perfect – he was the rock star, I was the dancer. I tried to stay with him, tightened around him and shifted my hips. The room blurred; my breathing roared in my ears.

'Yeah, baby. Dance on me.'

His words, but I wasn't dancing, was barely holding on, whispering his name, teeth dragging on his neck, nails along his back, working against him. Heat building, so wet I could hear it.

And I lost my voice in a sudden, hard wave. Straining. Squeezing him so hard I couldn't breathe, shaking too hard to stop, creaming on him in hard, helpless spasms. I started to fall back and he caught me; bruised my lips with his as he took my mouth again.

His rhythm slowed and he eased back, letting me down from him, stepping back – clearly still ready; unfinished – zipping up with unsteady hands. 'I ... I've got another set,' he said, and I shivered at the low rasp of his voice.

'Yeah,' I murmured. 'I know.' I shifted forwards and shoved at my skirt, trying to get it back into place. Stood. Glanced up at him through the fall of my hair.

He was watching me, a slow smile on his lips. 'How about we finish up back at home, baby?'

The same thing he always asked. My rock star. Mine.

I smiled and pushed my hair back to meet his look, the way I did every time. 'Yeah.'

The best part of your favourite song was in knowing how it would end.

WICKED WORDS ANTHOLOGIES –

THE BEST IN WOMEN'S EROTIC WRITING FROM THE UK AND USA

Really do live up to their title of 'wicked' – Forum

Deliciously sexy and explicitly erotic, *Wicked Words* collections are guaranteed to excite. This immensely popular series is perfect for those who enjoy lust-filled, wildly indulgent sexy stories. The series is a showcase of writing by women at the cutting edge of the genre, pushing the boundaries of unashamed, explicit writing.

The first ten *Wicked Words* collections are now available in eye-catching illustrative covers and, as of 2005, we will be publishing themed collections beginning with *Sex in the Office*. If you never got the chance to buy all the books when they were first published, you can now complete your collection and be the envy of your friends! Look out for the colourful covers – guaranteed to stand out from everything else on the erotica shelves – or alternatively order from us direct on our website at www.blacklace-books.co.uk

Full of action and attitude, humour and hedonism, they are a wonderful contribution to any erotic book collection. Each book contains 15–20 stories. Here's a sampler of what's on offer:

Wicked Words

ISBN 0 352 33363 4
£6.99

- In an elegant, exclusive ladies' club, *fin de siècle* fantasies come to life.
- In a dark, primeval forest, a mysterious young woman shapeshifts into a creature of the night.
- In a sleazy midwest motel room, a fetishistic female patrol cop gets dressed for work.

More Wicked Words

ISBN O 352 33487 8
£6.99

- Tasha's in lust with a celebrity chef – it's his temper that drives her wild.
- Reverend Billy Washburn needs salvation from Sister Julie – a teenage temptress who's set him on fire.
- Pearl doesn't want to get married; she just wants sex and blueberry smoothies on her LA poolside patio.

Wicked Words 3

ISBN O 352 33522 X
£6.99

- The seductive dentist – Nick's encounter with sexy Dr May turns into a pretty unorthodox check-up.
- The gender-playing journalist – Kat lusts after male strangers whilst cruising as a gay man.
- The submissive PA – Mandy's new job fulfils her fantasies and reveals her boss's fetish for all things leather.

Wicked Words 4

ISBN O 352 33603 X
£6.99

- Alexia has always fantasised about being Marilyn Monroe. One day a surprise package arrives with a sexy courier.
- Bridget is tired of being a chef. Maybe a little experimentation with a colleague is all she needs to get back her love of food.
- A mysterious woman prowls the back streets of New York, seeking pleasure from the sleaziest corners of the city.

Wicked Words 5

ISBN O 352 33642 O
£6.99

- Connor the tax auditor gets a shocking surprise when he investigates a client's expenses claim for strap-on sex toys.
- Kate the sexy museum curator allows a buff young graduate to make a thorough excavation of her hidden treasures.
- Melanie the interior designer and porn fan swaps blokes with her best mate and gets up to nasty fun with the builders.

Wicked Words 6

ISBN O 352 33690 O
£6.99

- Maxine gets turned on selling exquisite lingerie to gentlemen customers.
- Jules is stripped naked and covered in cream when she becomes the birthday cake for her brother's best mate's 30th.
- Elle wears handcuffs for an indecent liaison with a stranger in a motel room.

Wicked Words 7

ISBN O 352 33743 5
£6.99

- An artist's model wants to be more than just painted, and things get pretty steamy in the studio.
- A bride-to-be pays a clandestine visit to the bathroom with her future father-in-law, and gets much more than she bargained for.
- An uptight MP has his mind (and something else!) blown by a charming young woman of devious intentions.

Wicked Words 8

ISBN 0 352 33787 7
£6.99

- Adam the young supermarket assistant cannot believe his luck when a saucy female customer needs his help.
- Lauren's first night at a fetish club brings out the sexy show-off in her when she is required to wear an outrageously daring rubber outfit.
- Cat's fantasies about hunky construction workers come true when they start work opposite her Santa Monica beach house.

Wicked Words 9

ISBN 0 352 33860 1

- Sarah gets a surprise when she and her husband go dogging in the local car park.
- The Wytchfinder interrogates a pagan wild woman and finds himself aroused to bursting point.
- Miss Charmond's charm school relies on old-fashioned discipline to keep wayward girls in line.

Wicked Words 10 – The Best of Wicked Words

- An editor's choice of the best, most original stories of the past five years.

Sex in the Office

ISBN 0 352 33944 6

- A lady boss with a foot fetish
- A security guard who's a CCTV voyeur
- An office cleaner with a crush on the MD

Explores the forbidden – and sometimes blatant – lusts that abound in the workplace where characters get up to something they shouldn't, with someone they shouldn't – someone who works in the office.

Sex on Holiday

ISBN 0 352 33961 6

- Spanking in Prague
- Domination in Switzerland
- Sexy salsa in Cuba

Holidays always bring a certain frisson. There's a naughty holiday fling to suit every taste in this X-rated collection. With a rich sensuality and an eye on the exotic, this makes the perfect beach read!

Sex at the Sports Club

ISBN 0 352 33991 8

- A young cricketer is seduced by his mate's mum
- A couple swap partners on the golf course
- An athletic female polo player sorts out the opposition

Everyone loves a good sport – especially if he has fantastic thighs and a great bod! Whether in the showers after a rugby match, or proving his all at the tennis court, there's something about a man working his body to the limit that really gets a girl going. In this latest themed collection we explore the sexual tensions that go on at various sports clubs.

Sex in Uniform

ISBN 0 352 34002 9

- A tourist meets a mysterious usherette in a Parisian cinema
- A nun seduces an unusual confirmation from a priest
- A chauffeur sees it all via the rear view mirror

Once again, our writers new and old have risen to the challenge and produced so many steamy and memorable stories for fans of men and women in uniform. Polished buttons and peaked caps will never look the same again.

Sex in the Kitchen

ISBN 0 352 34018 5

- Dusty's got a sweet tooth and the pastry chef is making her mouth water
- Honey's crazy enough about Jamie to be prepared and served as his main course
- Milly is a wine buyer who gets a big surprise in a French cellar

Whether it's a fiery chef cooking up a storm in a Michelin restaurant or the minimal calm of sushi for two, there's nothing like the promise of fine feasting to get in the mood for love. From lavish banquets to a packed lunch at a motorway service station, this Wicked Words collection guarantees to serve up a good portion!